The Sunne in Gold

By Nene Adams

Shady Ladies Press, Inc.
34495 Branch School Rd
Laurel, De. 19956

©2000 Nene Adams
All rights reserved.
Published in the United States
By Shady Ladies Press, Inc.

All rights reserved. No part of this publication may be reproduced, stored in a retrieval system, or transmitted, in any form, or by any means, including electronic, mechanical, photocopying, recording, or otherwise, without the prior permission of the publishers.

ISBN: 0-9702127-4-0

All characters in this publication are fictitious, and any resemblance to actual persons, living or dead is purely coincidental.

Cover design by Douglas R. (Randy) McVey.
http://elfwood.lysator.liu.se/loth/r/a/randymc/randymc.html
mythic_art@webtv.net

Inquiries, orders and catalog requests should be addressed to:

Shady Ladies Press, Inc.
Rt. 3, Box 305 F
Laurel, De. 19956

To my other half, Corrie - my knight in shining armor, my dream, my soul -without whom life would be infinitely duller, infinitely plainer, and infinitely less worth living.

Nene Adams
October, 2000

*O goodly images of those antique times
In which the sword was servant unto right
When not for malice and contentious crimes
But all for praise, and proof of might
The martial brood accustomed to fight
Then honor was the meed of victory
And yet the vanquished had no despair*

–The Fairie Queen, Edmund Spenser

♦ Nene Adams ♦

CHAPTER ONE

ame a rush of ruddy dawn cascading down from white-shouldered mountains, and Castle Inishowen fell to siege…

Madrigal trembled in terror and tried to place her shackled arms over her head, but the chain that fastened her bonds to the massive bed was too short. Whimpering, she allowed her wealth of blue-black hair to cover her face and closed dark violet eyes tightly, wincing each time the castle walls shuddered beneath another blow from the attacking army's siege engines. The stone floor that grated against her knees was cold, but nowhere near as chilling as the terror in her heart. A wild cry echoed up from the courtyard three stories below: "The gate! They've breached the gate!"

Madrigal shivered again and jerked her leg against the cuff that fastened it tightly to the chain. Although only a slave, and her lord's bedslave at that, she had heard enough from the other servants to be nearly faint with horror at the

✦ The Sunne in Gold ✦

thought of being in the hands of the knight known as Blacksunne. Lord Francis had waxed eloquent about the dark knight, filling the slave girl's mind with a thousand terrors, that were about to come true, if what she were hearing drifting through the arrow-slits was any indication of the way the battle was going.

Please, she prayed as she shivered, *let me find a way to die before he comes...* Wrapping thin arms around her slightly swollen belly, Madrigal whispered brokenly, "Please..."

Dozens of masculine throats roared in unison, "The Sunne! The Sunne!" and the screaming began in earnest as the attackers pressed their advantage. In the midst of the roiling melee, one figure clad in black enamel-chased plate armor stood out like a Titan: immovable, implacable and incapable of defeat.

The black knight's high tenor voice carried over the sounds of battle, "May God damn you for a coward, Westfield! Show yourself!" he thundered, waving a massive broadsword overhead.

The battle surged on as the knight strode through it, seeming scarcely to notice the men he mowed down as if they had been mere wheat to his scythe. Blood splattered the peacock-blue surcoat he wore over his armor; the device on one shoulder–a stylized sun as black, as a raven's breast, set on a field of gold–stood out clearly. This was the dreaded Blacksunne: the knight who had never known defeat in battle and whose fame carried all before him; the knight who had ridden with King Richard the Lion-Hearted on Crusade to the Holy Land and received his spurs from the royal hand.

The sound of his name alone was enough to cause his foes to shudder aside in dread.

Blacksunne's voice might have resembled an unbearded boy's, but those who mistook the knight for an unblooded child soon learned otherwise, often as their souls were sent shrieking to Hell. "Westfield!" Blacksunne shouted, "Come, test your steel against mine! Come!"

Lord Francis Westfield was not in the midst of battle, rallying his rag-tag collection of men; he was not in the castle, seeing to its defenses; the lord and master of Inishowen was in the stables, trying frantically to saddle a recalcitrant mare. "Hold still, you damned jade!" he gritted, struggling to fasten a stubborn saddle girth.

I must get away, he raged inwardly, almost choking on bile. *There are those who've poured sympathy and friendship in my ear from the beginning of this business; I can use that to make alliances, raise a new army, sweep the countryside with rebellion and flames. When I return, t'will be at the head of a thousand skilled men and I'll crush Blacksunne like an inconvenient louse.*

A voice from behind made him start in fear and surprise.

"Going somewhere, cousin?"

Lord Francis turned his head slowly, and a sickly smile spread across his face. He did not have time to reply as a gauntleted fist drove into his mouth, and he tumbled down into sparkling darkness.

♦ The Sunne in Gold ♦

Lord Francis Westfield knelt on the cold stone floor of the Great Hall, directly in front of the dais where the new lord of the manse sat in a massive carved oak chair. Blacksunne had not yet removed his armor; nor had he removed his helm or lifted its visor. He sat at his ease, however, the great broadsword of the O'Cameron ancestors leaning against the arm of the chair within easy reach.

Lord Francis pulled at the bonds fastening his wrists behind his back and winced as the movement sent another jolt of pain through his head. "So, cousin," he spat sarcastically, "had I known you were coming, I'd have slain the fatted calf."

Blacksunne did not move, although one hand clenched into a fist. "I gave you every opportunity to surrender, Francis. You took what was mine and expected me to give it up without a fight? You're either a *very* brave man, or a fool."

"Is it foolish to be ambitious? Remember, Cousin, it was not *I* who left this place to go crusading with the Lion-Heart to the Holy Land. Five years gone, was it not? And poor Sir Giles, left all alone in his old age, his only child deserting him in his hour of need."

"Cease your damned lies!" Blacksunne's fist thudded on the arm of the chair and the armored figure leaned forward menacingly. "You have *always* coveted Inishowen, Cousin. Do not think I haven't heard about the way you invited yourself into the castle right after father became ill. You cozening bastard! Was he even cold before you started issuing orders?"

Lord Francis smiled, showing a missing front tooth; the wound still bled sluggishly, and the light beard around his mouth was stained, dark red against gold. "Possession is nine-tenths of the law, Cousin, despite what Sir Giles' will might have been. You were not here. I was. 'Tis as simple as that."

Blacksunne relaxed and casually rested a hand on the hilt of his sword. "Well, I possess Inishowen now. You and yours aren't made for war, Francis, more for raping serfs and terrifying sheep." The dark knight chuckled. "You should have stayed on your mother's estate in Cornwall."

"My mother's estate? You *must* think me mad. Cornwall is nothing more than a filthy boil on the buttock of the world, and my mother is the brazenest whore who ever lifted her skirts to a guardsman's dancing arse. Seeing Inishowen, who would *not* be tempted?"

"You should have known better. Cousin, you have known me long; our fathers were brothers and our families close. Did you truly believe I would stand aside and do nothing?"

"I'd honestly hoped you dead, but it doesn't really matter what I believed or dreamed. Come. Pronounce your judgment. I admit my crime willingly, if it is a crime to covet and not a sin I could be shriven for by any shave-pate priest."

Blacksunne rose. Both hands went to the helm that shielded his features. Lord Francis' hazel eyes darted back and forth; he searched for sympathy from the men who lined the walls of the Hall and found nothing but scorn and disdain.

The knight reached back and unclasped the hasp that held the two pieces of the war helm together, then drew it off in one smooth gesture. Long, dark crimson hair snaked across armored shoulders, and Lady Cathelin Brigit O'Cameron stood revealed, her molten amber eyes as haggard as a hawk's at bay.

"So, Cousin. You ask me for judgment. I desire justice. We shall see if the twain can meet."

Lord Francis's lips twisted into a sneer. "I'll not beg, Cat. Strike off my head with your bloody great sword, or do

♦ The Sunne in Gold ♦

whatever else you will. But do it quickly; I weary of kneeling here like a supplicant before a vengeful goddess."

Cathelin slowly walked down the stairs of the dais. "I should send you straight to a deserving Hell, Francis. But I respect your mother too much to kill her only son, thieving bastard tho' he is."

Turning to her chief man-at-arms, a taciturn older man with a figure like an ale barrel and a rusty red mustache, Cathelin said, "Cut off his right thumb. Then give him thirty pieces of silver, no more, no less, and escort him to the boundaries of Inishowen. And," she continued, swiveling her head to address the kneeling man, "if I ever hear of you befouling my land again, you pig-dog, I'll have no more mercy. I'll take your head and nail it to the doorpost to serve as an oracle." She smiled savagely, showing salt white teeth. "My wild ancestors would have done no less."

Lord Francis tried to spit but his mouth was too dry. The removal of his right thumb meant he would be unable to use a sword, unless he could transfer that skill to his other hand. The jibe about thirty pieces of silver burned in his soul like acid. *How like Cathelin to rub coarse, religious salt in to my wounds*, he thought with growing fury. *Why not just call me Judas and be done with it?*

As he was dragged roughly to his feet, Lord Francis worked his mouth, and gathered enough moisture to scream shrilly, "I'll have Inishowen someday, Cathelin! And revenge! *Remember* , Blacksunne, I will have my revenge!"

Cathelin shook her head as Francis was literally carried away, his hysterical screams and threats echoing along the stone corridors of the castle. When they finally died down, she motioned over a silent guardsman and said, "I'm going up to the master's chambers. Send a servant with wine, and have my squire fetched. I'll also want a bath; tell the cooks to start heating water."

♦ Nene Adams ♦

The man tugged his forelock respectfully. "Aye, m'lady," he replied before sprinting off.

Cathelin sighed wearily, shoulders slumping for a moment. The battle had been won, the dead dragged away for burial, and the injured sent to the abbey, a little ways apart from the village, that nestled at the foot of the castle mount. Now, she could rest until her seneschal had time to look at Inishowen's accounts and bespeak her the damage done to the castle's stores of goods and gold by that son-of-a-soul-crippled-sow the Good Lord had seen fit to inflict upon her as a blood relation.

She straightened up and began making her way to the stone staircase that spiraled up to her bedchamber, mentally making lists and wondering if the contents of the iron bound casket she had brought home from the siege of Acre would provide enough to outlast a harsh Irish winter.

♦ **The Sunne in Gold** ♦

♦ **Nene Adams** ♦

CHAPTER TWO

Much later, soaking in hot, herb-strewn water, Cathelin rubbed her aching shoulder and wished she hadn't sent her squire Thomas down to his supper.

The tub she soaked in was a huge wine cask that had been sawn in half; it was perfect for one, and even someone of Cathelin's more-than-ordinary height fitted comfortably inside. The water steamed gently, and despite the raw place on her hip where the padding beneath her armor had slipped, and bruises covering her from crown to heel, Cathelin relaxed for the first time since she had come home from the Crusades in Saracen Outremer; only to find her family seat usurped by Lord Francis, her father cold this last twelve-month, and, fortunately for her, vengeful allies on every hand, eager to help bring down Westfield.

Aye, she thought, *poor Francis. The boy would go and insult every neighboring laird in miles with his nose-in-the-air, wipe-my-arse Sassenach ways.* Luckily for her, those same neighbors had been willing to stand and fight with her

♦ The Sunne in Gold ♦

for revenge's sake, rather than concessions like cattle or sheep, neither of which could be spared if her people were to survive.

Despite her satisfaction, an unpleasant consideration continued to niggle. Francis might have made enemies but he might also have made friends. *There could be those who'd support my cousin should he decide to try and win the prize again*, she thought. *P'raps mercy was a mistake but by Christ! I'm mortal weary of blood and death.*

Well, no need to borrow trouble; there'll be time enough to deal with it if the day comes.

She dismissed her doubts, closed her eyes and lay her head back against the edge of the tub, strands of crimson hair billowing around her like exotic water weeds, and relaxed, until her trained ear picked up a sound that should *not* have been there–the sound of another person's breathing.

Cathelin's amber eyes popped open, and she leaped from the tub in one smooth motion, suppressing a wince as sore muscles protested. "Who's there?" she asked warily, her body in a half crouch. "Show yourself."

Only a whimper answered her.

Head cocked to one side and dripping water, Cathelin slowly crossed the room that occupied fully one-half of the western tower's third floor. She approached the shadowed corner–prepared for anything–except the sight that came into view as she cautiously peered around the high, canopied bed.

A woman knelt on the stone floor, mother naked save for a wealth of fine, blue black hair that puddled around her, all tangled and elf locked from miscare. Her enormous dark violet eyes were rimmed with red from tears, her sweetly rounded face slick with moisture. She shivered, but not with cold – with absolute soul killing fear.

With a start, Cathelin realized that the woman was manacled; heavy iron chains led from the cuffs on both wrists and ankles and fastened to one leg of the bed. She straightened up, and the woman whimpered again, bowing until her face was pressed against the floor.

"Christus! Who *are* you?" Cathelin did not mean to sound harsh, but the presence of another, when she thought she had been alone, startled her.

The woman shook with terror. "M-M-Madrigal, Mistress," she half-whispered.

Madrigal was nearly frozen with shock and fear. She had seen the other woman come into the bedroom as if she owned it. The slave had kept quiet, hoping that this woman with hair like the setting sun would ignore her; she would have crept away, silent enough not to be noticed, but for the iron bonds that kept her chained in place.

She must be Blacksunne's leman, Madrigal thought, and with further horror remembered every tale of Lord Francis' regarding the knight's sadism and cruelty. *His woman must be as terrible as himself.* The slave trembled, wondering what fresh horrors awaited her.

Cathelin was nonplussed. There had been no such servant at Inishowen when she had left. "Speak up, woman. What are you doing here?" For a moment, she wondered wildly if one of her men had intended this as a jape, then dismissed the thought. Although her preference for the female sex was known, none of her men would have so presumed on their lady commander's legendary temper.

Madrigal trembled some more. Keeping her face to the floor as she had been taught, she replied, "I... I was the Lord's bedslave, if it please my mistress."

Comprehension dawned on Cathelin's face. She knelt down, a careful arm's length from the other woman. "A slave, eh? From where?"

"Palestine, Mistress. But I was born in Bactria."

Cathelin put out a hand and cupped Madrigal's chin, forcing the other woman's face up so that dark purple eyes met amber gold. "I keep no slaves," she replied flatly.

✦ The Sunne in Gold ✦

Cathelin had seen too much during the destruction of Acre, things that still filled her nights with terrible dreams and visions of death and blood and screams. She needed no Saracen slaves to remind her of a time best forgotten.

Madrigal said nothing, although her eyes filled with tears again. Silently, she whispered to her unborn child, *I am sorry, little one. Perhaps Allah will grant His mercy on us both, and our deaths will be merciful and swift.*

The slave believed the sun-fire woman intended to kill her, and part of her welcomed the freedom of death. She lowered her eyes and waited calmly for the end, finding from some unknown depths the strength to accept the inevitability of her ending and the courage not to beg.

Cathelin saw emotions flooding across the slave girl's face: fear, regret, then acceptance. With a pang, she abruptly realized that the other woman expected to be butchered, in cold blood, as if she were some sort of animal. Cathelin wrenched her eyes away, breathing heavily.

They sat there for some time, the slave waiting patiently, the Irishwoman blinking back tears of her own. Finally, Cathelin rasped, "Where did he keep the key?"

Madrigal blinked, startled from her thoughts. "I," she began, then stopped. Tears spilled down her face as a tiny shred of hope blossomed. "The master kept it in there," she said at last, pointing to a small, decorative box with ivory inlay that sat on a nearby table.

Cathelin stood up, and, for the first time, Madrigal realized how magnificent this woman was, like a warrior out of legend–broad shoulders, smoothly rounded bulges in the arms, thighs as firm as tree trunks. The slave blinked again as Cathelin stalked away, momentarily fascinated, despite herself, by the play of muscles in the Irishwoman's buttocks.

Returning in a moment, Cathelin unlocked the cuffs, flinging them away as if they were trash. Muscles writhed beneath the skin along her jaw as she took in the raw, bloody places on the slave's wrists and ankles and saw for the first time the marks of the lash, some of them still oozing, that criss-crossed Madrigal's back.

Madrigal had stayed absolutely still while she was being freed; the moment Cathelin finished unlocking the cuffs, she prostrated herself, laying her face on the Irishwoman's bare foot and kissing it.

Had she seen the look of total disgust on Cathelin's face, Madrigal might have died of sheer fright. As it was, she flinched when the other woman said in a hard tone, "Get up."

The slave tried to obey, but long hours kneeling on the cold stone floors had left her too stiff. She struggled to rise, but nearly fell over. Crying out, Madrigal instinctively tried to protect her stomach and its precious burden, when strong arms reached out and caught her.

Cathelin grimaced, then with a grunt, lifted the astonished slave into her arms and laid her carefully on the bed. Madrigal tried not to cry when the wolfskin covering rubbed against the still tender flesh of her back, although she did let out a gasp.

"Stay there," Cathelin commanded, crossing to the door. Flinging it wide, she declared loudly, "Ho, a servant for your lady." Running footsteps echoed as a maidservant pelted along the corridor.

Reaching the door, the maid curtseyed and said breathlessly, "Mistress? You called?"

Cathelin waved a hand. "Have warm water, clean linen rags and my saddlebags brought up. Also, more wine and food."

The maid curtseyed again, then turned around and ran back down the corridor. The Irish were casual about nudity and had little body modestly; the maid no more noticed her mistress' undressed state than she would a child's.

Cathelin closed the door and turned back to the figure on the bed. "Roll over," she said shortly.

✦ The Sunne in Gold ✦

Madrigal obeyed, inwardly terrified. Thus far, the sunfire woman had offered her no hurt, but that command usually meant a beating. "Please, Mistress," she said, her voice muffled against the bed furs. "Have mercy. I am," she began but was interrupted.

"I'm not about to beat you, girl. Just lie still; I need to see to your hurts." Cathelin was more than a little exasperated and ran her hands through her still-dripping hair. With a curse, she snatched up a linen sheet and began to dry herself, mentally thanking God and Saint Brigit that it was high summer and the castle fairly warm.

Madrigal lay still, fearing to move, as Cathelin quickly tugged on a pair of breeches and a linen shirt that had seen better days. A discreet scratching at the door signaled the return of the maid, who entered with several other servants at her heels.

No one lifted a brow at the naked Madrigal's presence on the bed; what their mistress chose to do with Lord Francis' property was none of their concern, although most of them felt sorry for the girl. Silently, a table was pulled over; a wooden bowl of steaming water, clean rags, and a tray containing a flask of wine and a plate of food were left beside the bed. Cathelin's leather saddlebags, retrieved from the stables, were left as well. As silently as they had trooped in, the servants departed, leaving the two women alone.

Madrigal hissed softly through her teeth, fiery threads of pain lancing through her back as the other woman gently bathed it. The wolfskin coverlet beneath her was liberally bedewed with tears by the time Cathelin had cleaned the cuts to her satisfaction; then, the Irishwoman began tenderly washing the slave's wrists and ankles.

Cathelin noticed much older scars on the slave's back, scars that had turned silvery with age. Her amber eyes glowed with rage. Slavery was anathema to her; she had seen barely pubescent girls sold in the public markets of Antioch to white-bearded lechers, and she had personally witnessed the fate of harem girls at their master's hands. *Irizin,* she thought with a pang, then brutally put that memory aside. *That was then; this is now.*

Despite her anger, her hands were gentle as she removed a jar of green fresh-scented cream from her saddlebags and began to slather it on the cuts. Madrigal hissed again, this time in relief. The cream was cool, almost icy, and took much of the pain away.

Finally, Cathelin tied strips of linen around the slave's wrists and ankles, then stood up. She walked over to a massive oak chest and threw the lid open. Rummaging around inside, she finally came up with an old linen nightshirt, thin and threadbare with age.

Without a word, Cathelin helped Madrigal turn over and sit up, then pulled the nightshirt over the other woman's head. Madrigal swallowed. There was something she wanted to ask, but the stony look on Cathelin's face made her afraid. At last, gathering her courage, the slave said, "Mistress? Will I be required to serve Lord Blacksunne tonight?"

Cathelin's lips tightened. "I *am* Lord Blacksunne."

Madrigal's eyes glazed and she struggled for breath, heart beating against her chest like a caged bird. "I, I," she stuttered, then scrambled to her knees, ignoring the burning of cuts being reopened. Laying herself face down before Cathelin, she managed to get out, "Please forgive this stupid slave, Mistress." She did not know what to think about this revelation, but she was certain it boded ill for her and the unborn child she carried.

✦ The Sunne in Gold ✦

Rolling her eyes, the Irishwoman said, "I thought I told you I don't keep slaves. Get up girl, before you do yourself more harm."

Shaking with fear, Madrigal sat up. She kept her eyes lowered; in Palestine, a slave who presumed to stare into a master's eyes could be whipped to death. "Forgive me, Mistress. I beg you." It was all she could say as visions of torture, rape and mutilation spun through her head in rapid succession.

"I am *not* your mistress! Nor yet your master!" Cathelin was frustrated, distressed and beginning to get angry. "There are no slaves at Inishowen, and I'd not give a tarnished copper for what that bastard Francis told you. He is gone; you have no master save yourself. Now stop all that bowing and scraping, girl. I don't like it and I won't have it."

Madrigal whispered, "As you command, Mis–" She broke off, not willing to offend this half man-half woman creature. *Surely*, the slave thought, trembling in every limb, *this Blacksunne must be a djinn or a servant of Shaitan. No woman could wield weapons on the field of battle, and no man would allow one to command him.*

Cathelin sighed and ran her hands through her hair again. "Call me by my name, child. Cathelin. You *can* say Cathelin, can you not? Or call me Lady, if it pleases you more."

Hesitantly, Madrigal said, "Cathelin." Her slight accent gave the Irishwoman's name an exotic quality. "My Lady." This attempt was much firmer; the slave felt odd calling her mistress by her given name, and was more comfortable with an honorific.

"Good." Cathelin smiled. "Now, why don't you try and eat something." She indicated the plate of food. "But don't drink too much wine. You don't want a thick head tomorrow."

Madrigal reached for the plate, feeling as if she were in a dream. As Cathelin walked over to the fireplace to sit down and stretch her long legs out on the cold hearth, the slave began to eat, scooping up the cold beef and juicy summer greens with her fingers, astonished to find herself scraping the plate with a crust of bread in very little time.

Cathelin chuckled. "You've a hearty appetite for such a wee thing," she said. "Now, get you some sleep. Aye, sleep, Madrigal," she added as the other woman's eyes widened. "I know 'tis but a few hours past the nooning, but from the look of things, you're fair knackered."

Madrigal put the plate down and obediently curled up on her side, legs tucked up. She closed her eyes, but she could not sleep; she dreaded what the sun-fire woman might do.

Lord Francis had amused himself by spinning tales of Blacksunne, the tormentor; Blacksunne, the monster; Blacksunne, who lived and breathed only to subject young women to unimaginable tortures. Madrigal's fear was so great it was nearly paralyzing. That fear only increased when Cathelin crossed over to the bed and, with a weary sigh, lay down, rubbing her temples.

"I think I'll take a bit of my own advice," Cathelin said softly. "I'm mortal weary after such a day. Nay, girl," she added as Madrigal made to get off the bed. "Stay. We'll find another place for you later."

When Madrigal lay back down again, Cathelin relaxed and slipped into a light, restful sleep. Her warrior's trained senses were still on alert; she would wake up immediately if there were an emergency, or if someone attacked. The thought that Madrigal might be hostile she dismissed; the girl was unarmed and seemed too cowed to take foolish risks.

After a time, the regular rhythm of Cathelin's breathing convinced the slave that the other woman was truly asleep. Madrigal leaned up on one elbow, the better to study her new mistresses' face.

♦ The Sunne in Gold ♦

Cathelin was not classically beautiful; her nose had been broken more than once and was slightly askew. Her cheekbones stood out like ivory spars beneath skin that bore a light touch of the sun; elsewhere, Madrigal remembered, her skin had the color and sheen of fine cream. A small scar marred the underside of her chin; another scar, this one as jagged as a lightning bolt, ran from her right temple, through her hair and around the back of her ear. Madrigal noticed that Cathelin's ears had been pierced and was not surprised; the people of Ireland were fond of personal adornment.

There were other scars, of course. Tentatively, Madrigal traced a long, curving scar on Cathelin's forearm, marveling, despite her lingering fear, at the texture of the other woman's skin.

Around Cathelin's upper arm, Madrigal remembered, had been a dark blue band, like a wide cuff of twisting snakes within a braided border. It was done using the sacred woad; the slave had been shocked to discover that the marking was permanent, the pigment driven beneath the skin in an incredibly painful ordeal that was sometimes considered a rite of passage. Ireland might have been a Christian nation, but old pagan customs still clung despite the Church's best efforts. This was astonishing to Madrigal, who had been raised in the faith of Islam.

Madrigal's heart almost stopped when Cathelin's eyes opened. Those fierce amber orbs held a shimmering fire that both fascinated and frightened the slave. "I thought I told you to get some sleep, girl," Cathelin growled, but with a wide smile. "And stop staring at me like a goose-wit. Has the tip of my nose turned green?"

Madrigal shook her head frantically and lay down, cradling her head on her folded arms and closing her eyes. *Perhaps Allah has shown us mercy, little one*, she thought to her unborn child. *Perhaps the lady is not as terrible as the lord told me.* A very small part of her began to trust the other woman a little. But her natural suspicions were still very much alive.

Eventually, Madrigal fell asleep, her dreams filled with fire, thunder and the memory of Cathelin's smile.

Lord Francis sat cross-legged before a small peat fire, the acrid smoke stinging his eyes. Against his chest, he cradled his swollen right hand, wrapped in rough linen rags. The throbbing, raw agony of his missing thumb made him scowl and take a deep swallow from a horn mug filled with usquebha.

"At least that bastard of a butcher used a hot knife," he snarled to himself, watching shadows flicker on the walls of his hiding place. After Cat's man had hacked his thumb off with brutal efficiency and escorted him to the boundary of Inishowen, Francis had stumbled along in shock and pain, nearly choking on bitterness and gall.

He'd found a hedge witch willing to treat his injury for silver, and she had sworn her spells and herbal salves would keep the wound from mortifying. He had declined the splinter of the True Cross she had pressed on him, however; he would rather have purchased a curse to squeeze his bitch cousin's heart into a hard, black stone within her breast. The witch had refused, may God condemn her straight to Hell, and he had beaten her savagely before leaving her in the tiny, stinking hut to die.

No one will deny me my birthright, he thought as torment gnawed his lacerated flesh, *especially a woman. If they're not for me, they're against me, b'Christ. I will have*

♦ The Sunne in Gold ♦

Inishowen, and I will drink every night from Blacksunne's empty skull, and Heaven help the ones who get in my way.

Afterwards, his brain on fire, he had crawled like a shrinking beast to a place he knew well, to heal and nurse the injuries of body, soul and mind. No one knew he was here, save the only one he trusted.

As if in answer to his thoughts, a figure appeared at the entrance. "My lord?"

The side of Francis' mouth quirked up in an expression that was more sneer than smile, then softened deliberately. "Sorcha, my love," he said. The blonde woman came and knelt at his feet, gently taking his bandaged hand and examining it.

Francis put aside his mug and stroked her hair awkwardly with his left hand. "You managed to slip out. Were you noticed?"

Sorcha shook her head. "Nay, my lord. None noticed and none followed."

"Good." Francis' grip tightened on her blonde locks, and she gasped, a deep inrush of breath that owed more to excitement than fear. Slowly, inevitably, he pushed her head further and further down. "You know what I need, Sorcha," the lord said in a hard tone that brooked no refusal. Despite the hot streaks of agony that flashed up his arm, he was hard as an iron bar.

The memory of the witch's bleeding face, her broken whispers for mercy, had merged with fantasy, and in his mind's eye, he saw Cathelin kneeling there, battered by his fists, ready to serve her master abjectly before dying, his sword hacking down again and again until his bitch cousin dissolved in a mist of blood.

Sorcha gasped again. "Yes, my lord," she said, voice husky with passion. "I know exactly what you need." Her fingers fumbled at the cord that fastened his breeches.

♦ Nene Adams ♦

Francis threw his head back, eyes squeezed shut, pleasure mingling with pain.

His mouth moved, lips forming shape without sound. Cathelin, he repeated silently over and over. Cathelin.

When the moment came, he roared in triumph, the enemy he hated and cursed having died a thousand times within the vaults of his mind.

The Sunne in Gold

♦ Nene Adams ♦

CHAPTER THREE

"**W***hat!*"

Cathelin's roar of rage startled Madrigal awake; it was early the next morning—she had slept through the day and night together, exhausted both by pain and the emotional upheaval she had experienced the previous day. For a moment, she lay perfectly still, although her heart pounded. Then Madrigal realized that her Lady's anger was not directed at her at all, but towards the man she knew as Michael Drury, the castle's seneschal.

Drury was not a small man; in fact, he was as tall as the lady herself—but in her larger-than-life presence, he seemed diminished. He held his loaf-shaped hat in his hands and twisted it with nervous fingers. "Please, Milady," he said, reaching up to pluck at his mustache. "There was nothing we could do. The old lord was dead, beggin' your pardon, may he rest in peace. Lord Francis claimed Inishowen in your absence. There were no other heirs to contest his claim."

♦ The Sunne in Gold ♦

"And so you allowed that worm to eat my father's food, slay my father's cattle, and spend my father's gold as if there were no tomorrow? By God, man! Did you not think of the people who *depend* on us, on Inishowen, to survive the winter? Or perhaps you believed the Good Lord would rain snow less harshly upon your heads since otherwise you'd starve? Feh!" Cathelin was seething; she had summoned Drury to bring the castle's accounts, and the news was not good.

Saint Brigit! she thought angrily. *In a year's time, Francis managed to run through every bit of Inishowen's wealth and stock; gold doesn't stick to his fingers, it runs through like shit through a goose.*

Cathelin plopped herself down in a chair and picked up the massive accounts book, waving it beneath Drury's nose like a weapon. "Why'd you not slit his weasel's throat while he was swiving some wench? Our neighbor folk would not only have thanked you with hosannas, they'd have helped you bury the bastard."

Drury gulped. The truth of the matter was, despite the fact that the castle people were all loyal to the O'Camerons, being left without a lord in residence had made them nervous and uncomfortable. To the majority, a bad master was better than no master at all.

Cathelin sighed. Loyalty was all well and good, but the castle's people depended on a lord to survive – she understood this and couldn't really blame her folk for their inaction . Without a lord's protection, they'd have been prey to every jumped-up baron with a court connection, looking to acquire Inishowen's lands. "All right, then. Pack your saddlebags, Michael. You're going to Cork."

Drury stuttered, "C-C-Cork? Oh, Milady, please don't turn me out! Please." The big man seemed on the verge of tears.

♦ **Nene Adams** ♦

"I'm not turning anyone out, you quake-buttocked fool. I brought some treasures back from Outremer, jewels and such. You're to go to the Jeweler's Guild, and the Goldsmith's; get every copper groat you can, then stock up on supplies. We'll need anything and everything come wintertime."

Drury's weathered face filled with relief. "Yes, Milady," he said, bowing his head.

"Take a list of foodstuffs, woolens and the like. Whatever we need. I trust you'll bargain well, since your family, as well as everyone else's, will suffer if you don't."

"Yes, Milady."

"And Michael?" Cathelin's voice was a dangerous purr.

Drury gulped. "Yes, Milady?"

"Don't forget the wine."

Drury nodded in relief and turned to go, knowing a dismissal when he heard one.

As the door closed behind the seneschal, Cathelin rubbed a hand through her crimson hair and sighed. *And I truly believed retaking the castle would be the hardest part*, she thought ruefully.

A few moments later, a discreet scratching on the door made her sit up straighter and call, "Enter!" somewhat impatiently.

This uninvited visitor was the second in command of her army, a dark-haired Scottish warrior named Wolf McLeod. The mustache that drooped above his upper lip hung down to the sharp angle of his jaw, and his eyes were the icy blue of sunlight reflected in a mountain loch. His cool gaze swept around the room, registered the slave on the bed, and came to rest on Cathelin's face.

"I thought ye'd be wantin' to know about Owain Kilkenney," he said. Years in Ireland had not erased the

♦ **The Sunne in Gold** ♦

Highland brogue from his tongue. "I've word from the abbey."

Cathelin drew in a sharp breath and let it out slowly. Owain was a young, good-natured kern whose pretty face, blonde curls and merry manner made him very popular.

"Does he yet live?" she asked without much hope. The only one of her men to sustain a serious wound, Owain had taken a swordblade through the gut during the melee against Francis' men.

Wolf shrugged his burly shoulders. "Nay. The monks say the lad was shriven and died peaceful enow."

Cathelin sat in silence a moment, gut churning with anger and guilt. Owain was a sweet, quick-witted lad who had survived the trials of Outremer, only to be cut down by his own kind in a battle that should have never taken place. *That is another debt I owe you, cousin*, she thought bitterly.

"Have the body washed and laid out," she ordered when she thought she could speak calmly. "He'll be buried with arms and armor on the morrow in the abbey cemetery. Tell the Mistress of the Hearth to prepare cold meats, sallets and bread for a funeral feast to be served in the kern's quarters. Small beer and ale only."

Wolf nodded. "The lad had no kith or kin hereabouts, nor wife nor sweethearts to be mournin'."

"Then Owain Kilkenney will mourned by the O'Cameron clan." Cathelin's guilt was subsiding; as a war chieftain, she had learned that death was inevitable. A young man stricken down on the battlefield was tragic but she could not allow herself to be paralyzed by grief. No warrior could and hope to lead her troops to survival and victory.

"Aye, well, 'twas a light toll to pay for the retakin' of the castle," Wolf said philosophically. He, too, would miss Owain, but years of soldiering had left him more accepting of the consequences of war. "The other wounded are doing well and with the Good Lord's luck, will be braggin' of their scars come the fortnight. I'd best be goin', milady. There's much to do afore the lad's delivered safe to Jesus' arms."

He took his leave with a brusque bow.

She stared at the door for a long moment after McLeod's departure, lost in memories of the laughing, bright-eyed lad who now lay cold and silent. She shook herself, turning back to the needs of the living.

The Irishwoman caught sight of Madrigal's prone figure on the bed, and noted that the slave's eyes were open.

"So you're awake, eh?" Cathelin said. "Are your wounds paining you?"

Silently, Madrigal shook her head. Cathelin stood up, pushing the matter of Owain aside – there would be time enough to grieve the dead but now it was the living who had priority. She crossed to the bed and sat down on the edge, noticing the other woman's barely perceptible flinch. "Softly, girl. I'm not going to hurt you. I just want a look at your back." Cathelin reached out and carefully peeled the nightshirt up, seeing with satisfaction that the cream had kept the linen from sticking to the wounds.

The lash marks seemed less inflamed already. Cathelin nodded with satisfaction. "Well, I think you'll survive. That cream's a marvel, I tell you. Bought it from a healer in Antioch. Many's the man I've seen die of wound rot; but this stuff prevents it. I paid a king's ransom for the secret of its making, too."

Madrigal wasn't sure how to respond, so she settled for whispering, "Yes, Lady."

"You'll be up and about in no time, you'll see. But you can't run around the castle in a nightshirt. Have you no proper clothes?"

Madrigal's deep purple eyes filled with tears. "The lord did not see fit to give me any. He preferred me..." She stopped and spread her hands apart helplessly.

♦ The Sunne in Gold ♦

Cathelin's nostrils flared with anger. *Francis, you've a great deal to pay for*, she thought. *And I wish to God I'd extracted every pound of flesh you owed.* Despite her anger, she smiled slightly for the girl's sake. "Well, *that* will not do. I suspected you had little, but... My sister Marguessan, may God rest her soul, was about your size. I've asked the Wardrobe Mistress to bring you a selection, and what you like, you can keep."

Madrigal was frankly astonished. The notion of anyone *giving* a slave a *choice* was beyond comprehension; but she kept silent with the stoic resignation of someone who has no will of their own, save their master's.

Cathelin said gently, "Have *you* no questions? You seemed mortal surprised that Blacksunne and myself are one and the same."

Madrigal said softly, "What you wish me to know, you will tell me."

The Irishwoman snorted. She had bound her dark crimson hair into two braids that swung on either side of her face; the waist length plaits were fastened at the ends with wrapped leather thongs. "'Madri," she said, "if you wish to know more of me, of my life, you must ask." Her amber eyes twinkled. "I know you've a tongue in your head, lass. Use it."

For a moment, the slave was lost in thought. Cathelin swung her long legs up on the bed and reclined on one elbow, watching the other woman's face intently.

After a while, Madrigal asked hesitantly, "How did it come to pass that you are the Blacksunne?"

Cathelin blew out a breath. "A long tale, Madri. But suffice to say, my mother, Lady Ydris O'Cameron, married Sir Giles Forthwright, an English knight. Ah, they were very much in love," she mused. "Soon after their marriage, I came along, then my sister Marguessan–she died of a fever when I was seventeen–and then no more. My father desperately wanted a son, but God chose not to grant him his dearest wish.

"After mother died, he fell into despair; he truly loved no other woman, and would not sully Ydris' memory with another marriage. So, he decided that if the Good Lord would not give him a son, he would *make* one."

Cathelin stopped, momentarily caught by the memory of her father's strong arm guiding her own, his hand atop hers as she wielded her first sword against the pells. Swallowing, she continued, "I trained for years, but not the normal girl's pursuits. 'Twas the arts of war I learned, and there was no better teacher than my father. To our mutual surprise, I think, I proved to have a talent for it."

During the Irishwoman's recital, Madrigal listened carefully, not only with her ears but with her soul, trying to find the tiniest lie, the slightest hint of falsity, but to her surprise, found none.

Cathelin continued, "My ancestors founded this village two centuries ago, fleeing enemies in Scotland, and the O'Camerons have lived and died here since. But I was restless, and as some would have it, reckless. I left for the Holy Land five years ago, joining the crusade against the infidel under the banner of King Richard Lionheart. His mother, Eleanor of Aquitaine, was a great childhood friend of my father's, so 'twas only natural that I sought service with him and no other.. Of course, the King had no idea I was a woman, and neither did his men. My own kerns knew, but were sworn to silence on the matter."

The Irishwoman chuckled, recalling the priceless look on the King's handsome face when he had discovered her not to be a comely lad, as he had thought, but a lass full grown. *Aye*, she thought, *he'd come to my tent that night for a bit o' seduction, and ended up playing draughts with me until dawn.* Despite the earlier embarrassment, the two had grown close.

♦ The Sunne in Gold ♦

"'Twas Richard himself who knighted me, giving me spurs with his own hand. He also gave me the title Blacksunne, deeming it best that few as possible know a woman fought within the black armor. Little did I know that minstrels were already composing songs about Blacksunne; it was mortal embarrasin' to climb off the boat in Calais, and find that the deeds of Cathelin O'Cameron had been credited to a mysterious knight of unspeakable bravery and fame.

"It's quite a riddle. In my own country, and to my own men, I am now and forever will be Lady Cathelin O'Cameron of Inishowen; but to the English, I am Lord Blacksunne. Two persons in one body; you'd think it would get a wee bit crowded, would you not?" Cathelin chuckled. "And that is the end of my tale, Madri. P'raps you've one of your own you'd like to share?" Cathelin concluded, cocking her head to one side and staring at Madrigal expectantly.

While her Lady had spoken, Madrigal came to the conclusion that it had been her former master who lied. *After all*, she thought, *the Lady has not offered me any hurt, she has fed me and tended my wounds, and certainly, her people have respect for her.* As a slave, Madrigal was intimately acquainted with the difference between fear and respect.

It was with something approaching relief that the slave surrendered the worst of her fears, and began to believe, for the first time, that she might survive this experience after all.

Clearing her throat, Madrigal said, "What is this 'Madri' you call me? Is that to be my new name?"

Cathelin's amber eyes widened. "No, no, I will call you what you wish. 'Madri' is but a small-name, an endearment, of sorts."

"Ah." Madrigal had finished considering; *now*, she thought, *it is time to act.* The woman sat up, gracefully kneeling on the bed, her hands clasped together in her lap. The glory of her long hair spilled like a waterfall of dark indigo around her. "Please forgive me, Lady, but a slave has no past worthy of interest."

The Irishwoman's golden amber eyes flashed with barely suppressed anger. "I told you, you are *not* a slave!" she began hotly, but was silenced when Madrigal raised a slender hand.

"Forgive me, Lady, but I *am* a slave. I have known nothing else most of my life. Although you have removed my bonds, I am, nevertheless, your property."

Cathelin blinked, dumbfounded. "B-b-but," she stuttered, but again was, with exquisite politeness, interrupted.

"You own this castle, do you not?" Madrigal asked. When Cathelin nodded, the slave continued, "And you own all the property within? I am a slave; I was purchased by the Lord Francis and now, like the castle itself, I belong to you. There is nothing else. There can *be* nothing else. That is the way of the world, and all is as Allah wills."

Cathelin thought furiously. It was becoming obvious that nothing she could say was going to convince the other woman that she was free. Finally, the Irishwoman gave up. "Very well, tho' you've a stubborn streak in you I've rarely seen in mules, much less lasses. If you insist you are a slave, I'll argue no more. Of servants I have plenty; what skills have you to earn your keep? I can keep no idle hands about; we'll have a hard enough passage through winter as it is."

Madrigal was not modest about her accomplishments; they'd cost her much in time, and sometimes pain. "I can play many instruments, and my master's have told me I have a good singing voice. I have made paper, dyes and inks; I can weave, sew and embroider. I have been taught to cook, bargain at the marketplace, and I know many amusing tales and poems to entertain you. I am also," and she hesitated, then continued bravely, "highly skilled in the arts of love."

"What?"

♦ The Sunne in Gold ♦

Madrigal gave the astonished Irishwoman a shy look. "When I blossomed, I was sold to a harem-master in Palestine. I was given a pleasure girl's training; some of my teachers had been great beauties in their time, and I learned much. Lord Francis praised my skills highly." *When he was not beating me for failing to rouse him,* she added silently, *but that was as Allah willed.*

Cathelin swallowed, overcome for a moment by the memory of another harem girl: Irizin, whom she had met at the village well, so long ago in the Eastern lands; Irizin, whose dark eyes had flashed with promise, and more, above the veil that swathed her unbelievably beautiful features; Irizin, whose master had left her broken and bleeding body in the Irishwoman's tent when he had discovered his concubine's infidelity.

Madrigal waited patiently, although inwardly she cringed at the haunted look on the Lady's face. She hoped she had not been too forward; some of her worst whippings had been because she had overstepped the bounds of propriety between master and slave.

Finally, Cathelin spoke slowly, "So, it seems to me a shame to waste such talent in the kitchen, or in the laundry, or about the common household. At the moment, I have no servant to tend to my personal needs; if you are willing, Madri, I would have you tend my wardrobe and see to other such things." *I cannot turn the poor weevil out*, she thought. *She'd starve inside of a week.* A tiny corner of her mind was incredibly curious about just *how* skilled her new servant was, but Cathelin ruthlessly suppressed that thought.

Madrigal drew a deep breath and bowed from the waist until her forehead touched the coverlet. "As my Lady commands," she said calmly; inside, she nearly wept with relief.

The Irishwoman smiled slightly. *P'raps one day she'll realize she's free to do as she pleases*, she thought, *but in the meantime...* Aloud, she said, "All right, girl. Enough of that. Have you anything else to tell me?"

The slave straightened. One of her father's favorite sayings had been, 'As well be hung for a sheep as a lamb'. Now, she gathered her courage together; her pregnancy would be the most difficult thing to confess. "My Lady," Madrigal began.

But was interrupted by a small, furious, female form that burst through the chamber door like a whirlwind.

Sorcha O'Reilly stood framed within the doorway, green eyes snapping with indignant sparks. "Well?" she demanded outrageously. "P'raps you'd care to explain why Michael Drury is down in my kitchen, pokin' about the stores and askin' questions of my folk that he has no business doin'?"

Madrigal flinched, expecting an explosion. But, to her surprise, Cathelin laughed at the other woman's effrontery. "Ah, Sorcha," she said to the infuriated blonde. "Gracious as always. Glad I am to know that despite advancing years, my memory is as keen as ever."

Sorcha ignored Cathelin's sally. "I am the chatelaine here, Cat. Appointed by your father of blessed memory, in case you've forgotten. Unless you intend to give Michael Drury the keys, then I'm tellin' you to order him to keep his long nose away from my duties and stick to his own business."

Now Cathelin frowned. As willing as she was to accommodate Sorcha's moods, this discourtesy was beginning to irritate her. "As far as Drury, you may rest contented knowing that he does no more than my will, nor less besides."

Madrigal watched this sparring in wide-eyed wonder. Sorcha, the slave knew well. Sir Francis had encouraged the chatelaine's subtle, and not-so-subtle abuses; Madrigal also knew that the blonde woman and her former lord had been secretly betrothed. She wondered if her Lady knew of this,

♦ The Sunne in Gold ♦

but decided she did not. *Nor will I reveal the tidings*, Madrigal thought, suppressing a shudder. *My Lady may not be as savage as I first thought, but surely she would strike down the bearer of such ill news.*

Meanwhile, Cathelin had risen from the bed, nostrils pinched white in anger, in response to Sorcha's shrill rantings. "You may be distant kin of mine, Sorcha O'Reilly," she rasped, "but by Saint Brigit, you will *not* dictate to me what I may, or may not, do in my own household!"

Sorcha stumbled back, face pale. Cathelin's eyes were brighter than molten gold with fury; Sorcha dared not defy the mistress of Inishowen any longer. *But some day*, the blonde chatelaine thought sullenly, *when I am wed to Lord Francis, it will be she who dares not try my wrath.*

Sorcha swallowed her pride and said humbly, "Forgive me, Cat. I've overstepped myself. Of course, if Michael Drury is actin' on your own orders, I'll give no more protest."

Cathelin snorted, anger subsiding. "You're forgiven, Sorcha. Have a tray sent up for Madrigal; no doubt she's perishin' hungry. And tell the hetman, Fergus Niall, to come up from the village. I need to speak to him about the harvest."

Sorcha threw a scathing, hate-filled glance at the figure of Madrigal on the bed behind Cathelin. Not a few of the whip-marks on the girl's back had been made by the chatelaine; in truth, she had enjoyed it mildly, but had been mostly content to leave the chit be. But for a slave to have witnessed her humiliation... Sorcha bowed her head in acknowledgement of Cathelin's dismissal, and inwardly vowed to be revenged on Madrigal, any way she could.

Cathelin sighed as Sorcha left, and walked over to the clothes chest, selecting a dark red tunic, gorgeously embroidered along the sides, cuffs and neckline with black and gold oak leaves, and a pair of knitted black hose. She turned to Madrigal. "There's a tear in the seam, here," the

Irishwoman said, pointing to one side of the tunic. "Do you think you feel well enough to fix it for me?"

Madrigal smiled and sat up, brushing her hair away from her face. "Of course, Lady," she answered. "I feel much better today."

While Cathelin waited, Madrigal carefully sewed up the torn seam, taking impossibly tiny stitches that could barely be detected with the naked eye. It was only a matter of moments before the tunic was as good as new.

Cathelin observed all this in wonder. She herself had never mastered the art of needle and thread; in Outremer, her squire Thomas had taken care of her clothes. "Marvelous!" she breathed, turning the tunic over in her hands; the damage could not be detected now. "You've a fine light touch, Madri."

The slave blushed slightly and returned the precious steel needle to its ivory case, then tucked it back inside the small wooden sewing box. Madrigal slid off the bed and padded over to Cathelin. For the first time, the Irishwoman realized how tiny the former slave was; the top of her head barely came to the level of her own breasts.

"Please, allow me," Madrigal said politely but firmly, taking the mended tunic from Cathelin's hands and laying it carefully aside on the bed. The Muslim girl quaked at her temerity, but if she was to be the Lady's servant, she would perform her duties to the best of her ability.

While Cathelin struggled to hide her amusement, Madrigal removed the taller woman's old linen shirt and battered trousers. She then helped her don the thigh-length tunic and hose, carefully pulling up the latter to avoid baggy knees, and tying the leather laces tightly enough around Cathelin's upper thighs to keep the hose in place, but not so tight as to impair circulation. Finally, she took a clean loincloth from the clothes chest and fastened it around Cathelin's hips.

✦ The Sunne in Gold ✦

As she drew one end of the long cloth between Cathelin's legs, Madrigal was acutely aware that her face was only inches away from the flaming thatch that crowned the other woman's mount. She averted her eyes as she tucked the free end back into the wrapped waist and pulled it tight; the sight of those softly curling locks, as ruddy as the hair on the Lady's head, caused strange stirrings in her lower belly that made Madrigal flush slightly.

Madrigal looked up into Cathelin's amber eyes and asked, "What footwear does the Lady desire?"

Cathelin bit her lip to hide a smile. *I've not been waited on so since I was a wee child*, she thought. *I could grow to enjoy this.* Aloud, Cathelin said, "The brown boots, if you please."

Madrigal retrieved a pair of knee-high leather boots from an iron-bound oak chest, then knelt gracefully at Cathelin's feet. "If my Lady will permit?"

Cathelin sat down on the edge of the bed and allowed the dark Muslim beauty to draw on her boots. Then the Irishwoman stood up and stomped a few times, settling her feet.

A discreet scratching came from the door; a few seconds later, it was opened by a stout, florid faced woman with iron-gray hair and dark blue eyes that twinkled merrily. "'Tis only myself, Lady," she said, sweeping into the chamber with several dresses flung over one arm. "I've brought you the things you asked."

Cathelin gave the older woman a brilliant smile. Meagan MacAvera, the Mistress of Wardrobe, was one of her favorite people. Mistress Meagan had been serving Inishowen since before Cathelin had been born; her duties were to see to all household linens and woolens, and included supervising the yearly weaving and dyeing, as well as overseeing the creation, maintenance and management of clothing worn by all of Inishowen's people. She had also acted as a second mother after the death of Ydris, and had been a vast source of comfort after the death of Cathelin's sister, Marguessan..

"Come in, Mistress," Cathelin said warmly. "'Tis grand to see you again."

Mistress Meagan laughed heartily. "Aye, and grand it is to see you as well, colleen. Well, then, here's the dresses you asked for; are they for wee Madrigal?"

Madrigal smiled tentatively at Meagan and rose from her kneeling position. She, too, felt the Wardrobe Mistress to be a friend; the cheerful Scottish woman had always had a kind word for the slave.

"Yes," Cathelin replied, "I thought she and Marguessan might be of a like enough size, and I've since learned the girl has nothing of her own."

Mistress Meagan raised a brow but forbear to comment. "I think you've the right of it, lass," she said to Cathelin. "Come here, Madrigal, there's a good girl. Try this one on; I think it will suit you nicely."

Madrigal shyly took the dress from Meagan's hand; it was linen, floor length and dyed a rich blue. Though simple, the dress had an embroidered cloth belt that could be tied around waist or hips, and the tasseled ends dangled nearly to the floor. Madrigal had never had such a fine dress before and she was close to tears.

"Well?" Cathelin prompted. "Are you trying it on or standing there all amort 'til sundown?" A generous smile took the sting out of her words.

Madrigal stripped off her nightshirt, wincing slightly as the wounds on her back were stretched; fortunately, there was no tearing. She slipped the dress over her head and swiftly tied the belt around her hips, pushing the length of her blue-black hair out of the way. The sleeves were a little long, but otherwise, it was a perfect fit.

Meagan said, "That's fine, just fine. I'll have Tom Cobbler make up some shoes for you. I think we've nothin'

✦ The Sunne in Gold ✦

that would suit in the stores, save perhaps some slippers for indoors."

Cathelin nodded. "Attend to it, Meagan, and soonest." She reached out one hand and grasped Madrigal's shoulder gently. "Let me see," she said.

The Irishwoman carefully spun Madrigal around and caught her breath at the depth of the other woman's beauty. *She'll be driving the lads insane before too long*, Cathelin thought... *or the lassies.*

There were a few women, and men, in the ranks of the warriors and craftspeople who served the Lady that were of her own mind; they preferred their own sex, and despite the Church's official ban on such things, marriages and bondings still took place as usual. The parish priests turned a blind eye, knowing that in some things, it was best to let the people do as they wished, and add some extra penances or prayers. The Church's hold on the Irish was not as firm as the bishops wished; the Celts had a way of borrowing what they liked, changing what they did not, and throwing out the rest with a casual shrug.

"Very nice. Still, it needs something," Cathelin murmured. She went over to a small, pearl studded box that stood on a table and opened it, stirring the contents around with one finger. Finally, she came back with something glittering between her two hands.

It was a light silver chain, the links as delicate as woven cobwebs. Dangling from the chain was a purplish-red agate that had been carved in the shape of a phoenix–the crest of Sir Giles Forthwright's family. Cathelin placed it carefully over Madrigal's head, pulling her loose hair out of the way, and adjusted the lay of the agate charm against the Muslim's bosom.

"There," the Irishwoman said in satisfaction, while Meagan beamed. "I think that much better, myself. Keep it,

Madri, as a welcome gift; you're one of my people now and deserving of much better than you've gotten before."

Madrigal laid one hand on the charm and began to cry softly. The dress, her new status in the household, and now this gift... She could not help but cry. For so many years she had dwelled in a place of utter loneliness, where no one cared whether she lived or died; where no man or woman would have lifted a finger to help her; where her worth was valued, not as a human being, but as property. To know that the Lady felt that she belonged, truly belonged to her own tight-knit clan, was more than Madrigal could bear. Hot tears coursed down her face and she bit back a sob.

Instantly, she was swept into strong arms–arms that had the potential to kill, and had often done so, but at this moment were as gentle as a mother lioness with her cub. "Shhhhh," Cathelin crooned, pressing Madrigal's wet face into her chest, braids tickling the other woman's neck. "Softly, sweetling, softly. It's all right, now. I'm here."

Meagan tiptoed out of the door, leaving the other dresses draped over a chair. As she closed the door carefully behind herself, she wiped at threatening tears of relief and sympathy. Sending up a silent prayer to ask for peace to be given the slave who had endured so much, Meagan went back to her duties with a much lighter heart. Cathelin held Madrigal, rocking the smaller woman in her arms until the sobs changed to sniffles. She drew back a little and looked down into the slave's face. "All done, sweetling?" she asked kindly. Cathelin had more than an inkling as to what Madrigal was going through; her experience in Outremer had given her a unique perspective on the effects of slavery.

Madrigal wiped her eyes and stared at the wet stain on Cathelin's tunic. "Oh!" she exclaimed in horror. "Your tunic!"

Cathelin looked down and chuckled. "It's all right, Madri. It'll dry itself in a bit. But how are you?"

♦ The Sunne in Gold ♦

Madrigal sniffed. "I'm fine, Lady," she replied. "I just..." For a moment, the Muslim girl hovered on the verge of a fresh outbreak of tears; she swallowed the lump in her throat and controlled them with an effort. "Thank you," she said simply.

"My pleasure, sweetling," Cathelin said. "Now, if you're all right, I must be going to my meeting with Master Niall." Then she paused, as if remembering something. "Where's that food I ordered?" she asked of the air. Turning around, Cathelin opened the chamber door and shouted, "Ho. A servant for your Lady."

A male servant appeared almost as if by magic. "Yes, Lady?" he asked, bowing his head and tugging his forelock.

"I ordered a tray of food sent up from the kitchens some time ago," Cathelin snapped. "Where is it?"

Tiny beads of sweat broke out on the servant's forehead. The man had been cautioned by all the other servers of their Lady's temper; the tales they had told him, while sniggering behind their hands, had him terrified of this warrior queen. "I-I-I," he stammered, then caught hold of himself. "I will inquire, Lady," he said, and turned, running headlong down the hall to the great stone staircase that lead down from the tower to the lower floors.

Cathelin's lips twisted. By the standards of the day, she was quite lenient with her people; as Lady of Inishowen, she literally held the power of life and death over them, although she rarely exercised this privilege. Other lords might discipline with torture or hangings; she preferred a glove of velvet over a fist of steel.

This did not mean that Cathelin allowed laxity or disrespect; indeed, nearly every servant at Inishowen had, at some time or another, been exposed to the Lady's fierce temper, and once was usually more than enough.

Madrigal had sat down in a chair next to the fireplace, smoothing the fabric of her new dress with both hands. She looked at the fuming Lady. "Perhaps it was forgotten?" she asked, trying to placate her mistress; one of her duties in the harem had been to attend to the needs of the other wives and concubines, and she had often been complimented on her peace-making skills.

Cathelin clenched her jaw. "If it was…" she replied ominously, but did not voice the threat; she spied the servant scurrying back along the hall, out of breath and panting heavily.

"Well?" Cathelin growled.

The servant bowed and struggled to control his breathing. "It comes, Lady. The Chief of the Hearth, Mistress Shevaughn, sends her apologies."

Cathelin was annoyed, but controlled her anger. It was not *this* man's fault her orders had been ignored. She dismissed him and turned back to Madrigal.

"Your tray will be here soon, Madri. If it is not, send Meagan to find me. I'll not be defied in my own house, by God!" Cathelin had a fairly good idea of what had happened. Sorcha had deliberately not conveyed her orders to the kitchen staff, a petty gesture of defiance. She made a mental note to deal with the vixen later; she had no time at the present. The hetman, or overseer, of the village, Master Niall, would be waiting.

Madrigal nodded, saying softly, "Yes, Lady," although she would never have complained. *It is not my place*, she thought. *I have no wish to make trouble. Allah has been kind thus far; it is best to avoid angering anyone, the lowly or the high.*

Cathelin left the chamber, cutting a magnificent figure in her embroidered tunic and boots, braids of dark red hair framing her handsome face. She did not even bother to carry a light sword; unarmed, the Irishwoman would be more than a match for a man her own size.

✦ The Sunne in Gold ✦

After she left, Madrigal busied herself going through the contents of the clothes chests, sorting and evaluating the numerous tunics, breeks, hose, shirts, vests, and other items of apparel. Some, like a breastband that was heavily stained and full of holes, she laid aside–these would be given to Mistress Meagan to be cut up as rags. Others, like a gorgeous teal blue tunic with intricate silver thread knotwork that had been picked in places, she put in a pile to be mended.

As she worked, Madrigal softly hummed an old romantic air she had heard played often in the harem by blind eunuch musicians. A tray of food, bearing a loaf of still warm bread, cheese and a slice of tender lamb, came and was devoured. As the child within her grew, Madrigal knew that she would be eating more and more; she hoped that she could gather up the courage to tell the Lady of her condition before it became too obvious.

CHAPTER FOUR

It was late afternoon before Madrigal was satisfied with her work. The enormous clothes chest had been organized to a fault, and all the mending had been done, except for the teal-blue tunic; she would have to ask the Lady for silver thread before that job could be finished. Madrigal had also strewn the chest with bundles of dried lavender gotten from Mistress Meagan, both to sweeten the clothing and to keep away devouring moths.

Then the Muslim woman had bustled about the room in a flurry of cleaning and dusting. As a final touch, she emptied the cressets that hung on the walls of their burden of ash–the pierced iron vessels provided both warmth and light, were far cheaper than candles and cleaner than rushlights–and scrubbed away their coating of soot and rust.

Now, Madrigal sat quietly, trying to finger-comb tangles from her incredibly long hair. A carved horn comb stood on the Lady's table in front of a bronze mirror, but the Muslim girl did not want to use it without permission.

✦ The Sunne in Gold ✦

During her cleaning frenzy, Madrigal had removed her fine new dress and worked naked, it being easier to remove dirt from skin than cloth. She had also ventured from the confines of the Lady's chamber; although she had both dreaded and feared her reception, the other servant's had, at the least, been distantly polite. It was clear that her new status in the household had become common knowledge by some mysterious means.

In truth, that was Mistress Meagan's doing. Before Cathelin had left, she had drawn the Scottish woman aside and told her to make sure that everyone at Inishowen understood–Madrigal was her personal servant and ranked as a lady's maid; anyone who offered her offense because of her former enslavement would face Cathelin's wrath. Meagan had gleefully done as she was bid, smiling broadly after seeing the crestfallen expression on Sorcha's face.

After gathering a basin of cold water and quickly sluicing off the worst of the dirt, Madrigal had put her dress back on and sat, patiently waiting for her Lady.

Smiling to herself, Cathelin entered the door of her private chamber and stopped dead in her tracks.

When she had left that morning, the chamber had been, frankly, a mess. And it had not smelled very pretty, either; the lidded pot behind the screen in a corner had not been emptied, the fireplace had been full of clinkers and ash, the cressets emitting a feeble light at best. The fine tapestries that hung on the stone walls to keep out the cold were full of dust and spider-webs; the chairs strewn with bits of clothing; the floor filthy and full of trash.

Now, Cathelin's amber gold eyes were wide with amazement. It was, as if in her absence, a miracle had been wrought.

The floor was not only clean, but sported a few bright rag rugs; the room smelled of lavender instead of stale piss; the cressets gleamed; even the furniture had been given a good coating of beeswax. Madrigal sat by the fireplace, her dark eyes shining.

Gracefully, Madrigal rose and crossed to Cathelin. "Are you pleased, my Lady?" she asked shyly, lowering her eyes.

Madrigal was stunned when Cathelin placed a gentle kiss on her forehead and whispered, "More than pleased, sweetling."

Cathelin put her arm around the smaller woman's shoulders and gestured. "'Tis nothing short of amazing, Madri. I should make *you* the chatelaine; at least, you've proved you have no fear of hard work."

Madrigal's heart almost burst with pride. Searching for something to say to keep this moment from ending, she replied, "All your clothing has been mended and aired, my Lady. But I need silver thread to fix one tunic; the knotwork has come undone in many places, and it cannot be mended until I have it."

Cathelin gave her a friendly squeeze. "Ask Meagan in the morning," she said. "Surely we've a bit of silver thread squirreled away somewhere. Ah, you've done a fine job here, sweetling. I feel as if I'm truly at home, instead of dwelling in a pigsty."

The Irishwoman let her arm drop away from Madrigal's shoulders and crossed to the other side of the room where a long oak table served as a desk; unlike many of her peers, Cathelin could both read and write in Latin, and preferred to do her own correspondence instead of relying on the services of a paid scribe or priest.

The account book for Inishowen was there; all her papers had been neatly stacked, and a new quill sharpened for her use. As Cathelin sat down, Madrigal immediately appeared at her elbow with a mazer of spiced wine; the square metal goblet, set with chunks of amethyst, was

✦ The Sunne in Gold ✦

Cathelin's favorite and had been hers since she was a teenager.

Cathelin nodded her thanks and began to write a letter to Sir Alan Eoghain, one of her neighbors; she would write letters to all the nearby lords, hoping she could hammer out agreements to take any surplus stores they might have at the end of the harvest in exchange for future favors.

As she labored, Cathelin unconsciously rubbed the back of her neck; the muscles were rigid with tension and fatigue. Niall had been pessimistic; the fields had been allowed to lay half fallow, a quarter of the new calves had been lost due to disease brought on by fouled water, and the vegetable harvest, planted nearly too late, would be scanty at best.

Cathelin tensed when she felt someone creep up directly behind her, but within a heartbeat she knew it was Madrigal. Soft but strong hands glided across her shoulders. Cathelin held her breath as those hands began rubbing, gently but firmly, skillfully teasing the knotted muscles into relaxation.

Madrigal massaged her Lady's neck and shoulders, softly humming to herself. She had noticed the Irishwoman's discomfort, and, wanting to be as thorough in her duties as possible, decided to massage away her mistress' pain. It was something she had been taught as a child, when she was a servant in the household of a physician.

Cathelin closed her eyes and bit back a groan, as Madrigal's hands kneaded the stiff muscles in her neck. She let her head fall forward, letter forgotten, as little by little, the wire-tight tension she had felt all afternoon faded beneath the Muslim girl's ministrations.

Cathelin was acutely aware of how close Madrigal was to her; even through the linen tunic, she could feel the other woman's body heat against the skin of her back. Finally, however, the massage ended; those wonderful hands slid away, and Cathelin was left relaxed, but with a different sort of tension coiling in her lower belly.

Firmly, the Irishwoman thrust that thought away. Madrigal had been a pleasure slave; no one knew better than she how such wretched girls were treated. Cathelin would never force herself on an unwilling woman, especially one who believed she had no choice and would submit out of fear. *Better to sleep in a cold bed*, Cathelin thought, *than hurt the poor girl any further.*

Besides, she thought, *if it's company I'm needing, there are a few down in the soldier's barracks who'd be happy to share a jug of wine and a tumble with me.* Cathelin found herself thinking about a freckle-faced kern, with short cropped hair, a beautiful smile, and the nicest heart shaped arse she had ever seen. *What was her name? Aoife*, Cathelin thought with a mental purr.

Cathelin stood abruptly and stretched. "Er, Madri?" she asked, turning around. "I'll be off now. You can eat in the kitchens, if you like, or else have a tray fetched up. Don't wait up for me, sweetling. Take to bed when you've a mind."

Madrigal stopped trying to work a particularly difficult tangle from her blue-black hair. "Yes, Lady," she answered. "Have you found another place you wish me to stay?"

Cathelin was startled for a moment. "Well," she began, "I've been a wee bit busy of late, but if it's another bed you're wishing for, I can —"

Madrigal interrupted shyly, "No, Lady. Do not trouble yourself. Please, I am content."

Cathelin shrugged. She did not mind sharing a bed; she had done it before, and with lice-ridden men, too, in Outremer. "Whatever you wish." She watched Madrigal trying to pick out the knot in her hair, then scooped up the wooden comb from the dressing table. "Here, lass. This may

♦ The Sunne in Gold ♦

work better," Cathelin said, handing the comb to the other woman.

Madrigal took it tentatively, then bestowed such a beautiful smile on the astonished Irishwoman that her heart nearly stopped. "Thank you, Lady," Madrigal murmured.

Cathelin cleared her throat. "I'll be off now. Don't stress yourself too much, Madri. You still need to rest."

Madrigal bowed her head in acknowledgement, and Cathelin left, relieved to be away from the slave girl's presence. *Saint Brigit,* Cathelin thought, hurrying to the soldier's barracks. "Glad I am to have her here," she said softly to herself, "but when the Good Lord spoke of temptation, I truly believe he had no idea."

Madrigal went down to the kitchens and met Shevaughn, Chief of the Hearth. She was an enormously tall woman and nearly as broad, with a round, red face and a booming laugh. Some of the other servants treated Madrigal coolly–in fact, Sorcha ostentatiously took her wooden bowl of stew and left the room with a sniff as Madrigal sat down–but at least, no one dared offend her outright.

Shevaughn was frankly astonished at Madrigal's command of English. "An' ye've been in this country only a few years?" she asked, absently smacking a pot boy as he tried to sneak a meat pastry from the cooling rack.

"Yes, Mistress," Madrigal answered. "On the boat from Palestine, my former master insisted that I learn his language as quickly as possible." Privately, Madrigal thought that being lashed each time she made a mistake was a good incentive to learn quickly.

Shevaughn shook her head, jowls wobbling. "Sweet Jesus," she said. "Ye've a good head on yer shoulders, lassie. No doubt, the Lady thinks the same. But here I am, natterin' on like a lack-wit. Eat, child. Eat."

Madrigal finished the meal in silence, and Shevaughn, noticing her appetite, dished up seconds and even thirds without being asked. When the Muslim girl offered a shy compliment, the hearth chief swelled with pride. "I can see ye appreciates good cookin' when ye sees it, lassie. Yer welcome in my kitchens anytime." Shevaughn glared fiercely at the other servants, obviously daring them to contradict her.

No one did; Shevaughn was as feared in her smoky realm as Cathelin was on the battleground. Only last year, a drunken kern of Francis' had tried to roughly woo the hearth chief in her own domain; there was still a gouge on the heavy oak kitchen door where she had pinned him to it with an accurately thrown knife.

Shevaughn beamed at Madrigal. "Ye see? My folk likes ye as well."

Madrigal choked back a chuckle. Rising gracefully, she replied, "Many thanks, Mistress, for the meal and the company. Now, I must return to the Lady's chambers and await her return."

Back upstairs, Madrigal removed her cherished dress and pulled on her nightshirt, wishing Cathelin were there to change her bandages. The cuts on her back were no longer as painful, but every time she moved, the Muslim girl could feel the fragile skin stretching uncomfortably.

At last, covering the cressets with their wrought iron lids and banking the fire, Madrigal pulled the wolfskin cover off the bed and slipped between the cool sheets. It was not too long before she fell into a deep sleep.

✦ The Sunne in Gold ✦

Sorcha left her bowl of stew on a cabinet as she left the kitchen, her presence gone unnoticed by the others. Having that little eastern whore behave as if she were the Lady of the Manse was more than she could stomach.

Aye, and when I've come into my own at last, she thought angrily, *t'will be the heathen slavey that's first to go.* The blonde chatelaine patted her pocket, the faint rustling of the parchment note giving her a pleasant sense of anticipation. When Francis took his rightful position, he promised she would be at his side. Then these wretched, disrespectful servants would learn what it was to have a *true* Lady at their helm. All she had to do was find Blacksunne's weak spot.

Sorcha's eyes narrowed into thoughtful slits. Cathelin seemed quite fond of her Muslim slavey. Overfond, perhaps.

A faint smile curved her lips. Perhaps the heathen slut would prove useful after all.

Cathelin reeled up the stairs, her tunic slung over one muscular shoulder. In one hand, she held an nearly empty wine jug; with the other, she supported herself against the stone wall as she bumped from stair to stair. Cathelin O'Cameron was drunk as an earl, sated on both wine and love.

♦ Nene Adams ♦

Sweet, sweet Aoife, Cathelin mused. The guardswoman had been quite enthusiastic to the idea of a tumble in the hayloft above the stable, and Cathelin was sure she would still be picking straw out of strange places come morning.

The Irishwoman staggered into the darkened bedchamber, striking her shin against a table leg. Cursing, she lost her balance and stumbled across the room, arms windmilling, the wine jug forgotten until it landed with a crash against the hearth, and, finally, she fell over a chair with a bump and a vile oath.

Madrigal sat up, clutching the sheet to her bosom. In the dim light from the banked embers of the fireplace, she could see Cathelin sprawled over a chair, clutching her aching leg in both hands and swearing softly.

Madrigal hastily got out of bed and stirred up the fire, lighting a cresset with a flaming splinter of kindling. That done, she hurried to Cathelin's side. "Lady?" she asked, "are you hurt? Ill?"

Cathelin grinned at her crookedly. Her dark crimson hair was unbound and sprinkled with bits of hay; the exposed skin of her torso was blotched and sweaty. With a start, Madrigal realized the purpling bruise on one breast was a love-bite, and she blushed.

Cathelin crooned, "Pretty, pretty Madri." She gave the astonished and embarrassed slave girl a wink. "Have some wine, sch… sch… sweetling. S'good wine. S'over there, I'm thinkin'. By're Lady!" she exclaimed, looking mournfully at the shattered wine jug on the hearth, "What a waste; and a good swallow left, too."

Madrigal realized with a sigh that her Lady was drunk. She stood and put one of Cathelin's arms around her shoulders, pulling the inebriated Irishwoman up with an effort that left spots dancing in front of her eyes. *Allah!* Madrigal thought, nearly wheezing. *She's as heavy as a she-camel.*

♦ The Sunne in Gold ♦

The two women staggered over to the bed, Madrigal's face red with strain, and Cathelin softly slurring a bawdy song under her breath. Finally, Madrigal managed to get Cathelin seated on the edge of the bed and knelt down to remove her boots.

After tugging on one boot unsuccessfully, Madrigal sat back with an exasperated sigh. Cathelin chuckled. "Nay, Madri. That's no how it's done. Turn around an' grab it from behind."

Madrigal did as she was bid, straddling Cathelin's outthrust leg and bending over, the boot held tightly in both hands. With a start, she felt Cathelin's other boot on her backside.

"Now, lassie, pull," Cathelin shouted, giving the Muslim woman's buttocks a shove. The boot popped off, and Madrigal nearly fell face-first into the floor, only avoiding disaster by catching herself with her hands. The scene was repeated for the second boot, and Madrigal hastened to untie Cathelin's dirty hose and remove her loincloth. The Irishwoman did not make this an easy task; she lolled on the bed, giggling and singing to herself, while Madrigal sweated and struggled.

After much effort, and not a few Arabic curses muttered under her breath, Madrigal finally got Cathelin settled beneath the sheets and banked the fire again, smothered the cresset, and lay her Lady's clothes neatly on top of the clothes chest. At last, the weary slave girl climbed into her own side of the bed and lay awake for a while, listening to Cathelin's soft snores.

Sleep, when it finally came, would be all too brief.

◆ Nene Adams ◆

CHAPTER FIVE

Cathelin dreamed.

Thick clouds of dust swirled over the battlefield, obscuring the hot yellow sun. The screams of horses rivaled the hoarse pleas of wounded men as the battle raged, twin smells of blood and bowel-stench heavy in her nostrils.

Blacksunne wielded her mighty broadsword with skill and hatred. The siege of Acre had broken; the desperate Saracen army had poured from the walls, wailing and shrieking to their god, each one determined to die on the battlefield to secure his place in the heathen Paradise.

To Cathelin, it seemed as if a red haze obscured her vision. Only four days ago, her lover Irizin had died in her arms, tortured and beaten to death by her master. Each one of the men who died, spitted on her blade, bore the face of Irizin's murderer. Behind the visor of her war helm, her teeth were gritted, face a mask of murderous rage as she swept

♦ **The Sunne in Gold** ♦

through the Saracen ranks, leaving a path of utter destruction in her wake.

One after another, they came, and one after another they died. She lost count of the men she killed; she battled in a trance of insane blood lust, lopping off heads and limbs with an almost casual skill that left even her own allies chilled with fear.

At last, she wrenched off her helm, crimson hair nearly black with sweat and filth. She took a waterskin from her squire, Thomas, and squirted the lukewarm water over her face and head. The battle was over; two thousand seven hundred Muslim prisoners had been taken, and the city of Acre belonged once again to the Crusaders.

With indifference, she noticed that her broadsword's blade was clotted with blood and notched all along its length from the violence of her blows. Thomas handed her a cloth, and she began to wipe down the steel. Cathelin felt detached; it was as if all her emotions, having been caught up in a whirlwind of hate and fury, had subsided completely, leaving her empty and drained of all.

A figure strode through the swirling dust; it was King Richard, his own once-gleaming armor of blue steel fouled and dull. He pushed back his visor, revealing the handsome Plantagenet face; his blue eyes were dark with exertion, but an inner fire burned there. Unlike some Crusaders, Richard fought, not for personal gain, but for the glory of God.

"The Saracens would not surrender; they asked for no quarter, and none shall be given. When you have rested a while, O'Cameron, come join the other men. Every one of the prisoners will die, as a gesture to Saladin that we shall brook no denial of our quest–to free Jerusalem, or to die." Richard's voice was deep and self-assured; the King doubted nothing, his faith in God rock firm.

♦ Nene Adams ♦

Cathelin nodded her acceptance. "Aye, Your Majesty," she rasped. "Kill them all. Let God Almighty sort them out."

Richard chuckled. "Then I take it you will have no difficulty serving your term on executioner's duty?"

Having gotten the blade cleaned to her satisfaction, she rammed the broadsword back into its scabbard and looked at her King for the first time. Even he, the bravest man in Christendom, flinched back from the flames that twisted and burned in Cathelin's amber eyes. "Count on it, my liege," she said huskily, and her lips stretched over her teeth in a wolf's hungry grin. "Just as soon as I sharpen my sword."

The Muslim prisoners died–by the dozens, by the hundreds, and by the thousands. Several priests from Richard's own household went down the endless line, asking each prisoner if he would renounce his heretical faith and join his destiny with the Christian God. None did, but it would not have saved them anyway. The King was determined that every Saracen would die; if any had converted, they would have been shriven before execution to ensure their place in Heaven.

Day wore into evening, then into night, and into morning again, and the battlefield outside the city was soaked in blood, strewn with the bodies of the dead. Vultures had already begun their work when Cathelin took up hers; the broadsword of the O'Camerons rose mechanically up and down as she mowed through the line of kneeling prisoners, neatly beheading each one. When her aching arm could lift the sword no more, she stopped, panting, face speckled with blood, and turned back, her smile of savage satisfaction dying.

Her amber eyes widened as she looked...

At the headless bodies sprawled on the ground, some still quivering.

✦ The Sunne in Gold ✦

At the faces of the men who had not yet died. Some had clearly accepted their fate and waited with dignity; others babbled prayers and pleaded with Allah for mercy. Some were mere boys, not yet bearded, while others were wrinkled and brown, dark hair sprinkled with gray.

At her fellow knights, who drank and laughed and mocked the death throes of the Muslims, making faces and telling jokes, spitting and reviling, each one trying to outdo the other in cruelty and vicious humor.

At King Richard, who knelt, hands clasped, eyes closed, as he prayed for God to lend him strength for the coming battle, and to speed the souls of the heretic Outremer Saracens to Hell.

The enormity of what she had done finally struck Cathelin like a hammer blow. Her senses reeled as long-denied emotions rushed to the fore–guilt for Irizin, guilt for her own slaughter, sorrow and bitter rue; her hand clutched the hilt of her broadsword convulsively. Unable to stand, she fell to her knees; her heart ached and burned, throbbing in her chest like a wound. She was a soldier; her duty was to kill at the King's command, but she had become a butcher, no better than the man who had ordered Irizin's death.

She had killed those men like cattle, men helpless and bound, and, against all her oaths of chivalry and knightly vows. She had not only done the deed, but she had *enjoyed* it, reveled in death and the taste of hate, laughed in the depths of her soul as the blood of her enemies, heady as wine, flowed across her lips, a sweet, coppery taste she could still sense in her own mouth.

She could not deny any longer. On her knees, the sword of her family lying forgotten in the blood-drenched dust, Cathelin wept like a child for the loss of life, wept for the sheer waste of it all, wept for her butchered Irizin, and at long last, wept for her own lost innocence.

♦ Nene Adams ♦

Madrigal was wakened by a whimper from the woman who lay next to her. Propping herself up on an elbow, the Muslim girl carefully leaned over, trying to see if the Lady was ill from her drinking bout.

Cathelin's head thrashed on the flat pillow, face greasy with sweat. Madrigal could see her eyes rolling beneath the closed lids, and Cathelin's fists clutched the sheets in a deathgrip.

"No," Cathelin whispered, panting in desperation, "Not again. No more. Please."

Ah, Madrigal thought, *the Lady rides the Night Mare, and from the sound of it, the journey is not a pleasant one.*

Madrigal's heart swelled with compassion and she suddenly felt close to tears. To see one as mighty as the Lady suffer, caught helplessly in the grip of evil dreams, roused the slave's pity. Although she had known Cathelin only a very short time, already Madrigal felt an enormous sense of trust. It was as if she had discovered a thing she had already known, something that had lain just out of reach in her former life, but was now within her grasp, if only she dared reach out her hand.

With great daring, praying to Allah that her trust had not been misplaced, Madrigal began to croon a lullaby in Arabic, one she had learned as a child, and with her hand, traced lazy patterns on the Irishwoman's brow.

"Come, little one," Madrigal sang softly, "the evening draws near. Come, little one, and have no more fear. Climb up in your bed, and lay down your head, while I sing the western wind away."

♦ The Sunne in Gold ♦

That simple song had more effect than Madrigal could have ever hoped for. Cathelin calmed; her breathing evened out and grew more regular, her hands relaxed their hold on the sheets. The battleground of Acre faded, and she slipped back into true sleep, nightmare visions soothed away.

Madrigal continued to sing until she was sure that the other woman was no longer plagued by the Horse of Evening Ill. She withdrew her hand and settled back on her side, listening to Cathelin breathe.

She had nearly fallen asleep herself when she felt a long, muscular form mold itself to her back. Cathelin snuggled up against Madrigal with a sigh of pure contentment, putting one arm around the Muslim girl's belly and drawing her legs up against the other woman's. Madrigal's eyes widened when she felt Cathelin's face buried in her hair, warm breath against the back of her neck.

The dark-haired woman tried surreptitiously to free herself, but her efforts only caused Cathelin to mutter restlessly and tighten her grip. Madrigal gave up and closed her eyes, feeling warm, cherished and oddly comforted by the closeness of her Lady.

When Madrigal woke the next morning, Cathelin was seated at her desk, eating a meat pastry and scratching on a bit of parchment with a quill pen.

A pair of servants entered, rolling the wine cask tub along the floor. After they set it up in a small alcove, a seemingly endless parade of servants trooped in, carrying buckets of steaming water, which they emptied smoothly, spilling not a drop. In a little while, the tub was full; one final servant scattered a double handful of dried herbs across the surface of the water, laid out a clay jar of soft soap, linen rags, a small bucket of hulled oats, and a copper dipper. He then departed, leaving the two women alone.

Cathelin put down her pen and stood, stretching with the boneless grace of a cat. Madrigal gulped when she saw the muscles rippling beneath the surface of the Lady's smooth skin. Cathelin was nude; sunlight struck sparks from her dark crimson hair, and the fiery curls between her thighs glowed like rubies. The sight dazzled the slave into speechlessness.

"Well, the lay-abed's finally awake, eh?" Cathelin asked with a smile, amber eyes twinkling. "You'd better hurry, lazybones, or the water'll be colder than a witch's tit."

Cathelin had wakened with the Muslim girl cuddled in her arms. For the life of her, she could not remember if "something" had happened or not. She had lain awake a long time, studying the other woman's features–sweet, heart-shaped face, delicate cheekbones and chin, and a nose straight from a Grecian urn. The angle of Madrigal's jaw made her profile as clear as a line of flame, and just as hypnotic.

The few locks of blue-black hair that feathered across her face made her creamy skin seem even paler. Madrigal was, quite simply, the most stunningly beautiful woman Cathelin had ever seen, and she hoped fervently that she had not done Madrigal an injury; Cathelin was feeling a little nervous as she waited for the other woman's reaction.

The Irishwoman walked over to the bed and handed Madrigal a flaky pastry. "Here. Eat this, sweetling. Then you can wash and soak a while with me." Cathelin watched carefully for any sign of repugnance or fear, but Madrigal sat up and took the pastry with a smile of thanks, and Cathelin breathed a silent sigh of relief.

The smell of the pastry in her hand was, at first, appealing. But suddenly, the scent turned Madrigal's belly inside out. Dropping the meat pie, Madrigal stumbled off the

◆ **The Sunne in Gold** ◆

bed and fell to her knees beside the chamber pot, heaving and retching convulsively.

Cathelin was instantly at her side, pulling back the Muslim girl's long hair and supporting her. "What's wrong, Madri?" Cathelin asked anxiously. "'Tisn't pig, you know." *May God damn me for a selfish swine myself,* she thought savagely, *if 'tis aught that I've done to provoke this.*

Just the thought of pork, the forbidden meat of her faith, made Madrigal's stomach rebel again. She retched helplessly, acrid taste of bile making her even sicker. Finally, though, just when she thought she would die, the nausea eased. Madrigal sat back on her heels, wiping her mouth with one hand, the other clutching her stomach.

Cathelin tenderly wiped her face with a damp linen rag. "Are you well again, sweetling?"

Madrigal nodded, not trusting herself to speak. She put her hand on Cathelin's arm and tried to rise, but the Irishwoman prevented her.

"No, no, sit here a while 'til it passes. Did I..." Cathelin hesitated to ask the question that was burning inside her. Taking a deep breath, she said, "Did I do something to you last night, Madri? Quite the head I had, and when I woke up..." Her voice trailed off. She could not continue.

Madrigal looked at the Lady, dark eyes filled with an expression of puzzlement. "Do, Lady? You came in and hit your leg, the wine jug was broken, and I helped you into bed. That is all I know." Privately, Madrigal did not want the Lady to know that she had seen her riding the Night Mare. It would embarrass the warrior to know that her vulnerability had been witnessed, so Madrigal vowed to keep silent on the matter.

Cathelin was relieved again, but now she found herself concerned about the cause of Madrigal's illness. "Good. Now, I know you've not eaten this day, unless you raided the kitchens in the night, which I doubt. Here, rinse out your mouth," she said, handing Madrigal her own mazer of clean spring water. As the slave girl did as she was told, spitting the water into the chamber pot, Cathelin continued, "So it can't be tainted food or poison. Unless... What did you eat for supper?"

Madrigal whispered, "Stew. Like the others."

"And you had nothing special? Mind you, Madri, I'll not be angry. I know Shevaughn too well." *And Sorcha*, she added silently. "Give her half a chance, and she'll stuff you like a Solstice goose." Cathelin helped Madrigal back to her feet and kept one arm around the smaller woman, who swayed. "No, Lady. I had the same as the others." Madrigal put a hand to her forehead and closed her eyes as dizziness swept through her. She truly did not feel well at all.

Cathelin shook her head. "Well, I confess to being baffled, sweetling. I'll have one of the men run down to the Abbey; Brother Ignatius is a fine apothecary. I'd trust him afore I'd trust anyone else. P'raps you've only eaten too much and made yourself sick by it, but I'd rather be sure."

Madrigal weakly protested, but Cathelin was firm. "'Tis the same as I'd do for any who look to me, Madri. I've made up my mind, and what's done is done. Now, do you feel well enough for your bath?"

Madrigal nodded, feeling exhausted and not a little apprehensive. She knew full well why she had gotten sick; she had suffered from morning illness nearly every day, sometimes even into the afternoon, when the child first began to grow. She had hoped to be past that time, but it was obvious that Allah had not yet finished with his trials. *And I pray this priest of the Christ is not as learned as the Lady believes*, Madrigal thought fervently.

She knew it would not be much longer before her pregnancy was obvious, but she wanted to put off telling her Lady as long as possible. *Once the Lady sees how well I perform my duties*, Madrigal thought, *then perhaps her wrath will be softened.* She did not really fear being killed any

♦ **The Sunne in Gold** ♦

longer; instead, she hesitated to place another burden on the already heavy load she knew her Lady carried on her broad shoulders. To know that a child conceived of the hated Lord Francis dwelled beneath Inishowen's roof. Well, such a child could be the focus of the Lord's further ambitions.

No, it was best to keep silent and wait, Madrigal decided. *No need to concern my Lady now.*

The master's chamber was so large that the tub sat by itself in splendid isolation in an alcove, steam rising in wisps from the enormous oaken cask. Cathelin steered Madrigal to the tub and helped her off with the nightshirt, carefully peeling away the stained bandages on her back, but stopped Madrigal from getting in.

"Nay, sweetling. Wash first, then soak. Here, I'll help you." Cathelin dipped hot water from the tub and poured it over Madrigal's shoulders, then scooped up a little soft soap from the jar onto a linen rag and sprinkled a bit of oats over it. When Madrigal looked curiously at this ritual, Cathelin explained, "The oats'll help scrub off the dirt. 'Tis marvelous good for the skin."

Madrigal stood absolutely still as Cathelin rubbed the rag across her shoulders, scrubbing gently, her touch dispassionate yet caring at the same time. Down her back, mindful of still tender scabs; across both small, firm buttocks; massaging the backs of her thighs, the sensitive hollows of her knees. Madrigal closed her eyes as tiny ripples of pleasure flowed through her with each firm glide of the slippery cloth. Then she shuddered as Cathelin dipped more hot water and let it cascade over the other woman, rinsing away soap and oats and grime.

Madrigal gasped when Cathelin poked her with one finger. "Here, Madri," Cathelin said, her face expressionless. "You can wash your own front; I need to wash my own self afore the water turns cold."

♦ Nene Adams ♦

Cathelin turned her back as she began her own scrubbing. The Irishwoman's heart was pounding. She had meant to be kind and helpful, but had found herself growing increasingly aroused by Madrigal as she had washed her.

The Muslim girl's skin was like velvet, soft but with a firmness beneath that gave lie to her seeming fragility. Kneeling on the floor, ignoring the harsh stone beneath her knees, Cathelin had smelled the other woman, Madrigal's scent like honey and musk, and had felt her own desire roused to near fever pitch. She had to stop; Cathelin knew that if she had continued, the washing would have quickly turned to seduction, and she was determined to leave the former slave strictly alone.

I'll not force her, the red-haired woman thought. *She's been through enough as 'tis.* Cathelin scrubbed quickly, hoping the cool rush of air against her wet skin would help chill her ardor.

For her part, Madrigal was feeling both disappointed and relieved, but also a bit self-conscious. She washed herself, wondering why her Lady had stopped. *Perhaps I have done something to offend her*, Madrigal thought, and wondered what it could have been.

Then a revelation struck the Muslim girl. *Of course*, she thought, *I am blind. I am the servant here; it is not seemly that the Lady wash me as if I were her own child. I should be washing her. Foolish, foolish slave*, she chided herself, rinsing quickly. *Your ignorance of duty will be your downfall. Just because the Lady has been kind does not mean you may ignore her needs.*

Quickly, Madrigal asked, "Lady? Do you wish me to scrub your back?"

Cathelin stood stock-still and took a deep breath. She forced herself to calm. *Easy, woman*, she thought. *The girl's only trying to be helpful.* Cathelin said aloud, "Why, yes, Madri. Thank you kindly."

✦ The Sunne in Gold ✦

Cathelin handed the cloth to the Muslim girl, who eagerly began scrubbing Cathelin's back, hoping by enthusiasm to be forgiven for her lapse. Madrigal marveled at the scars on the other woman's skin; so many, and some had obviously been deep wounds, and yet her Lady had survived. That she was a great warrior, the slave had no doubt. But until this moment, she had not realized *how* great.

Madrigal felt a sudden flush of pride. She had heard it said that the status of the master reflects upon the slave; she had never felt this way herself, and had not truly understood what it meant until now.

To bask in the shadow of the mighty is a wondrous thing, Madrigal decided. *To know that I stand in the presence of one who has braved untold dangers, and faced death in battle, the greatest warrior in the world, and I am trusted with her very life. For does she not allow me to sleep in her bed, serve her food, be closer to her than any other living being? Truly, Allah has blessed His servant. This is a mistress I can be proud of serving.*

Little by little, Madrigal's confidence was trickling back. She made a mental vow to help her Lady as much as possible. *If I can draw away some of her burdens, then I will be a true servant – the Left Hand of the Master,* she thought, remembering the title given to slaves who were so trusted and loyal, they were given a status nearly equal to a family member, and at death, were honored by a place in their owner's own tombs.

Cathelin shuddered a little as Madrigal, in her newfound pride, scrubbed all the harder, seemingly determined to buff her mistress' skin until it gleamed. It was not painful; in fact, it was just the opposite. Finally, Cathelin could stand no more. "Thank you, Madri," she rasped, eyes closed tightly, "But I think my back can get no cleaner."

Madrigal smiled. "Yes, Lady," she replied as she rinsed Cathelin with dippers of hot water. "Now, we soak?"

♦ Nene Adams ♦

"*Yes.* We soak." Cathelin helped Madrigal into the tub and then climbed in herself, mentally thanking God that the heat of the water would conceal the flush of desire that covered her skin.

It became obvious that both women would not fit comfortably facing one another; with a sigh, Cathelin motioned for Madrigal to sit between her spread legs and rest her back against the taller woman's torso.

Madrigal leaned back, her head pillowed against Cathelin's neck. One of the Irishwoman's arms was around her waist, helping support her. Madrigal rested her arms on the sides of the wine cask, eyes closed and utterly relaxed, feeling a little drowsy.

Cathelin rested her chin on top of Madrigal's head, closing her own eyes. The water was hot enough that she felt herself beginning to relax; even with the other woman's closeness, the slide of skin against skin, Cathelin's breasts rubbing against Madrigal's back, the Irishwoman felt desire slipping away, replaced by calmer contentment.

They soaked a while, then, while the water was still warm, Cathelin asked Madrigal to wash her hair.

Delighted, Madrigal complied; then nothing would do but for Cathelin to wash Madrigal's own blue-black locks.

Madrigal's eyes were squeezed shut against the soapsuds dripping into her face, as Cathelin's fingers massaged her scalp. Then she heard the Lady's voice, amused: "Hold your breath, sweetling," and that was all the warning she received before Cathelin pushed her head beneath the water.

Madrigal came up sputtering, arms flailing wildly, fingers scrabbling to find purchase on the rough sides of the tub. *Drowning!* Fear and panic swept through the Muslim girl; she kicked out with her legs, whimpering and retching, all rational thought gone in the instinctive animal's struggle to survive.

✦ The Sunne in Gold ✦

In the first few seconds, Cathelin thought it was a jest, an excuse to get into a water fight. But the instant she realized Madrigal's distress was not a joke, Cathelin grabbed her, holding the thrashing woman tightly, ignoring the minor pain of nails raking across her shoulders, legs flailing wildly against her thighs. Madrigal tossed her head back and forth, strings of wet black hair clinging to her face. Her eyes were open but unseeing; she was panting with exertion and panic.

"Madri!" Cathelin said urgently, "Madri, you're safe! You're safe, sweetling. Softly, Madri, softly. Shhhh," the Irishwoman crooned, "You're safe now. I've got you."

Madrigal's hands tightened convulsively on Cathelin's shoulders as, with a shudder, she began to cry.

Cathelin held her for a moment, tucking the other woman's head against the side of her neck. *I'd better get the both of us out of this water before we catch our death of cold*, Cathelin thought.

Not loosening her grip on Madrigal, Cathelin gathered her legs beneath her and stood, powerful muscles uncoiling, sheets of water slopping over the side of the tub. She held Madrigal in her arms, carrying the slave like a child, while hot tears continued to scorch the skin of her neck.

Cathelin persuaded Madrigal to loosen her grip long enough to be wrapped in a dry sheet and tucked into a chair near the hearth. Ignoring the water droplets sprinkling her skin, Cathelin crouched down and built up the fire, tossing a few bundles of dried herbs on the wood to sweeten the smoke. Despite the summer day, the interior of Inishowen was a little chilly; the thick stone walls did not absorb heat very well.

Finally, Cathelin dried herself off briskly, then pulled on an old tunic, not bothering with underclothes or hose. She picked Madrigal up from the chair like a doll, and sat down, tucking the other woman in her lap.

♦ Nene Adams ♦

Madrigal's face was shiny with tears; wrapped in her linen sheet, soaking wet hair slowly drizzling a puddle on the floor, dark purple eyes rimmed with red, she looked as forlorn as a lost child.

Cathelin settled Madrigal's weight more firmly against herself, took one of the miserable girl's hands in her own, and sighed. "Well, if I'd know you'd take my jape so ill, sweetling, I'd never have done so. Surely you did not think I meant to drown you?"

Madrigal shook her head. Now that the panic attack was over, she felt nauseous, headachy and very much ashamed. "Forgive me, Lady," she whispered. "I, I," The Muslim girl shook her head again, her throat constricted by remembered fear.

"Tell me." Cathelin's voice held calm command; Madrigal looked into the Lady's amber gold eyes and realized that in this, she would not be denied.

Bowing her head to hide her shame, Madrigal did as she was bid. She began her tale with her new master, an English knight, purchasing her in Palestine.

"I was purchased by the Inglizi Lord from the Palestine slave market; the Chief Wife of the merchant prince I belonged to took exception to her husband's growing interest in me, and had me sold." Madrigal's voice was soft and steady, if a little rough from swallowing the bathwater; the hand still clasped in Cathelin's grasp was cool and dry.

Madrigal continued, "The Inglizi Lord kept me for a few days in Palestine. Then, we went to the ship which would take us to England." As the Muslim girl continued, still speaking calmly of the Inglizi's casual brutality, Cathelin's lips compressed into a tight line and her nostrils whitened in suppressed fury.

Madrigal spoke of daily beatings, whippings and rapes; the Inglizi had broken her ribs, smashed his fists into her face, kicked her savagely when she lay helpless on the

✦ The Sunne in Gold ✦

ground, retching in terror and pain. His methods when it came to teaching her English were equally brutal; each time she made a mistake, he whipped her with a pony lash until the blood ran.

"One day, I displeased the Lord. He had been drinking much; he was very angry that I had forgotten some small chore. The Lord decided that I needed to be taught a lesson."

And that was one lesson Madrigal would never forget. Hauling the weeping, pleading young woman by the wrists, the Inglizi had dragged her to the stern of the ship and ripped off her simple linen shift. Standing there naked, shivering in the wind, face wet with tears, Madrigal had been sure the Lord intended to offer her to the sailing men, who had prowled around the scene like animals close to being maddened by blood scent.

Instead, the Inglizi had something more diabolical and sadistic in mind. He had wrapped hempen rope around Madrigal's wrists, tying her bonds so tightly they drew blood. Then he drew back his leg and brutally kicked her off the stern.

Madrigal would never forget that horrible moment. Sailing through the air, all the breath driven from her lungs as the sea came up to meet her with a hammer blow. Being dragged behind the sailing vessel, helpless, twisting in her bonds, one minute below the ocean, the next above, in so much pain she would have screamed if she had been able, arms nearly wrenched from their sockets. In a state of absolute terror, she had gasped for air, inhaling seawater, which only made her panicked state worse. Finally, after a time, which had seemed an endless eternity in Hell, she had been hauled up like a fishing catch, dripping and half dead from near drowning and fear, and dumped back on the deck.

The Inglizi's eyes had betrayed his excitement as Madrigal had lain there, shivering, almost mindless with terror.

♦ Nene Adams ♦

Madrigal stopped speaking. She kept her eyes downcast, staring at the pattern of threads in the linen sheet that was wrapped around her.

Long minutes passed, broken only by the hoarse sound of Cathelin's breathing. Finally, Cathelin asked, "What's his name?"

Madrigal shivered. "I," she began, then stopped as a lump in her throat prevented speech. She had a superstitious dread of the Inglizi and thought he was an evil djinn; even the mention of his name might be enough to put her in his power again.

Cathelin's voice was as hard as the steel of her broadsword, and just as sharp. "Look at me."

Madrigal raised her head and stared into her Lady's eyes. They were molten pools of gold, so bright they dazzled. Cathelin said again, "What is his *name?*" The Irishwoman was very nearly in a killing rage; the only thing that prevented her from grabbing a sword from the wall and hacking the room apart was the thought that Madrigal needed comforting, not more fear. As she waited for a reply, Cathelin slowly disciplined herself to a calmer state.

Softly, praying that her Lady was strong enough to protect her, Madrigal replied, "Wallace. Alexander Wallace, my Lady."

Cathelin pulled Madrigal to her chest and held her tightly. "I'll make you a Solstice gift of his head, sweetling. That worm-riddled bastard doesn't deserve to breathe the same air as you." She gently kissed the Muslim woman on the forehead. "I may even go hunting afore Samhain. He'll no more hurt you, Madri. On my honor, I swear it."

She wanted to do nothing more than leap on the first horse and track this Wallace down, but schooled herself to wait. Cathelin had heard of him; he was reputed to be a mediocre swordsman, with a mean streak wider and longer than the road from Cork to Dublin. *I'll find him soon enough,*

♦ The Sunne in Gold ♦

the Irishwoman thought, *and I'll bury his worthless carcass face down and unshriven. Surely, if any go to a deserving Hell, 'twill be Alexander Wallace.*

Madrigal, greatly daring, put her arms around Cathelin's neck and laid her face against the other woman's throat. "Do not trouble yourself over me, Lady," she said. "I am well enough."

Roughly, Cathelin said, "No. If I had known…" She could not finish. Cathelin's heart was filled with pity, and more than that, for the sweet young girl she held in her arms. To have survived all that and not be made bitter by it was a matter of amazement and profound respect. Madrigal was far braver than many soldiers and knights Cathelin had met; she doubted any of her own kerns could have suffered so and survived.

They sat together, each taking comfort from the other's presence, listening to the sound of each other's heartbeats and the soft rhythm of their breathing.

Finally, Cathelin rose, cradling Madrigal in her arms. "Sweetling, I must go," she said regretfully as she carried the Muslim woman to the bed and set her down carefully. "I hope to be back afore the evening meal. In the meantime, you rest. I'll have someone run down to the Abbey and fetch Brother Ignatius."

Madrigal had forgotten about the holy man. "I feel much better, Lady," she said, hoping to forestall the monk's visit. "Perhaps it was only the rich food. I am not accustomed to such fare."

Cathelin snatched the old tunic over her head, dropping it on the floor, and pulled on a pair of dark brown knitted hose. "I'd feel better knowing Brother Ignatius looked at you anyway. Don't fret yourself, sweetling. He's a kindly old man who'll treat you like his favorite daughter, so there's no reason to be a-feared. " Cathelin felt Madrigal's protests were the result of her terrible experiences; she wanted to reassure the other woman that Ignatius was no threat.

Madrigal bowed her head in acceptance of the unavoidable. "Yes, Lady," she replied. "I will make the holy man welcome."

Cathelin quickly ran a comb through her dark crimson hair and braided it up into a long queue that fell down the middle of her back to her waist; then she drew on a light tan, sleeveless tunic, embroidered with running stags around the square neckline, armholes decorated with whipped leather stitches. The tunic exposed her lightly tanned, muscular arms, and the color contrasted sharply with the dark tattoo that snaked around her upper left bicep. On top of the tunic she put a simple leather vest, and pulled on her boots.

With a smile, Cathelin went to the door and opened it. "Be well, Madri," she said. "I'll try not to drink too much wine tonight."

Madrigal smiled in return as Cathelin left.

Sighing, the Muslim girl surveyed the watersoaked floor, the crumpled linens, the scattering of damp oats; unwinding the sheet that covered her, the Madrigal began her day's chores.

♦ **The Sunne in Gold** ♦

♦ **Nene Adams** ♦

CHAPTER SIX

Madrigal walked carefully down the winding stone stairs, holding up her skirts with one hand. It was another of her new dresses–pale green, the color of new leaves in the spring, and decorated with carved wooden buttons and dark gold ribbons threaded through the wide sleeves.

She had begun exploring her new world. Mistress Meagan had welcomed her help in the sewing room, where she and her circle of women wove, dyed and sewed the clothing that was used by the people of Inishowen; Madrigal had even been persuaded to go to the barracks by a friendly kern, to entertain the soldiers with songs.

In fact, they had given her a little harp to play on; it was her most treasured possession, aside from the necklace she had gotten from the Lady. She had also begun showing Shevaughn, the hearth chief, how to prepare some of the dishes of her former homeland using spices brought back by the Lady from her sojourn in Outremer.

♦ The Sunne in Gold ♦

Madrigal had begun to think of Inishowen as home. And with that thought, another came.

It had been three weeks since the monk's visit. Brother Ignatius, an ancient man with a fringe of silvery hair fluttering around his ears, had reminded Madrigal of a friendly bat–his enormous ears were nearly pointed and stuck out sharply on either side of his head; his beaky nose bent down at the end in an exaggerated curve.

Brother Ignatius had prodded and poked, muttering under his breath, and at last pronounced Madrigal with child. The Muslim woman had hastened to explain to the holy man about her circumstances, hoping against all hope that he would have compassion for her dilemma.

To her surprise, he had.

"I'll no be tellin' a soul, so dinna fash yersel'," Ignatius had said, blue eyes twinkling. "But ye'd best be thinkin' on how ta tell Lady Cathelin; ye'll be no more hidin' yer state, I'm thinkin', fer more than another month er two more."

He had given her a pouch of herbs to make into a tea, to combat the baby-ill in the mornings. Madrigal had to admit that they helped greatly in calming her stomach.

Unconsciously, her free hand went to her belly and she patted the growing bulge. *My child*, she thought, *Allah has been kind. Now, my happiness would be complete if only He would visit his vengeance on another.*

But she refused to finish the uncharitable thought. For the past three weeks, Sorcha O'Reilly had been intent on making the slave's life as miserable as possible. There were daily pranks, such as still-steaming horse droppings smeared on the bed after Madrigal had left the room to carry dirty sheets down to the laundry; or waiting until Madrigal had gone out on some errand and throwing rancid grease and stale piss all over the floor. That had taken the Muslim nearly four hours of hard, down-on-her-knees labor to clean up.

♦ Nene Adams ♦

Madrigal had no proof, but she was sure it was the chatelaine's doing. Without such proof, however, she had no intention of telling the Lady anything. *I do not want to destroy her faith in one of her servants*, Madrigal thought. *Not unless the evidence is unclouded, so that her judgment may be.*

The Lady's nightmares still plagued her; when they did, Madrigal sang to her softly until the journey was past. Each morning, the slave awoke with her Lady's arms around her, a cascade of bone-straight crimson hair blending with her own blue-black. Often, Madrigal would lay awake unmoving, cherishing those few moments of utter safety and comfort in the gray dawn.

The slave was so intent on her thoughts that she failed to notice the smear of shiny grease midway down the stairs until it was too late. Her foot slipped, throwing off her balance. With a cry, she fell forward, instinctively trying to roll into a ball to protect her precious burden, tumbling down the unforgiving stone stairs.

A blur of visions: flashes of stone; red-black sparks of pain; a servant's face seen upside down, his expression one of comical shock; the floor rising up in disjointed, nauseating leaps.

With a crack, the back of Madrigal's head struck the last step, sending an explosion of agony down her spine and then the peace of darkness and oblivion. The Muslim woman lay unconscious, a pitifully crumpled heap on the cold stone floor at the bottom of the stairs, blood staining the pale green dress she had worn so proudly a few moments before.

✦ The Sunne in Gold ✦

When Cathelin entered the Great Hall, she was whistling a jaunty tune, a brace of partridges slung over one shoulder. Her hair was half down, clothing ripped and stained, but her expression was one of triumph. She had gotten permission to hunt on one of her neighbor's lands, and her men had taken several bucks, wild boars and more. The meat was in the courtyard now being dressed, and Cathelin's mouth watered at the thought of a juicy haunch of venison for supper instead of mutton.

The Irishwoman stopped dead when she heard the voice of Mistress Meagan raised in a bellowed shout, "Dinna move her, ye lack-wits! Wait fer the litter, b'Christ!"

The partridges sailed through the air and fetched with a thump on the floor as Cathelin moved with inhuman swiftness to the source of that voice. At first, all she could see were the backs of the household servants standing in a rough semi-circle around something at the foot of the stairs; heart in her mouth, Cathelin roughly shoved them aside until she was clear and saw...

Madrigal. Unconscious and obviously badly injured. That sweet face was papery white, lips slightly blue, and her breathing was labored and raspy. Meagan squatted next to her, trying to assess the girl's injuries with hands that shook slightly.

Cathelin drew a deep breath and knelt down beside Madrigal. "What happened?" she asked Meagan, voice tightly controlled.

The Scottish woman did not look up from her delicate probing of Madrigal's skull. "I dinna know. One of the servants, Tom Swann, saw it happen. He says she just fell."

Cathelin's molten amber eyes narrowed and sought out the unfortunate witness; he gulped, prominent Adam's apple bobbing up and down. "Well?" she growled.

♦ Nene Adams ♦

Swann gulped again. "Aye, Lady," he said nervously. "'Tis as I told the Mistress. She was walkin' down the stairs, and all of a sudden-like, she just fell down. I swear it."

Meagan finished her examination. "The girl's skull's no cracked that I can tell, but she's had quite a fall. I've sent fer Brother Ignatius; she's got broke ribs and I don't know what all else. We'd best be careful."

Cathelin nodded agreement. "Where's that litter?" she asked the crowd in general, who gave a collective shudder at the tightly reigned rage in her voice. Almost immediately, a litter appeared, carried by two men.

Carefully, paying heed to Meagan's instructions and feeling their Lady's hot gaze on their backs, the men loaded the unconscious slave and began carrying her up the stairway. Halfway up, one of the men slipped and nearly fell, but caught himself in time to keep Madrigal from tumbling off the litter.

His ruddy face paled in fear as Cathelin flowed up beside him. She bent down and wiped one finger across the step; the expression on her face took on a wolfish appearance, lean and narrow and lusting for blood.

Not trusting herself to speak, Cathelin nodded for the men to continue, then caught Meagan's arm when the woman passed. "Grease," she said shortly.

Meagan caught her breath. "Sweet Mary and Joseph!" she whispered. "Who?"

Cathelin shook her head. "I don't know, but by God, I intend to find out. And when I do…"

Meagan shuddered at the promise of slow, agonizing death in Lady Cathelin's amber eyes. "The lass'll be all right," she said, patting the other woman's arm. "I'm sure of it."

Cathelin's expression was bleak. "She had better be," she replied harshly, then turned and walked up the stairs heavily, hands shaking and teeth clenched so hard her jaw hurt. *If anything happens to my Madri*, she thought savagely,

♦ The Sunne in Gold ♦

the tortures of Castille will not *equal what I'll be doing to whoever's responsible. Aye, and with my own hands, too!*

The servants watched their mistress with heavy hearts. Most of them had gotten to know the sweet Muslim girl, and although a few still disapproved, the majority had come to like her for her sunny ways and friendly smile. She was always willing to lend a hand at any task, had a way about her that was completely disarming, and the other servants prayed for her recovery with compassion and pity.

But one pair of cold green eyes watched with ill-concealed glee, and one pair of thin lips stretched into a tiny, triumphant smile.

Sorcha O'Reilly slipped out the postern gate behind Inishowen and ran through the kitchen garden to the stable. Once there, she coaxed a wild-maned mare to allow her to mount bareback, then she rode away, dark brown cloak flying back behind her like ragged wings.

Six miles away lay her destination—a cliff that overhung the pounding sea. The cliff face on the landward side was riddled with caves, and it was to one of these that she pounded up, the mare's sides flecked with foam.

Sorcha slid from the horse's back and ran lightly to the cave mouth. "My Lord?" she asked, peering into the darkness. "'Tis Sorcha."

A ragged figure appeared in front of her. Francis Westfield was no longer the spoiled, finely dressed lordling he had been. His beard had grown wild and straggled across his face; hazel eyes sunk deeply into bruised sockets; his frame had become gaunt, mere whipcord over bone. But his eyes burned with a mesmerizing fire–a look Sorcha recognized. It was the madness of a fanatic, and Lord Francis' hatred of his cousin had become an obsession that had pushed him well beyond the bounds of sanity.

"Well?" he rasped.

Sorcha drew a breath, excitement warring with fear in her breast. Since his exile, Lord Francis had become a figure of infinite fascination for the chatelaine; not the least because the vengeance he labored for had become her own. "'Tis done. The wench is dead."

"Good," Francis nodded. "How?"

Sorcha reached up and patted a blonde braid. "I greased a step. 'Twas a simple enough doing. It'll be thought an accident; all the castle knows how careless the chit was, popping up and down the stairs all blessed day."

Francis took a step forward and grabbed Sorcha's arm in a steely grip that made the woman shudder in pain and arousal. "And Cathelin?" he asked, tongue flicking out to moisten his dry lips.

"I wish you could have seen her face, my Lord. Why, she was paler than new curd, that one. Being deprived o' her bed wench should set the high and mighty Lady back a notch or two."

"Excellent." Francis roughly pulled Sorcha to his chest and kissed her savagely, deliberately hurting her, then released her with a sneer.

Sorcha stumbled back, one hand to her bloody lip. Her green eyes were dark with fear and desire. "Aye, my Lord," she said huskily, then flowed up to press her full breasts against him. "And how goes your own venture?"

Francis idly toyed with one of Sorcha's blonde braids. "Well enough," he replied. "I've gotten some like-minded men who agree that Blacksunne needs to be taken down. In a few months, we'll strike." His hazel eyes narrowed. "Are you sure the slave's dead?" he asked with mock casualness.

✦ The Sunne in Gold ✦

"Oh, still breathin' she was when I left, but I doubt that'll last for long," Sorcha replied airily, tilting her face back for another kiss.

Instead, Francis gathered her long braids in both of his hands and twisted them brutally, wringing a smothered yelp from the woman. "Did I not tell you to be sure?" he asked in a dangerously calm tone.

"Aye, my Lord, aye! But I came straight away to tell you." Sorcha's green eyes were filled with tears.

"Go back," he commanded, emphasizing each word with a yank, "Go back and make sure. That bitch has to die, do you hear me? She has to die!"

Francis reserved a small portion of his hatred towards the slave he considered had betrayed him. When Sorcha had first told him of how Madrigal had not only been freed, but raised to household status, he had nearly choked on bile; since then, the chatelaine's acidic reports of Cathelin's and Madrigal's growing closeness had made the flames of anger burn even hotter. Sorcha believed the two were lovers and so did Francis. The thought of his slave finding happiness in his cousin's arms was more than Francis could sanely bear.

If I could, he thought, ignoring the blonde woman's agonized protests, *I would take my little slave and teach her a few lessons in humility. Too bad she wouldn't live long enough to learn everything I want to teach her.*

"Please, my Lord!" Sorcha screeched, trying to fall on her knees but prevented by Francis' grip on her hair, "Please! I'll go, *I'll go!*"

Francis released her, and Sorcha fell to the ground, her head aching and scalp raw. "See to it, my beloved," he said with another sneer. "I want that heathen whore dead by nightfall."

"Aye, my Lord," Sorcha answered, rubbing the top of her head, "She'll not breathe another moment after I return. And then, shall I be coming to you again? P'raps tonight?"

♦ Nene Adams ♦

The blonde woman's voice held a note of eagerness; she relished Francis' lovemaking–it was violent and passionate, filled with a pain she found arousing beyond anything she had ever known.

Francis paused on his way back to the cave. Without turning around, he replied, "Yes," and then disappeared back into his sanctuary.

Sorcha climbed back aboard the mare, more determined than ever to see the slave girl buried and Cathelin writhing beneath a burden of hurt that could well nigh crush her. The chatelaine laughed softly to herself as she wrenched the mare's head around and started back to Inishowen. *Aye,* she thought, a small smile twisting her lips. *The Lady will know what it is like to be deprived of the one she loves this very night.*

The pounding of the mare's hooves echoed for a long time after Sorcha had gone, intent on her murderous errand.

Brother Ignatius' wrinkled face was grave as he wiped his bloody hands on a rag. "Aye, two broke ribs, but I bent 'em back and strapped 'em down, so that'll be no difficulty; should heal well. Skint up as well; like to have took off all the hide twixt knee an' hip. Her brain pan's no cracked, but she took quite a knock. The wee lass'll probably be out fer the day, at least. But," he added, blue eyes staring into Cathelin's amber, "there's more, an' it's no good news I'll be tellin'."

Cathelin stared at the still form on the bed and her mouth worked. After a moment, she rasped, "What is it?" Her face was pale and her hands clenched and unclenched at her sides.

♦ The Sunne in Gold ♦

Brother Ignatius studied the woman in front of him. "Sit ye down, Lady, an' have a swaller 'er two o' wine first."

Cathelin turned on the old monk, amber eyes blazing. "*Tell me*, damn you!" she shouted. "Or by Saint Brigit..."

Ignatius held up one hand. "Dinna threaten me with damnation, Lady. Do as I say, or not another word I'll be tellin' ye."

Infuriated almost beyond her control, and sick to her stomach at the sight of Madrigal's unnaturally pale face, Cathelin whirled around and threw herself down in a chair. Brother Ignatius padded over, brown robes swaying, and poured them both mazers full of wine from a nearby decanter.

He waited until she had taken a long swallow, then said, "Madrigal's with child. And very close to losin' it, she was. No all the blood on yon dress was on count o' her scrapes. But the bairn's secure for the nonce."

Cathelin stared at him in shock, the metal mazer clutched so tightly in her hand it creaked. Then she swallowed. "With, with child?" she stammered, trying to force her reeling brain to absorb the information. "But how?"

"The usual way, I'm supposin'," Ignatius chuckled. Then he patted Cathelin's hand. "I knew, o' course. When I come up afore to see to her belly-gripes, I could feel the bairn movin'; but the wee gal asked me to tell no one, includin' yerself."

Cathelin blinked. Rapidly, she brought up and rejected scenario after scenario of Madrigal dallying with one of the castle servants or even a kern. Suddenly, with a sinking feeling in the pit of her stomach, she *knew*. "Francis," she breathed.

"Aye. So Madrigal said." Ignatius took a gulp of wine and wiped his lips on one long sleeve. "'Tis my belief that the Good Lord was watchin' o'er her this day, but she's no out of danger yet, Lady. Rest is what the lass needs; she should no more be clamberin' up and down the stairs all day. Not until the bairn's born."

Cathelin's lips tightened. "May God *damn* you straight to Hell, Francis," she said aloud; then her face grew troubled. "Brother," she said, "why did she not tell me?"

Ignatius looked into Cathelin's eyes, the gold now clouded with pain. "As to that," he replied kindly, "I believe she meant to tell ye, Lady. But she was afeared."

"Afraid?" Cathelin shook her head, wild locks of dark crimson hair fluttering. "What has she to be afraid of? Surely she didn't think–"

"She knew how much ye hated Lord Francis, Lady Cathelin, may God forgive us both fer the thought."

Cathelin frowned, toying with the mazer. "But I cannot believe..." Her eyes abruptly filled with tears as the full depth of Madrigal's stressful situation struck her. "Oh, my poor Madri!" she exclaimed, biting back a sob. "All this time, and I never knew."

"Dinna fash yersel', Lady. The lass was happier these few weeks than I'd e'er seen afore. 'Twas your doin', no mistake."

Cathelin burst into fresh tears. Brushing past Brother Ignatius, she flung herself down on her knees next to the bed, taking Madrigal's small hand in her own. "Can you forgive me?" she pleaded quietly. "Please, *please*, wake up, sweetling." *I'm here*, she added silently. *Don't leave me.*

Brother Ignatius gathered his things and prepared to go. "While ye're down on yer knees, Lady, remember–a prayer or two won't hurt."

Cathelin nodded, still crying, as the old monk left. *I've been blind, so blind!* she castigated herself. *I knew something was troubling her and I did nothing!*

She remembered teasing Madrigal about her growing weight; although her frame was still slender, the Muslim had filled out some. Cathelin had noticed the growing bulge of the

♦ The Sunne in Gold ♦

other woman's belly, and put it down to rich foods and Madrigal's enormous appetite.

And all the while she was with child, Cathelin thought, berating herself for a fool. *What a burden to have to carry on her shoulders, and I, who should have been helping. I've been acting like a fornicating swine, I have, and 'tis a wonder and a marvel to me that Madri hasn't left my bed afore now.*

Although Cathelin had sternly resisted the urge to make her growing feelings of attraction evident to the other woman—she would not force herself on someone who was incapable, by her past slavery, of refusal—nevertheless, waking up in the morning with Madri snuggled in her arms had quickly become Cathelin's favorite part of the day.

She found herself thinking about the Muslim when she was outside the castle, hunting or harvesting, or helping her people; and her servants and kerns adored Madrigal, despite her faith and origins. *She's certainly made herself at home*, Cathelin thought, *and for that, I'm glad.*

And whenever she came home, Madri was always there with a smile, a cup of wine, and those delicate, thoughtful attentions; in fact, it had come to seem as if Madri was able to anticipate Cathelin's needs, always on hand instantly with whatever was required.

Aye, Cathelin thought, *she's very nearly my own right arm, she is. And I'll never forgive myself if she comes to harm.*

Tears streamed down Cathelin's face as she bent her head and humbly whispered a fervent prayer to God and Saint Brigit not to take Madri away.

Madrigal's eyelashes fluttered as she slowly rose from the well of darkness and into the light.

Gradually, she became aware that her hand was being held gently, that her Lady was there; she could hear the other woman's voice, whispering. Madrigal's free hand went instinctively to her abdomen and she was reassured by the still-bulging presence of her child.

"Lady?" she whispered.

Cathelin's face immediately swam into her vision as the Irishwoman leaned over her. "Madri?" she asked, a tentative smile lighting up her red-rimmed eyes. "How do you feel, sweetling?"

"Thirsty," the slave rasped, and a mazer of cool water was touched to her lips. Madrigal drank, the water sliding down her throat more welcome than the nectar of Paradise. The cup was taken away and she whimpered, wanting more, but Cathelin soothed her.

"No more, Madri. You'll be sick." Cathelin wiped Madrigal's face with a damp cloth. "You fell down the stairs, sweetling, and fetched your head and ribs quite a crack, but Brother Ignatius says you'll be fine."

Madrigal's head was pounding as if a horde of djinns had taken up residence and were tunneling through her skull. "I," she began, then gulped as a wave of nausea swept through her.

Cathelin hastily fetched a basin in time and supported the other woman while she retched helplessly. Laying Madrigal back down gently, Cathelin wiped her lips and perched carefully on the edge of the bed. "I know you're with child, Madri," the Irishwoman said simply. "Brother Ignatius told me."

Madrigal closed her eyes, feeling depleted and drained. At any other time, she might have been panicked, but now... She waited, her emotions exhausted, mind numb, head dizzy and throbbing with pain.

✦ The Sunne in Gold ✦

Cathelin took Madrigal's hand again and squeezed it carefully. "'Tis all right, sweetling. You've not lost your place here; I still want you," she hesitated a moment before finishing, " to serve me, if you'd like. You do still want to stay, don't you?" she asked anxiously.

Madrigal opened her dark eyes. Her long hair had been braided up loosely, and a few stray locks curled onto her cheeks. A tear trickled down her face. Her Lady was looking at her with those amazing amber gold eyes. "Yes," she whispered. "Yes, Lady, I want to stay."

Cathelin put the back of Madrigal's hand against her face. "Well, you're to rest, sweetling, at least for a few weeks. 'Twas a near thing on those damned stairs; you like to have lost the babe, and your life besides. So, no more cleaning, no more gallivanting about; stay in bed. All right?"

Madrigal nodded carefully. "Yes, Lady," she said. A warm glow suffused her soul; she felt like dancing, felt like singing, but the pain was too great for that now. She had no more fears–the Lady had spoken. She and her child were welcome in this place she had come to regard as home.

As Madrigal closed her eyes and sank slowly into the bliss of peaceful sleep, she felt her Lady's lips brush tenderly against her brow, and the slave smiled.

Cathelin walked downstairs to the dining area. The hall was vast, with high ceilings; the banners of her family's enemies hung on the walls, as well as their swords, axes, shields and spears. The long, T-shaped table was crafted of heart oak, so dark with age it seemed almost black in the uncertain light of rush torches in the iron cages that lined the stone walls.

Wolf McLeod was waiting for her. Her second in command bowed his head respectfully, murmuring, "Lady?" He was not quite as tall as Cathelin, but more powerfully built, as muscular as a young bull. A torc encircled his thick neck, the finialed ends set with cabochon beryls. He was dressed in a tartan kilt that exposed scarred knees, and a billowing-sleeved shirt beneath a leather vest. The vest was covered with bone buttons–they would not be enough to stop a sword blade, but would suffice to turn aside a knife thrust.

"Wolf, I have a task for you," Cathelin said as she joined her kern at the table and poured them both goblets of wine.

Wolf wet his lips with the spiced drink and waited politely.

Cathelin took a long swallow of wine. "You've heard of what happened to Madrigal earlier today?" When Wolf nodded, she continued, "Well, what's not generally known is that the step was greased."

Wolf raised a black eyebrow at this information, and rumbled in his deep, gravelly voice, "Assassin?"

"Aye." For a moment, Cathelin's amber eyes flared with anger, but she immediately regained control. "I want the one responsible found. And soon."

"Could it have been meant for another?"

Cathelin shook her head. "Nay. The servants go up and down those stairs all day. Whoever it was knew what time Madrigal usually came down to help Meagan in the sewing room. It was meant for her. And I want that person found!" Her fist slammed the top of the table hard enough to make the goblets jump.

Wolf reached out a hand to steady his cup and looked at Cathelin with steady blue eyes. "Aye," he said, "Me as well. With your permission, Lady, I'll get to it directly. We're

✦ The Sunne in Gold ✦

all rather fond of wee Madri in the barracks; there'll be no dearth o' volunteers for a turn at the rack when we catch the bastard who hurt her."

He and Cathelin exchanged a savage smile. Madrigal had endeared herself to the fighters when one of them had heard her singing. At his request, every day after that, Madrigal took time in the afternoon after weapons practice to sing to the men and women of Cathelin's private army. Although at first shy, after being presented with a small, battered hand harp, she had grown in confidence, blossoming under the kern's surprisingly gentle attentions.

Wolf knew that neither man nor woman of the Phoenix would harm Madrigal; in fact, just the opposite. "Well, Lady, I'll be taking my leave," he said, rising. "Have I permission to question the house servants?"

Cathelin waved a hand. "Of course, of course. Do whatever is necessary Wolf. 'Tis a free reign I'm giving you. Only, do not fail me in this. I want him." Her lips skinned back from her teeth in a wolf's grin. "Or her."

After Wolf left, Cathelin sat at the table for a moment, absently adding water to the wine in her goblet. It wouldn't do to get drunk; she had too much to do. Abbot Benedict was waiting in her father's office–a rarely used room since she herself preferred to do business from her master chamber.

Cathelin got up, shoving the bench with a thrust of her knees, and stalked away, resentful of any time she had to spend away from Madrigal.

Abbot Benedict was a tall, beautiful, infinitely proud man with a mop of silver hair, a high ivory forehead and a patrician nose that seemed built for his cold gray eyes to stare down. "I wish to discuss the matter of the heathen slave, Lady Cathelin," Benedict said in his round-toned voice as soon as Cathelin walked in the door.

Cathelin sat down and crossed her legs at the knee. "What *about* Madrigal?" she asked, irritated. The Irishwoman and Abbot Benedict had never gotten along; he was convinced that his destiny was to be Archbishop, and so he assiduously sought out sin, as avid in his self-proclaimed duties as a starving rat catcher. Only once had he attempted to chastise Cathelin for her sexual proclivities; after Bishop Rudolphus, his direct superior, received the rich gift of an emerald crucifix with the Lady's compliments, Benedict had been instructed to leave Cathelin strictly alone.

Benedict looked down his long nose at the woman he privately termed the "Whore of Inishowen."

He despised Cathelin, not the least because she refused to allow one of his own priests to take over the parish duties in her own household, preferring a doddering old man named Father Paul who had been young in her grandfather's time. And, of course, because she was a sinner of such magnitude, she would surely roast in Satan's own fire; but she got away with flaunting it in what Benedict considered the most brazen manner imaginable.

"It has come to my attention that Brother Ignatius has been treating your slave; this will stop." The abbot crossed his arms, sliding his hands within his sleeves. His gray eyes were as hard as river stones.

Cathelin stared at Benedict, her own eyes beginning to catch fire. "She's no more a slave than you are, Father Abbot. Less, in fact, since she does not bind herself to a vengeful and intolerant God. What of the compassionate God? The Lord of mercy who suffers the little children to come to Him?" Cathelin raised a brow and waited; she and Benedict had chewed this old bone before and it was a major point of contention between them.

Benedict's eyes flashed. "Do not speak of the Lord, Our God so blasphemously!" he chided, then stopped and composed himself. "But I am not here to chastise you for your many sins, Lady Cathelin. Brother Ignatius is bound to obey *me*, and it is my will that he come to Inishowen no more, if his patient is to be a Saracen heathen."

Cathelin drew in a breath. "What of Christian charity, Father Abbot?" she asked mildly. The calm tone was a sham; inwardly, the Irishwoman was seething.

"I'll not have Ignatius wasting his time, talents or anything else on some bed slave," Benedict replied, and the scathing disapproval in his voice was like a spark on oil-soaked kindling.

Cathelin stood up. "Exactly what do you mean by that?" she asked, stalking towards the silver-haired abbot. Her blazing amber eyes met Benedict's gray, and the older man shuddered a little, but rallied.

"I mean, Lady," he said with thinly veiled sarcasm, "that you will have to hire a leech to tend to your lightskirt. Brother Ignatius will not be coming here any longer."

Abbot Benedict turned to go, but Cathelin's hand on his shoulder stopped him in his tracks. The voice behind him was a deadly purr. "Leaving so soon, Father Abbot?" she said. "We've not yet finished this matter."

The taller man was spun around; Cathelin's grip on his shoulder tightened until it wrung a gasp from Benedict. "Now, you'll be listening to *me*, Father," Cathelin continued through gritted teeth. "Your abbey squats on land my ancestors donated for the purpose. Be assured, Benedict, if you defy me in this thing, the King–who is a very good friend and a comrade at arms–will not hesitate to grant me back the use of my own property. And what use has Our Holy Mother, the Church, for a priest who lost her a valuable tract of land, and hope of more besides?"

Benedict's gray eyes widened. "Surely you would not," he faltered, then gulped when he realized she would. This, this, this foul, unnatural bitch-whore, with her red lips and redder hair and sword skills, would not hesitate to take over the abbey's land grant and toss all the brothers out on their ears, himself, especially. And what would the Bishop say? The Archbishop? Indeed, what would Rome Herself say?

Sullenly, Abbot Benedict yielded, mentally vowing to flagellate himself more thoroughly than usual tonight to cleanse himself of the Whore's contaminating touch. "As you wish, Lady," he said with freezing dignity, "I will not forbid Brother Ignatius. *But* he must not miss any Masses, and he will be required to carry out his normal duties."

"Fair enough." Cathelin released the Abbott's shoulder. "And *do not* think to threaten me again, Father Abbot. I have far more friends at court than yourself, and that's including your own Bishop. Now," she drawled, adding a final insulting touch as Benedict turned to leave, "you have our permission to withdraw."

Benedict hissed through his teeth and gathered the skirts of his brown robes in both hands, hurrying from the room with the shreds of his tattered dignity gathered around him. As he swept away from the scene of his humiliation, he renewed his vow to see to it that Cathelin suffered and soon. He did not see Sorcha, hidden in the shadows, who watched him go with a small, satisfied smile.

And no one saw Sorcha later slip out to the back corner of the courtyard a few moments later, to the pigeon cote where she carefully tied a small cylinder to one particular bird's leg and released him to the sky. The messenger bird circled the castle three times before heading

The Sunne in Gold

off into the northeast, winging its way homeward and to Lord Francis.

Cathelin grimaced. She had disliked the pompous Benedict ever since the old abbot, Father Sulien, had died. *Why Bishop Rudolphus appointed such a self-righteous jackass is beyond my ken*, she thought, then scrubbed her face with one hand and sighed.

A glance at the thick striped candle that quietly marked time in one corner showed her it was nearing the night meal hour. Cathelin stood and stretched; she would be taking Madrigal some of Shevaughn's rich venison broth. *And feeding every drop to her with my own hands, is what I'll be doing*, she thought with a smile.

Cathelin left the room, in a far better mood than she had been when she entered.

CHAPTER SEVEN

A month passed.

To Sorcha's consternation, Cathelin kept herself so close to Madrigal that the chatelaine had no opportunity to carry out her Lord's deadly instructions. The greased stairs had not only failed,, but the eastern whore was now closely watched and protected. She could not even poison the slave's victuals; one of Cathelin's kerns tasted every dish. Sorcha had endured Lord Francis' fury at Madrigal's recovery–indeed, she still shuddered when recalling his inventive displeasure–but then, when she had told him of the pregnancy, he had smiled.

Sorcha rubbed her hands up and down her arms and shivered. That smile. He had told her to leave Madrigal alone for now, but his hazel eyes had burned with an insane fire. It was clear that he had other plans for the slave. The chatelaine could almost have felt sorry for the girl, if she had not hated her so.

✦ The Sunne in Gold ✦

Sorcha had also told Lord Francis of Abbot Benedict's hatred of Cathelin; the two men, united in this cause–with Sorcha acting as intermediary–were plotting the overthrow of the Lady of Inishowen.

The fiery blonde had received a message from the Abbot that morning and was on her way to deliver it to Francis. As Cathelin's blood kin, she was given a great deal more leeway in the performance of her duties than a common servant. Slyly, Sorcha had established a pattern of taking long rides in the early afternoon, claiming the need for fresh air and time alone before the crazed bustle of serving dinner.

The first few times she had gone out, Sorcha had been shadowed by outriders – no doubt kerns sent to spy by either Cathelin or her lackey, Wolf McLeod. Realizing they must suspect her role in Madrigal's 'accident,' the chatelaine had calmly trotted up and down the bridle path, the perfect image of a lady on a pleasurable outing, and pretended not to notice the spies. The ruse worked – she was no longer followed so closely. Although it was still too dangerous to see her beloved Francis in person, a lightning blasted oak in the woods just off the path served as a discreet depository for letters. The tree was not visible from a distance and she made sure no eyes were watching when she rode there.

Sorcha was particularly excited by today's message from Abbot Benedict. He had found some powerful men who were willing to ally themselves to her lord – three sworn enemies of the O'Cameron clan and Cathelin in particular. These new friends would soon unite their armies under Francis' leadership and together, they would grind her hated cousin and that heathen slut into the dirt where they belonged.

She collected her horse from the stables and spent an hour leisurely cantering down the bridle path in case there were any watchers. The chatelaine was so exhilarated that she wanted to spread her arms to embrace the sky and laugh out loud until the very hills rang and echoed to her gaiety.

♦ Nene Adams ♦

Soon, it would all be hers. Francis, the castle, the lands, the respect of the people, vengeance against Cathelin, everything. Her dreams were on the verge of coming true and she was having a hard time concealing her triumph.

Reaching the place where the withered tree stood, she dismounted and stretched before walking up to the oak and thrusting her hand inside the scorched hollow. Paper crackled against her fingers. Snatching the letter out, she shoved her own message into the hole, pushing it well down to make sure it was concealed from casual view. Francis' communication was hidden in her bodice and she remounted quickly, turning the horse's head back towards the castle.

The chatelaine could hardly wait to return to Inishowen. Francis' letter seemed to burn the delicate flesh of her breasts, a flaming ember that also ignited a pleasurable itch between her thighs. It had been nearly four weeks since the last time she had given herself to her lord; his violent lovemaking left her bruised, breathless and utterly fulfilled. He was a *real* man and she gloried in the mingled pain and pleasure he inflicted on her heated flesh.

Frustration was making her snappish and more ill tempered than usual. Patience had never been her strong point and it was difficult not to crow in triumph and tell Cathelin all, if only to see the expression on her face when the bitch realized how thoroughly she had been betrayed.

Sorcha smoothed her long blonde braids and smirked, promising herself that somehow, she would be there when Francis paid her cousin in full for every slight.

The issue of the slave was more troubling. It was clear that her lord had some plan for the hussy – knowing his seed was firmly planted in Madrigal's swelling belly was almost enough to drive Sorcha mad with jealous rage – but what? Surely, he couldn't prefer the dark whore's charms to the purity of her own love! Repeated questions only made him angry, so the chatelaine swallowed her objections and bided

♦ The Sunne in Gold ♦

her time. He wouldn't be so eager to warm the Moorish slut's bed if her nose, ears and tongue were removed with a hot knife.

The letter in her bodice continued to burn. She could hardly wait to open it, read it again and again, search for subtle clues and reassurances. This was something best done in the privacy of her rooms, however. Trembling with excitement, Sorcha clapped her heels to the horse's sides and urged it into a gallop, clinging like a burr to the saddle and laughing for the sheer joy of it all.

They will pay, she thought, her heart pounding. *Oh, aye... every last God-rotting one of them will pay!*

Sorcha passed down the hall quickly, skirts fluttering, and nearly ran into Wolf McLeod, who shot a narrowed blue glance at her retreating back. Both Wolf and Cathelin suspected Sorcha of playing a large role in Madrigal's accident; however, without proof, she could not be bound over for justice, and thus far, the Lady had forbidden a confession by torture. The warrior gripped the hilt of his sword tightly and renewed his vow to keep searching and to keep a very close eye indeed on the pretty blonde chatelaine.

Those afternoon jaunts of hers are mightily suspect, Wolf thought grimly. He'd assigned a pair of kerns to follow Sorcha for several days and they'd come up with nothing. Still, the warrior did not think it was a waste of time. He had stopped the surveillance to give Sorcha confidence, to allow her to think she was safe from prying eyes and drop her guard.

♦ Nene Adams ♦

Aye, give the lass rope enow and she'll hang herself for sure. 'Tis time again to set the hounds on the scent and see if they can bring this vixen to ground.

He walked purposely towards the barracks, kilt fluttering around his scarred knees.

Up in the master's chambers, Madrigal's forced convalescence–at Brother Ignatius' strict orders–had nearly driven her to tears of frustration more than once.

For the past month I have lain here, the Muslim thought, picking at the fur coverlet. *I feel well; my head no longer aches, I am no longer ill, my child grows well. But still the Lady treats me as if I were a sickly infant.*

In truth, Cathelin was fully enjoying the role reversal. She waited on Madrigal hand and foot when she was there, and had appointed one of her own kerns to act as bodyguard and nurse–a curly-haired girl with a charming gap between her front teeth named Becca Llediath, or Half-Tongue, because she had taken a sword stroke across her face in Outremer that had carved a piece from her tongue and left behind a hideous scar.

The injury did not prevent Becca from speech; in fact, Becca talked incessantly, and from her, Madrigal learned many of her new land's oldest tales, including the hair-raising story of Lludd and Llefelys, about fierce dragons, the heroic myth 'The Wooing of Etain, and many others.

Madrigal had passed her time by listening to Becca; singing and practicing on her little harp; and sewing and mending, the only two chores Cathelin and Brother Ignatius would allow. But now that she was feeling better, she wanted

♦ **The Sunne in Gold** ♦

to do more than sit, or take small walks in the garden. She longed to go back down to the sewing room with Meagan and her women, to talk and gossip of small matters; to go to the soldier's barracks and see her old friends, to show Shevaughn how to prepare more of her country's spicy dishes, and, most importantly, to take care of her Lady again.

Madrigal sighed as Becca nattered on. The Lady had not slept in the same bed with her since the accident, having a rope cot brought in for her use. The slave found that she missed her Lady's presence in the night, the feel of strong arms wrapped around her, the warm breath against her neck.

"Madrigal?" Becca asked anxiously, "Are you feelin' all right? I swear, you've not heard a word I've said in the past five minutes."

Madrigal sighed again. "Forgive me, my friend," she replied. "I am well. It is just that…" She spread her hands out helplessly.

Becca grinned, showing the gap between her teeth. "Aye, I know how you feel, truly. When I got this," she waved a hand at the thick scar that ran from her left temple, across cheek and lips, and ended at her chin, "I was with the bone barbers for weeks. Nearly went mad, myself."

Madrigal nodded. "Yes. But the Lady…"

Becca grinned again, this time conspiratorially, and her brown eyes twinkled. "Well, if you're of a mind, I suppose I could escort you downstairs myself. But you have to promise the minute you get tired to come back up. Lady Cathelin'll have my head on a pike if you strain yourself. Mind you, I only do this on count of she's not here."

Madrigal threw the bedclothes back eagerly. "Oh, yes," she said, swinging her legs over the edge of the bed, "Please. I would be so grateful."

Becca helped her rise. Madrigal's pregnancy was far more advanced; thanks to good food–Shevaughn had outdone herself in providing delicacies for the Muslim's burgeoning appetite, much to Sorcha's disgust–and much loving care. Brother Ignatius thought the child would be born sometime after the next three moons, before the winter Solstice. Cathelin privately thought her Madri was waxing like a new moon, and was determined to see her delivered of the child safely.

The kern helped Madrigal don a dress whose front panel had been let out to accommodate her growing belly; the weather had turned cooler, and the gown was of lightweight wool, dyed dark gold. The Muslim had embroidered a pretty pattern of black and crimson running hares all over the bodice and around the sleeves and hem. Madrigal smoothed her skirts, while Becca twisted up her hair into three braids held together at the ends with a carved wooden slide; the braids hung below her knees.

Cathelin had left Inishowen on an errand for a few days, leaving the seneschal, Michael Drury, in charge. The harvest was in, and soon it would be Samhain, the pagan festival still celebrated by many of the Irish, despite the Church's frowning on such activities. Madrigal was looking forward to the autumn celebration–there would be singing and story-telling contests, and she would play a special song for the occasion.

Despite Madrigal's protests, Becca made her sit down on the edge of the bed while the kern pulled soft house slippers of tanned deerhide on the slave's feet. Then Becca rose and offered her arm jauntily. "Where to first, mistress?" she said with a grin. "The sewing room? The kitchen? Or the garden?"

Madrigal took the offered arm and rose with a grunt. She had less of her usual grace; the small of her back often ached, and when she couldn't sleep, Cathelin massaged her with warmed oil. Although Madrigal enjoyed these attentions, they still made her uncomfortable. *I should be serving my*

✦ The Sunne in Gold ✦

Lady, she thought, abashed. *I am her slave, not the other way around.*

Cathelin's nightmares were becoming less and less frequent, although Madrigal still sang to her Lady in the night watches. But the Muslim missed her Lady's smiles when she performed some service that pleased or surprised her, and mostly, she missed feeling as if she were part of a community that revolved around the strong figure of Lady Cathelin.

"The kitchen, I think," Madrigal replied aloud, and was rewarded with another cheeky smile from Becca.

"Now, why did I think you were going to say that?" Becca said, cocking her head to one side. "The babe must be hungry again. He's all stomach, that one."

The two women walked from the chambers, and Becca kept a careful grip on Madrigal's arm as they descended the stone stairs. Cathelin had not let Madrigal walk down the stairs since the accident; she carried her, much to the other woman's embarrassment and everyone else's amusement.

The Chief of the Hearth, Shevaughn, beamed when Madrigal and Becca entered the steamy kitchen. "Well, look what the cat dragged in," she said, laughing so hard her jowls shook. "If it 'tisn't wee Madrigal. Here, child, come an' sit a while," Shevaughn continued, hastily clearing off a bench near a small table.

Madrigal started to sit down, but was prevented by Becca. The kern re-arranged the table and bench so that the dark-haired woman would sit with her back to a corner; then Becca took a chair and sat down at an angle to the slave, to keep her own self between Madrigal and the rest of the world.

Shevaughn watched these proceedings with a frown. "Are ye thinkin' that's so necessary, Becca?" she asked. "Surely none'd harm wee Madrigal in my own kitchens."

Becca shrugged. "I take no chances, Mistress," she replied, "I've no wish to be chopped into dogsmeat by Lady Cathelin, nor Wolf McLeod besides."

Shevaughn considered that a moment, then laughed again. "Aye, ye've the right o' that," she said, black eyes twinkling. The hearth chief's salt-and-pepper hair was cropped short around her face, leaving only a small tail in the back that was kept tightly braided and wrapped in leather thongs. She turned back to the fireplace, basting a haunch that was being turned slowly on its spit by a pot boy.

"How goes the gathering of winter's food?" Madrigal asked. She was worried, but only because Cathelin still fussed over the state of Inishowen's supplies.

"Well enow," Shevaughn answered, sprinkling a simmering iron pot with a dusting of herbs, "'twill be a hard winter, no doubt o' that, but Master Drury brought back a plentitude o' foods and such, an' the harvest was not near as bad as first thought ta be."

Madrigal sighed with relief. She knew, from what she had heard from her Lady and others, that Inishowen's folk were not only the castle servants and villagers. Small farmers and woodsmen lived in cottages sprinkled throughout Inishowen's vast tracts of land; Cathelin had worried that they might not survive the winter, and had been working diligently to make sure the castle's supplies could bear an influx of people, if the season were particularly harsh.

Shevaughn continued, shrugging her massive shoulders, "'Tis thankin' God I am, that the neighborin' lairds allowed the Lady to hunt on their lands. We've put up meat a-plenty, both dried, smoked an' preserved; 'twill be enow."

"What price did she have to pay for these favors?" Madrigal asked curiously.

The hearth chief opened her mouth to reply, then stopped and bellowed at a hapless undercook, "Nay, ye mincin' foplocked mullet! Make the sallet, *then* stuff the

The Sunne in Gold

partridges!" The man began hastily slicing roots, and Shevaughn muttered, "Saints preserve me from madmen and fools." She shook her head, then replied to Madrigal's question, "No price as yet. The debt to be repaid in four years time, or so I've heard. We need time to replenish the herds an' such."

Suddenly, Madrigal's stomach growled loudly, causing her to cover her lips with one hand in embarrassment.

Shevaughn had heard the rumble, however; the ultimate mistress of her domain, she missed nothing. "Oh, ho," she said loudly with a smile, "I hear a hungry babe."

As Madrigal blushed, the other kitchen servants laughed, even the disgraced undercook.

Shevaughn quickly scooped a bowl of honey-sweetened porridge from the soot-encrusted pot that hung in the back of the fireplace, and slid it in front of Madrigal. In a moment, the Muslim also had a plate of spiced venison sausage rolls, a chunk of sharp cheese, and a mazer of light ale.

As Madrigal ate, Sorcha swept into the kitchen, the jangling chain of her office with its many keys fastened around the waist of her dark brown dress. "Mistress Shevaughn," she said self-importantly, "'Tis time for the monthly inspection of the pantry."

Sorcha noticed Madrigal and shot her a poisonous look from deadly green eyes. Becca immediately shifted her position on the chair and stared back at the blonde chatelaine, one hand lingering on the hilt of her belt knife. Her steady gaze said, *That far. No further.*

Sorcha patted her braids and decided to ignore both kern and slave alike. "Well?" she asked the hearth chief, "I haven't all day, you know."

Shevaughn, who topped Sorcha by a good head, and outweighed her by more than half again besides, sucked in a breath through her nostrils. "Aye, *Mistress* Sorcha," she said sarcastically, "If ye'll wait but a moment, I'll be with ye presently."

Sorcha tossed her head, hands on her hips. "Nay," she retorted, "I've much to be doin' afore the day's end. 'Tis now, I'm thinkin'. Or would you rather I fetched Master Drury and told him you neglect *your* duties? A whippin' 'twill bring you down a notch or two, *common cook* as you be."

Shevaughn stiffened. She reached out a massive arm—beneath the layers of fat there was a foundation of surprisingly solid muscle mass—and wrapped her strong hand around Sorcha's upper arm. The chatelaine winced as the hearth chief's fingers bit into her flesh. "Missy, ye'll no be talkin' ta me suchly in my own kitchen," Shevaughn hissed. "Now, away wit' ye. *If*, and I say only *if*, I have the time tomorrow, I'll gladly open my pantry. But for now *get ye gone*!" she finished with a roar that made the copper pans on their hooks rattle against the walls.

Sorcha tore herself from Shevaughn's grasp, green eyes alight with rage. "'Tis payin' fer that you'll be," she said, rubbing her bruised arm. "Someday when my Lord comes…" Realizing she may have said too much, the chatelaine broke off with a gasp, whirled around and fled the kitchen, hot tears of anger on her cheeks.

Becca watched Sorcha leave with a thoughtful expression. *Now,* she thought, *where might the McLeod be at this time o' day? I'm thinking he'd be very interested in what I've heard.*

A few days earlier, Cathelin had announced to Madrigal that she was summoned to settle a yeoman's dispute

♦ **The Sunne in Gold** ♦

on the extreme edge of Inishowen's lands. It was a common enough duty for a conscientious overlord, and although the Muslim was not overjoyed at the separation – in fact, she felt quite the opposite – she understood the necessity and accepted it with good grace.

Taking a small retinue of kerns, Cathelin had ridden out and left Wolf McLeod in charge of the castle until her return.

However, a petty feud was not the real reason behind the Lady's journey. She had lied to Madrigal, and indeed the only ones who knew the truth were her hand-picked men and her Scottish second. Cathelin had hated deceiving her love, but to spare Madrigal pain and worry, she would have committed grosser sins than telling lies. Later, when she judged the time aright, all would be revealed. For now, she kept the secret sewn up tight and had taken pledge from her kerns and McLeod to do the same.

Cathelin was riding to bring Madrigal's tormentor, Alexander Wallace, to justice for violating his oath as a Knight Crusader of the Order of St. John of Jerusalem.

A crisp wind billowed her cloak behind her; the horses' hooves were muffled on the leaf strewn road that wound to the south towards Dublin – the traveler's trail called *Slige Midluachra*. Cathelin was on fire with purpose and impatient to get to the city, but she also kept her anger carefully controlled. As much as she might like to wring out Wallace till his hair bled, such a course of action would have severe consequences.

Aye, I've no need for grudge wars and clan squabbles to follow me home, she thought, body flowing easily in rhythm to her horse's canter. *Nor do I wish his Order to call grievance against me for slaying him outside the law. For what he did to Madri, the bastard deserves a slow death, but I cannot cry personal vengeance for her sake and have done. However much I love her, I have also my obligations to the clan to consider. Putting Wallace to the sword for oath breaking is enough of an excuse and lawful, besides.*

The city of Dublin – named after a *dubh linn*, or black water tidal pool – loomed close after several days of hard riding. She led her men down along a ridge and down to the *Ath Cliath*, the Ford of Hurdles, where they would cross the Liffey River on rafts. It was good luck that they had arrived at low tide, otherwise they would have had to camp on the mud flats and wait upon the morning.

Every day save Sunday was market time in the bustling trading town, and a seemingly chaotic mob of merchants, traders, wagon trains, sheep, cattle, horses, chickens, shouting peddlers, beggars and pilgrims swirled around the shallow wooden docks. Since the citizens of Dublin routinely dumped everything from dead cows to raw sewage into the river, the resultant stench was obnoxious enough to bring tears to the eyes of even the most hardened traveler.

Cathelin rode through the milling, roaring crowd, using her horse's greater weight to shove aside any opposition to her progress. When a band of merchants protested loudly, a show of her sword and rank badges kept them at bay. No one wanted to pick a fight with a heavily armed knight, especially not one who had a martial retinue at her back.

Choosing the sturdiest looking raft, she paid the pole-tender his fee – a silver penny per man and horse – and relaxed in the saddle once they were underway. Across the murky waters of the Liffey, she could see the stone walls that encircled Dublin, standing sullenly against a cloud-wracked sky. While they made their slow, steady progress, the Irishwoman reflected on her own knighting at the hand of Richard Lionheart, and the oath she had taken on that fateful day.

✦ The Sunne in Gold ✦

As a member of the Order of the Garter, her fealty had been pledged first to God and then to her King – in contrast with Wallace, who as a Knight Hospitaler, had vowed to uphold first God and then the Order of the Church. He had done neither and his own neglectful vice had given Cathelin the opportunity to dispense a richly deserved justice.

In her mind, she could hear King Richard's voice, a melodic baritone that had gifted the oath of the Order with all the solemnity of a holy sacrament. That moment, kneeling at his feet with the weight of armor on her back, was etched into the fabric of her soul. With very little effort, she could recall those words and let them echo in her heart.

"*Right mindful of your prowess on the field, and responsive to the wishes of your peers, we are minded to make you knight. Know that to wear the belt and chain of a knight is to hold a sacred trust; that the obligations of knighthood will demand your efforts every moment of your life.*

"*As a knight of the Order of the Garter, you must be respectful of all men, never offending the honor of another.*

"*As a knight, you must love your Kingdom and your province, and fulfill most faithfully your feudal duties to your Lord and your King.*

"*Your word must be dependable beyond doubt or question. You must never flee from the face of your foes. You must be generous to all.*

"*And, always and everywhere, you must be the champion of the right and the good.*

"*The Laws of the Order and the customs of the Kingdom require that a knight show prowess, as you have demonstrated upon the field of honor; that a knight be courteous, as you have shown yourself to be and as these noble gentleman attest; that a knight be humble before God, as you have shown in your vigil this night past, and that a knight be loyal to his Kingdom and the Order. Do you then desire to accept the burden of knighthood and swear fealty to the Crown?"*

She would never forget the King's brilliant blue eyes staring down at her, or the vows that had bound her in chains of tradition and honor. Foremost among these formal pledges was this – that as a knight, she was bound to respect all those who were weak or defenseless, whether because of age, infirmity, poverty or vow, and be steadfast in defending them.

Regardless of the Order to which they belonged, every knight had this obligation to help the helpless. When the white belt, spurs and chain of knighthood were conveyed upon them, each man additionally swore to uphold the honor of their rank; to forfeit their lives and position if foresworn; and to mete justice to anyone who dared break his oaths before the Almighty.

Cathelin's confrontation with Wallace was not to be a duel or a campaign to take land, title and riches from an honorable foe. She was under a holy obligation to commit the execution of an oathbreaker – a circumstance that could not have made her happier.

From all she had been able to gather from her father's contacts in Dublin, Wallace had been flagrantly flouting the rules of his Order for years. His ill-gotten wealth, plundered from the Saracens, had kept him safe for a while – every man had his price, and the Hospitalers were likely to turn a blind eye in exchange for fattening their coffers. Now a richly deserved punishment was about to fall upon him like a thunderbolt, and Cathelin likened herself to the Hammer of God.

Get you ready and hie to confession, sirrah, she thought, narrowing her eyes as a brilliant beam of sunlight lanced through the clouds and glinted off the waters, dazzling her sight. *Beg for the mercy of Christ, for by all I hold dear, you shall get none from me and mine.*

✦ The Sunne in Gold ✦

"Blacksunne, as I live and breathe! God's wounds, this is a merry surprise. What brings you to Dublin?" Wallace asked, an oily smile spreading across his face as he stepped aside to allow Cathelin to enter.

The Irishwoman looked around in distaste; filth was strewn about the floor, the rushes underfoot were soft with rot, and the place stank worse than a tannery. The house where Wallace lived was clearly expensive, sitting as it did in the shadow of Saint Audoen's Church, but from the interior, it might as well have been the meanest hovel in the poorest quarter of town.

Takes a pig to live like a pig, she thought in disgust, suddenly itching as if she could feel the fleas crawling into her armor. *The sooner I'm away from this sty the better 'twill be.*

Cathelin had dressed with considerable care that morning in the Coxcomb Inn, where she and her men had stayed the night. She wore her striking black-enameled armor, with the sky-blue surcoat of the Order of the Garter tied around her steel-clad torso. Her own sunburst insignia and the small red cross of the Templars decorated the front, while the big cross of a Knight Crusader returned from the Holy Land was emblazoned on the back. She had left her helm at the inn, preferring instead to cover her braided red tresses with a gilded steel cap. She looked every inch the powerful warrior, and had meant to impress upon Wallace the seriousness of her errand.

Her kerns carried naked swords and were dressed in ebony and scarlet leathers. The mail beneath their jerkins jingled with every step; with their scowling faces and fierce appearance, no thief or cutpurse had been foolish enough to molest their Lady.

Alexander Wallace made a pitiful contrast to his sleek visitors. Years of indulgence in wine, women and rich foods, and too little time in the practice field, had turned all of Wallace's muscle to flab and given him a sagging paunch. He wore a stained black tunic and trews patched with the white crosses of the Hospitaler order, all stained and splattered with unidentifiable muck. His skin was grimy, the creases in his neck ringed with dirt, and he smelled like a dungheap.

When he smiled again in his greasy manner and offered Cathelin a cup of wine, she could see flecks of meat stuck between his teeth and felt her stomach heave in protest.

A duel with this vile, repulsive, squalid swine would be an abomination. *'Twould be like spearing trout in a tun*, Cathelin thought. *Besides, I'd druther kiss the Devil's arse than pay him the honor of dying in battle.*

She gazed at Wallace, her lip curling in contempt, and spoke the words that would mean his doom.

"Alexander Wallace, once Knight of the Order of St. John of Jerusalem, I, Cathelin O'Cameron of Inishowen, called Blacksunne, do hereby declare and find you oathbreaker, abuser and vicious destroyer of the weak and defenseless. As a knight and a loyal subject of God and my King, I call these men to witness that I have fulfilled my oath and bring justice to one who has besmirched the very rank and estate of Knighthood. Make your peace with God, Wallace, for today you will face Him and your deeds will be weighed in the balance of His judgment."

A gray friar, clothed in the simple homespun robes of the Benedictines, stepped from behind the grim-faced rank of kerns. He held the tools of confession, sacrament and last rites in his hands. The friar's expression was calm. "Do you commend your soul to the everlasting and almighty God, my son? Will you die forgiven of your sins and in the sure

✦ The Sunne in Gold ✦

knowledge that with His compassion, you may yet redeem your immortal soul?"

Wallace blanched. "How dare you!" he screeched. His eyes darted to and fro, seeking any avenue of escape, but he was trapped in his own home like a cornered rat. "What is this farce?"

"I would not deny you the comfort of confession," Cathelin said in an implacable tone, "and you need not concern yourself with the disposition of your body, sirrah. I have already made arrangements to give your wretched carcass a Christian burial, tho' you deserve rather to be pitched in a ditch and devoured by dogs."

"You cannot do this." Runnels of sweat cut tracks through the grime on his face. "I have committed no crime. I demand you bring me to a magistrate at once, otherwise what you do is simple murder!"

Cathelin pursed her lips and glanced at the Benedictine. The friar explained, "You dwell in a 'liberty' of Dublin, Sir Alexander. In this area near the church, and in others, the normal laws of town and crown are suspended. Besides, this knight," he indicated Cathelin with a nod, "is acting well within his rights and according to the sacred vow of the Templars. He has adjuged you guilty and done everything properly within the rule of your Orders."

"Then give me sanctuary!" Wallace was desperate. "I demand sanctuary, damn you!"

"Even if you managed to reach the altar of Saint Audoen's, the good brothers cannot grant you their protection." Cathelin drew her sword with a steely rasp. "I filed a formal grievance and declaration of intent with the Order of St. John of Jerusalem and my own Templars at dawn. The master of your motherhouse is less than pleased at losing such a generous member, but in the end he had no choice but to admit my right. You *are* going to die today,

Wallace, and no amount of protesting will save your worthless life."

"I'll fight you," Wallace choked in fear, "You'll not take me easy to the slaughter."

Cathelin shrugged. "As you wish, man. You can bend your knee to the sword and die with dignity, or my men can truss you like a spring lamb and butcher you squealing. It makes no differ to me at all. You are an oathbreaker and the punishment is death, a lawful execution at the hands of your accuser."

Once again, Wallace looked about wildly for an avenue of escape. He found none. Slowly, the former knight's entire posture changed. His shoulders slumped, his head sank down to his chest, his hands dangled loosely. He seemed to sink into himself, growing smaller with each passing breath. Alexander Wallace was a broken man; his evil deeds had, at last, come home to roost, and he was forced to face the inevitable. He turned to the patiently waiting friar.

"Forgive me, Father, for I have sinned," he mumbled.

The Benedictine stepped forward, motioning the others back. It was his duty to minister to the dying, and Cathelin respected his authority.

"God does not distinguish," the friar said in a clear voice, anointing Wallace's forehead with oil, "He offers His mercy to all."

While the holy man did what he could to comfort Wallace, Cathelin grounded her sword in the floor and waited. The end of her quest was near; she could afford to be patient now.

✦ The Sunne in Gold ✦

As befitting an execution, Cathelin did not claim Wallace's arms or any part of his estate. She had stripped his body of all signs of rank and left it to the Benedictine brothers to see to his burial and notify his kin. She had even paid for the funeral out of her own pocket before taking her leave of Dublin.

She and her kerns rode back to Inishowen in quiet and solemn order. Wallace was dead, his blood on her hands, and she could find no cause for regret. That beast disguised as a man and a knight would never hurt anyone again.

On the *Slige Midluachra*, trotting north and to home, she wondered how best to tell Madrigal that the author of her nightmares was gone. In a move her wild ancestors would have approved, Cathelin had taken a single trophy from Wallace's body; even now, that bloody rag-wrapped item traveled at her knee, concealed in a leather saddlebag.

The Irishwoman hoped that Madrigal would appreciate the gift, when the time came for the truth to be told.

CHAPTER EIGHT

hen Cathelin arrived home several days later, riding easily on the back of a dun mare, Inishowen was in an uproar.

After riding through the massive iron studded gates, Cathelin dismounted and grabbed one of the milling, shouting throng. "What in God's name is going on?" she asked.

The man, a peasant farmer, recognized Cathelin immediately and hastened to tug his forelock in respect. "'Tis a hangin', Lady," he replied. "A witch, I heard."

Cathelin's amber eyes widened. *A witch?* she thought. "Who?" she asked, shaking his arm a little. "Who's been accused?"

The farmer's attention had been caught by a group of gossiping elders; he snapped his eyes back to Cathelin when he felt her grip tighten. "Why," he said, gulping, "some woman, I heard. A-castin' evil spells on the folk, or some such like. Maybe even dancin' naked an' temptin' the good

♦ The Sunne in Gold ♦

brothers of the Abbey." The man's eyes glazed and he licked his lips, clearly excited by the thought

"Feh!" Cathelin flung his arm away and led her horse through the mob in the castle's forecourt. Some enterprising businessmen had begun selling cheap clay mugs of cider and ale; others were hawking hot pastries and roasted potatoes. The scene reminded Cathelin of a festival, and her eyes grew hotter the more she took in the people's behavior.

Finally, Cathelin managed to push her way through to the stables. Flinging the reins of her horse to an astonished stable hand, she quickly passed out the back gate, and in a long, ground-eating lope, ran to the postern gate and into the kitchen.

The castle kitchen, at least, was an oasis of calm compared to the chaos outside. Spotting Shevaughn, Cathelin hurried over to the Chief of the Hearth, ignoring gasps and hasty bows from the other servants. "Mistress Shevaughn!" Cathelin yelled, getting the other woman's attention, "What's going on? Who's being hung? And *why*, for the love of God!"

Shevaughn wiped her hands on the sacking apron she wore slung around her neck. "Let's go someplace more quiet-like where we can talk," she said, and led Cathelin to a small room off the main kitchen area – the cool room, where stores were held in preparation of the day's cooking.

Clearing her throat and feeling distinctly nervous as her mistress' hot gaze burned, Shevaughn said, "'Twas like this, Lady," she began and explained about Sorcha's tongue-slip in the kitchens a few days ago.

Cathelin nodded. "Go on." Her face was grimy from road dust, and locks of dark crimson hair straggled down her back; the Irishwoman's dark brown tunic was stained, and her travel cloak muddy at the hem, but she presented a commanding figure nonetheless.

Shevaughn went on to explain how Sorcha had been questioned by Wolf McLeod, eventually confessing–when the kern gave the chatelaine a tour of the castle dungeons–to the attempt on Madrigal's life. She would not, however dire the threat, say why. And she had refused to reveal any more about her 'Lord.'

"An' so," Shevaughn concluded, "'twas the decision of Masters McLeod an' Drury to hang the woman for her crimes. Abbot Benedict, he protested somewhat strong, but 'twas to no avail. As soon as the people heard, well, you *know* how the folk are about a hangin'. An' as all the world knows, gossip an' rumor flies longer an' faster than geese to a hard winter's haven."

Cathelin nodded. Her people worked hard throughout the year just to survive. They'd take any excuse to stop their labors and have a festival; and a hanging–for whatever reason–was considered quite a treat. She did not condone such a party atmosphere, however. The application of justice was, and always should be, an occasion for solemnity and prayer. Cathelin made a mental note to have her kerns disperse the crowd in the outer courtyard.

Just as she opened her mouth to ask another question, Cathelin heard a familiar voice coming from the kitchen, and she recognized it as Madrigal's.

"Here," Cathelin heard her say, "Why do you not rest awhile, James? I can finish the pastry."

Shevaughn's black eyes widened and she flung out her hands at the look on Cathelin's face. "Nay!" she stammered, "The lass is fine, I swear it. Only, wee Madrigal was tired o' sittin' all day, an' anyhow 'tis no healthy for a bearing woman to be layin' about so, an'..." Shevaughn's voice trailed off as Cathelin spun about on her heel and left the cold room.

The hearth chief wiped her suddenly sweaty brow with the back of a hand. *Well-a-day*, she thought, *I've rarely seen Herself in such a mood.* Then her eyes widened again. *Sweet Jesus,* she thought to herself as she grabbed her skirts

♦ The Sunne in Gold ♦

in both hands and ponderously hurried from the room, *I'd best get there afore the Lady's spleen kills wee Madrigal.*

However, as Shevaughn rounded the corner, she slowed her pace, for she could hear that she was already too late.

"*What are you doing out of bed?*" Cathelin roared.

All was utter silence in the kitchen as the echoes of the enraged Lady's shout rolled back from the walls.

Madrigal laid aside the rolling pin and dusted her floury hands on her skirts. "I am well, Lady," she replied respectfully. "There is no need to be concerned." Although outwardly she appeared calm, Madrigal's stomach fluttered with anxiety.

Cathelin was not going to be so easily appeased. "Did not Brother Ignatius *himself* tell you to stay a-bed? Did not *I* tell you to stay a-bed? Saint Brigit, I'm gone only a few days, and my home is turned arse-over-crown, my chatelaine's about to be hung, and I find *you* in the kitchen laborin' like a common chop slut!"

Before Madrigal could reply, she found herself scooped up in Cathelin's arms, the Lady muttering, "Sweet Jesus, Mary and Joseph, Madri, stayin' off your feet you should be. No, not a word," Cathelin commanded. "I'll not hear excuses. Back to bed you go."

Madrigal put her arms around her Lady's neck as she was carried up the stairs. Part of her was still upset over having been caught disobeying orders, but another part marveled at the ease with which the extraordinarily muscular Lady was able to bear her weight up the stairs without even breathing hard.

Cathelin kicked the door of the master's chambers open with her foot and stood there a moment, staring. Becca was seated cross-legged on the floor, sharpening a knife. When she saw the Lady, she immediately leaped up and bowed. "G-g-good afternoon, Lady," the astonished kern stuttered. "Was your trip well?" she continued lamely, as Cathelin's scorching gaze swept her from heel to crown.

Finally, Cathelin grunted, "Well enough," and strode over to the bed, laying Madrigal down gently. "Now, p'raps you'll explain whyfor I see you sittin' on your poxy, lazy arse instead of stayin' with Madri *as you were* ordered?" the Irishwoman asked Becca, who flushed.

"Well," Becca said sheepishly, "I thought with Sorcha taken and all, 'twould be safe."

Cathelin's lips tightened. "Oh. You were *thinkin'* again," she replied scathingly. "'Tis a bad habit for a soldier. Might get you deaded someday."

Becca flushed again, the scar across her face silvery-white in contrast. "Aye, Lady," she said, bowing her head. "I am in the wrong. I should not have disobeyed." She sank to one knee, preparing to formally offer her apologies, when Cathelin stopped her with an upraised hand.

"I've no time for this now. Get you downstairs and fetch Master McLeod and the seneschal. And you're to tell them both that there's to be no hanging until I've sorted this bloody great mess out myself."

Gratefully, Becca rose and pelted out of the room.

Cathelin sank down on the edge of the bed next to Madrigal. "And as for you," she began, but was interrupted by a small moan.

Madrigal had one hand pressed to her swollen belly, and her eyes were closed. Hastily, Cathelin leaned over and asked, "Sweetling? Are you all right?"

A moment passed before the Muslim could answer. "Yes," she finally answered. "The child does well. Only..."

"Only?"

Madrigal chuckled at the anxious expression on her Lady's face. "Only he is very vigorous, this one. I think he finds his room too small and wishes to enlarge his quarters by kicking down the walls."

✦ The Sunne in Gold ✦

"Oh." Cathelin sat back, relieved. "Well, then, will you promise me to stay in bed, Madri?" she asked. "You should not be running about."

Madrigal sighed and interrupted. "I must," she replied. "The holy man is a marvelous healer, Lady, but he does not know much of woman's matters. I was a slave in the household of a physician. I have also been in the seraglio, where there were others who were both carrying and birthing children. My child is well, and grows strong; my ribs have healed, as has my head. Truly," she continued plaintively, "if I stay here much longer, Lady, forgive me, but I will go mad!"

Cathelin thought about that for a minute, then said resignedly, "All right. *But*," she continued sternly, despite the happy smile on Madrigal's sweet face, "No heavy laboring. No going down those stairs alone. And if you feel tired, Madri, for God's sake, rest."

Madrigal's dark eyes were shining. "Yes, Lady," she replied, then much to Cathelin's consternation, swung her legs off the bed and rose. "May I go back to the kitchens now?"

The Irishwoman sighed at the thought of all those steps, then reached out and dusted a smear of flour from the other woman's nose. "Aye," Cathelin said reluctantly, "but wait until Becca returns. I must bespeak Wolf and Drury, and sort out all this hanging business."

Becca returned shortly, accompanied by the tall seneschal and the smaller but bulkier warrior. Wolf nodded politely both at Cathelin and Madrigal, but Drury was twisting his loaf-shaped hat in both hands, obviously nervous.

As Becca escorted Madrigal out of the room, Cathelin said, "Well? Why is Sorcha to be hung? A man outside told me she was thought to be a witch, of all things. What, in Sweet Jesus' name, is going on?"

Drury looked expectantly at Wolf, then his shoulders sagged when he realized that *he* would have to be the one to explain. "Lady Cathelin," the seneschal said, "the kern Becca Half-Tongue overheard Sorcha make a remark about 'her Lord'. She seemed to imply that he would be revengin' her grievances–treason against you, Lady. So Master McLeod questioned her; she refused to tell us who this 'Lord' is, or what his plans are, but confessed to greasin' the step to kill Madrigal. So," he spread his hands helplessly. "I ordered her hangin'."

"I see." Cathelin crossed her legs and laced her fingers together over a knee. "And you, Wolf? Have *you* nothing to say?"

The warrior's blue eyes stared into Cathelin's amber without flinching. "Aye," he replied, "I suspected th' wench from most th' start, as did yerself. This 'Lord' business chills my bones, but I would nae order torture, since ye'd fain made yer feelin's on *that* subject clear."

Cathelin nodded. She could not condone torture; despite her initial rage at Madrigal's near-fatal accident, if she could have laid hands on Sorcha at that very moment, the worst she may have done would have been to kill her quickly. In Outremer, she had lost her stomach for such bloody work.

Wolf continued with a grimace, "I'd set some kerns to watchin' her, mayhap to sniff out her plans and discover the depth o' her treason. They intercepted a message – 'twas naught but a love letter - and her partner's name is nae mentioned, more's the pity. Her rooms have been searched but we found nothin'. I'm thinkin' she burned his answers and there's little use siftin' the ashes."

"Where is she now?" Cathelin asked.

"Locked in a storeroom, Lady," Drury said.

Cathelin rose and removed the silver brooch that pinned her cloak to one shoulder, allowing the garment to slip to the floor. "Take me to her," the Irishwoman ordered, amber eyes glittering. "I must speak to her afore orderin' any hangings, today or any day."

♦ The Sunne in Gold ♦

Both men bowed their heads in acknowledgement, then silently, led their Lady to the place where the chatelaine of Inishowen, Sorcha O'Reilly, awaited Cathelin's judgment and her own fate.

Sorcha was defiant. "So," she sneered, "'Tis the mistress herself come to pay a call. Well, Lady, had I known you'd be visitin' my humble dwellin's, I'd have laid out the Cloth of State." Her waved hand indicated the bare storeroom, holding only a rope cot, a chamberpot and a small, rickety table.

Cathelin sighed and motioned for Wolf and Michael Drury to leave her alone with the blonde chatelaine. After the two men left, shutting the door behind them, Cathelin crossed her arms over her chest. "Sorcha," she asked sorrowfully, "why?"

"Why did I try an' kill your little slavey?" Sorcha replied sarcastically, defiant although her hands twisted the folds of her skirt into a knot. "P'raps only because she was there. 'Tis quite blood mad I am, as all the world knows."

"Nay, Sorchi-fach," Cathelin said, using the other woman's childhood nickname, "I want to know the truth. What did Madri *do* to you that makes you hate her so?"

Sorcha's green eyes were brilliant with hatred; she had refused to explain to Drury or McLeod, but now that Cathelin was here. *Well*, Sorcha thought, *'tis best I get my vengeance where and how I can.*

"I despise that bit of heathen trash you keep for the warmin' of your bed, Cat," Sorcha said angrily. "Aye, I beat her afore, did you not know that? Quite a few of the marks on her back were made by my own hand. An' then, what do you do save make her think she's as good as the rest of us. Fah!" She spat, the gobbet of spittle just missing Cathelin's boot. "Takin' up with some poxy foreign whore when..." She stopped abruptly and turned away.

Cathelin moved closer to the other woman. "When what, Sorcha?" she asked.

For a long moment, Sorcha said nothing, just stared into space. Then, as if entranced, she replied softly, "When you could have had *me*."

Cathelin was stunned. She and Sorcha were distant kin, and despite the fact that the blood between them was not close, she had never considered that the blonde woman had any feelings for her other than familial ones. "Sorchi-fach, I sorrow that you feel this way, but why did you not tell me? We could have..."

Sorcha's shoulders quivered as she struggled to control her bile. "Nay," she interrupted. "You are *still* blind. I never loved you. *Never*. You were the golden child, the favored one, always havin' anythin' you wanted. An' me? I was nothin' more than a servant, tho' one of the blood. Oh, I *wanted* you, 'tis true. But only on count of you could give me more than I had. I wanted to be a grand lady, an' you could have given me that. But then, 'twas givin' it all to your precious slavey you were. I wanted her dead, Cat. Both for the insult an' to hurt you as well."

Cathelin's face was grim as a thought struck her. "Sorcha, how did Francis learn of my father's illness?"

The blonde chatelaine whirled around. "Why, for that I wrote an' told him myself," she replied with malicious glee. "I'd hoped you dead in Outremer an' Lord Westfield was *quite* grateful." She ran her tongue along her lips. "He was a far better lover than you'd have been, an' gave me more besides."

♦ The Sunne in Gold ♦

Cathelin felt sick. She had wondered how Francis had found out about Sir Giles' sickness; now she knew. It had been Sorcha who had opened Inishowen to Francis' greed, Sorcha who kept her enemy apprised of her actions, Sorcha who threatened Madri's life and child. Sorcha who had betrayed her position, her trust, her family. "Sorcha, do you know what you have done?" she asked. "'Twas bad enough to have tried to murder Madri, but this? 'Tis no less than treason, and you know full well the penalty for that."

Sorcha said nothing. She held her head high and stared at Cathelin with nothing but hatred, anger, frustrated ambition and insane envy glowing in her lambent green eyes.

"Who is this Lord you spoke of in the kitchens, Sorchi-fach?" Cathelin asked, wondering what else this women she had once trusted had done. "What have you knitted up now? Another plot?"

"I'll say no more, Cat," Sorcha replied. "*That* secret dies with me."

"I could have you tortured, you know," Cathelin said. She walked to the other woman and gently took one of her hands. "Tell me, kinswoman. Tell me what this means, and I promise to spare your life. Otherwise…"

Sorcha knew that Lord Francis would not be coming to her rescue. She had already resigned herself to her fate; death held no fear for her anymore. At first, she had wept and stormed and railed, but now, she was determined to protect her betrothed Lord to the grave. "Torture me then, Cat," she said defiantly. "Bring on the rack, the whips, the screws. I'll not betray my Lord, no matter what you do."

Cathelin flushed. Although Inishowen's dungeons were filled with the equipment necessary for torture, it had not been used in decades. In truth, she was filled more with sorrow and pity than anger. Sorcha had always been discontented with her lot; Cathelin felt guilty that she had not noticed how the discontent and envy had turned to bitterness.

"No," she whispered, "I cannot. I *will* not. Sorchi-fach, if you'll not tell me, I cannot force you."

Sorcha sneered, "No stomach for it then? I never took you for a coward, Cat, but I'm supposin' things can change."

Cathelin tasted bitter bile in the back of her throat. "So, you'd rather die than betray yet again? I find that passing strange, but no matter. God will judge you, Sorcha, not I."

Cathelin turned to go, then stopped with her hand on the latch. Without turning around, she said, "I'll have Father Paul come to take your confession. Make a full one, Sorchi-fach, and be shriven for your sins. You've left me small choice. Come the dawn, I must order your hanging."

Sorcha hid her trembling fists in the folds of her skirts as Cathelin left and the door banged inexorably shut behind her.

Madrigal hurried down the hall as quickly as she could, despite her somewhat waddling gait. She had heard that her Lady had confirmed Drury's orders for Sorcha's hanging. *Allah*, the slave thought, barely acknowledging the nods from other servants she passed. *She has ordered the death of kin.*

Cathelin had shut herself up in her father's office and refused to see anyone for any reason. She was in a savage temper; Michael Drury had already felt the stinging lash of her tongue and had fled in terror. Madrigal knew her Lady needed her, felt this knowledge in her bones, and hastened to answer the call.

♦ The Sunne in Gold ♦

Reaching the door, Madrigal took a moment to smooth her hair and brush off her skirts. Then she diffidently knocked, calling softly, "Lady? May I enter?"

There was silence, then Cathelin's voice croaked, "Nay, Madri. Go on, then. I'll be calling if I need anything."

Madrigal laid her face against the door. "Please, Lady, let me in," she pleaded.

Abruptly, the door opened and Madrigal nearly lost her balance, but Cathelin's strong arm caught her and put her back upright. The Muslim gasped at the sight of Cathelin's red rimmed eyes, elf-locked hair, and pale face. It was obvious that her Lady was in distress, and Madrigal ached to comfort her.

"Lady," Madrigal began, but was interrupted. "Go on, Madri," Cathelin said not ungently, "Go help Shevaughn or Meagan. Or practice your song. Go on now, sweetling. I need to be alone."

She started to shut the door, but Madrigal prevented it by shoving her full belly in the gap. As Cathelin's brows drew together in a frown, Madrigal laid a hand on her arm. "Please, Lady," the dark-haired woman said. "Let me in."

Cathelin sucked in a breath, then released it in a sigh. She opened the door wider and motioned for Madrigal to come into the room.

As the door closed behind her, Madrigal turned to face her Lady. "I have heard that you have ordered Mistress Sorcha to be hanged."

Cathelin sat down on a cushioned bench and leaned forward, hands dangling between her knees. "Aye," she replied heavily. "And aye, again. God knows I do not wish it. She hurt you, Madri, and I could not have forgiven her for that, but treason is treason, even if she is of the blood; she betrayed my father as well, and tried to steal a birthright that is not lawfully hers. I could have her quartered for it, or broken on the rack—I'd be within my rights as lord of this demesne—but hanging. 'Tis swift enough, I think."

Madrigal sat down beside Cathelin on the bench. "This decision must have been very difficult for you, Lady."

"Difficult? Ah, well, it could be put that way, I suppose." Cathelin's mouth worked a moment, then tears shimmered in her amber eyes. "I'm at least in part to blame for this, Madri. I've known Sorcha since we were children. She's always envied me my place. Father thought by making her chatelaine, 'twould be reward and rank enough."

Madrigal scooted closer to Cathelin and laid her head on the other woman's shoulder. "Envy is never satisfied, Lady," she answered, entwining her fingers with Cathelin's. "Had you provided Mistress Sorcha with the moon and all the stars, she would have asked why you did not give her the mountains and seas as well."

Cathelin chuckled in spite of her tears. "You've the right of *that*. But still, 'tis a hard thing, Madri, knowing that someone will die, and that by your own word and command. Oh, Sorchi-fach," she said softly, "had I only known."

Cathelin began to cry in earnest, guilt and sorrow etching her soul, like acid. She felt Madrigal's arms encircle her, pulling her head down to a soft breast, and felt the other woman's warm, firm belly pressing against her. Cathelin wept, tears of pity and rue, and Madrigal held her as if she were a child, rocking her gently and stroking her back.

Eventually, through the boundless agony in her soul, Cathelin was startled to hear a familiar song. Her hands tightened their grip in Madrigal's skirts as the slave sang a soft Arabic cradlesong.

Cathelin's head snapped up. Her face was shiny with tears, but her eyes glowed. "Madri?" she asked, "'Twas you?" *'Twas you who chased away my nightmares*, she added silently, not daring to ask aloud. *Your voice and your song*

♦ The Sunne in Gold ♦

that have helped me forget Acre. In my dreams, I saw Irizin, but it was always you.

Madrigal smiled shyly, then wiped her Lady's face with her hand. "Yes," she replied simply. "The Horse of Evening Ill often plagues you. I have tried to help."

"Oh, Madri," Cathelin whispered, "I never knew." She buried her face against Madrigal's neck, breathing the spicy scent of her blue-black hair. "Thank you, sweetling," she murmured, "without you..."

Madrigal placed a hand on the back of Cathelin's head and stroked her hair. "It was my duty, Lady, and my pleasure."

Cathelin sat up a bit, her face very close to Madrigal's. "You mean so much to me, Madri," she said softly, searching the other woman's dark purple eyes with her own. "I," she broke off, unable to continue, and began to cry again as sorrow welled up within her; first Sorcha, now Madrigal and Irizin. It was too much.

Madrigal held her Lady, pulling her face down again, crooning softly as Cathelin desperately whispered through her tears of another land, another time, and a woman named Irizin.

"I was young, so young and full of myself, a soldier of God in King Richard's army," Cathelin said softly, voice raw from weeping. "There was a village near where we camped. I would go there sometimes in the dawning to watch the women draw water from the well.

"They were so graceful, Madri, in their robes and veils, balancing clay jars on their shoulders, scooping clean water from the well in the lavender-gray light of early morning. They were more beautiful than anything I've ever known. And one was more beautiful than the rest.

"Her name was Irizin, and the headman of the village was her master. Irizin was one of his concubines, but the first time I saw her, my heart was no more my own, and I knew I could not rest until she became mine alone."

Cathelin stopped as she remembered that morning, the first morning when she had realized that the flashing black eyes above the light veil that shielded Irizin's features were staring back at her.

The Irishwoman sighed, and continued, "Oh, I'd been in love before, Madri. Or at least I'd thought so. But Irizin was different. Soon, she began bidding me good morning. How daring her actions were, I did not understand at the time. I truly did not know, but ignorance is no excuse. I am as much to blame for her fate as any other.

"Soon enough, we were doing more than bidding one another 'Good morrow.' Irizin would slip out of the seraglio at night and visit my tent; our sentries knew, of course, but that sort of thing was winked at. She was so beautiful, Madri. All fire and grace and beauty; I was out of my mind with love, and I begged her to stay with me. I had some wild notion, you see, that I could bring her back to Ireland. I was a fool," Cathelin said bitterly.

Madrigal said nothing; she had already guessed the ending of the tale, and her heart ached for both the Lady and her lover. She held Cathelin, silently offering support, as the Irishwoman continued.

"Well, I suppose the headman must have been suspicious. Irizin, she told me about the harem. All of it, Madri, and all of what I heard made me burn. I wanted to take her away from the pain, the slavery, the humiliation. Did you know she was circumcised?"

Madrigal closed her eyes. It was common in the East for a concubine to have her clitoris cut away; this was felt to guarantee faithfulness to her Lord and master. The circumcision of females was, thank Allah, something Madrigal had never had to endure herself, although she had known those who had been mutilated in that fashion.

✦ The Sunne in Gold ✦

But Cathelin was continuing, "The first time I saw her," she gulped. "I was shocked. I could not believe, and then I was so *very* angry, Madri. I wanted to take up the sword and paint the village red with the headman's blood. But Irizin was not bitter; she told me it was Allah's will, and although I did not truly believe she could be so complacent about it, I laid my anger aside.

"Then, well, I was a puffed-up peacock, Madri. So sure of myself until I came out of my tent one morning and found Irizin there."

Madrigal listened as Cathelin told her what she had seen. Irizin had been beaten savagely; the concubine was covered in blood, and there were signs of torture on her body. Her face had been left untouched as a final blow. Cathelin saw a bloody, mangled wreck of a human being and it bore Irizin's face.

Irizin had been alive, although just barely. She had died in Cathelin's arms, unable to respond to the other woman's desperate pleas.

"I went mad," Cathelin said dully. "I was prevented from killing the headman only by the direct command of the King. So, a few days later when Acre fell, I took up my sword with a vengeance."

Madrigal caressed Cathelin's back as a flood of jangled, horrible details about the battle poured from her. Cathelin's voice was a hoarse croak by the time she had finished.

"I did not want to live, truly," Cathelin whispered. "I took my leave of the King; he dismissed me from service, and I went to the headman's house. I took him out in the desert, Madri, and I made sure he was three days dying. For four years after that, I wandered through Outremer. Half mad I was, or more than half, drunk on blood and the sound of his screams, and Irizin's face until I met a monk named Father Timothy.

♦ Nene Adams ♦

"'Twas Father Timothy who helped me. He'd been a Crusader his own self, afore God called him to higher service. He listened, he understood, and he helped *me* understand that I was not a monster. And he gave me penance, which I sorely needed. I'd a goodly deal of gold and such from the siege; Father Timothy helped me send the bulk of it to the headman's family, to atone in part for their father's murder. The rest I've used for my own people's welfare; Father Timothy would take none himself."

Madrigal nodded. Such holy men in her own land wandered from village to village, helping the less fortunate and doing Allah's will. She knew many stories about such saints; she had no doubt that her suffering Lady had been visited by one of the Christian angels, or perhaps by one of Allah's own angelic servants.

Cathelin sighed. "Ever since, I've been plagued with nightmares about that time, Madri. I thought it was a punishment from God for my sins. But," she raised her head and looked deeply into Madrigal's eyes, "now I understand more clearly. God sent you to me, sweetling. I'm as sure of this as I'm sure of my own name. And I will spend the rest of my life taking care of you. I swear it."

Madrigal's heart nearly stopped and her dark eyes widened. "No, Lady," she said desperately, "You must not say such things."

Cathelin smiled. "Sweetling," she said, stroking Madrigal's cheek, "I cannot forget Irizin. I never will. But I believe God has taken pity on me at last. For did He not send you to me?"

Madrigal shook her head. This was wrong. She was a slave, a servant, and Cathelin a great noblewoman. "Lady, I…"

Cathelin leaned forward, the bulging curve of Madrigal's belly pressing into her own flat stomach. "Ah, sweetling," she said, amber eyes soft, "don't fret so. I, I love you, Madri. I

♦ **The Sunne in Gold** ♦

need you, like song and wine and air. I love you," she whispered, eyes wide and wondering, and her lips captured Madrigal's in a gentle kiss.

Madrigal was stunned. She could not move, could not breathe, as her Lady kissed her; not with passion, but with infinite tenderness and care.

Involuntarily, Madrigal's hands slid to Cathelin's broad shoulders, then she turned her head away with a gasp. "Please, Lady," she said shakily, "I am too far below you."

Cathelin chuckled. "Nay, sweetling. At the moment, you're in exactly the right place for me to kiss you again."

Madrigal put a hand across Cathelin's lips. "Lady," she said seriously, "I am a slave. It is not proper to love such as I; I am too humble, my station does not equal yours. It would be an embarrassment to you, a humiliation, and I do not wish you to be harmed on my account."

Cathelin slid off the bench and knelt before Madrigal. She felt as if a gigantic burden had been lifted from her shoulders; despite the lingering sorrow over Sorcha, despite her regret and guilt over Irizin, she knew this was right. Madrigal had helped to heal her as much as Father Timothy, but what she felt was not only gratitude. Cathelin realized that she had loved–*truly loved*–Madrigal for some time; she had just not admitted it to herself until a few moments ago.

"Sweetling," Cathelin said, "If I wished to take a sheep into my bed, my own folk would keep their wagging tongues to themselves. I've a fierce reputation, you know, and I give not a broken reed for the opinions of strangers." Then a thought struck her. "Madri," she asked anxiously, "I don't wish you to feel you *have* to do this. True, I love you, but if you feel you cannot… You are *not* a slave. You're free to do as you please. I'll not force you into something."

Madrigal interrupted. "And since I am free, as you say, what if I wished to tell you no?"

♦ **Nene Adams** ♦

Cathelin bit her lip. "As I said, I'll *not* force you. Oh, I'll woo you a-plenty, sweetling, if you've a mind to accept such. But if you absolutely want me to let you be, I will."

Cathelin held her breath as she waited for Madrigal's reply.

Madrigal was carefully examining her own feelings. She greatly respected and admired her Lady, that was true. But *love*? With a growing sense of disbelief, Madrigal realized that she had come to love her Lady with more than a servant's devotion.

I am happy when she is happy, Madrigal thought. *If I were able, I would take all her burdens on myself, to spare her the load. When she holds me in her arms, I have never felt safer or more cherished in my life. When she touches me, I feel the stirrings of feelings I did not know I possessed. When she is gone, it is as if a part of myself is gone as well. If this is love*, she thought, disbelief turning into wonder, *then I, too, am caught in its weaving.*

Madrigal made a decision; it was not an easy one. All her life, she had obeyed the commands of others, but this woman, her own Lady, waited patiently, not pressing or demanding, for her to make up her own mind. At the urging of her heart, Madrigal surrendered.

"Lady," she said at last, reaching out one hand to touch Cathelin's face, "I, I love you as well. I am still a little unquiet in my heart of hearts, but perhaps with time, that will pass." Seeing Cathelin's eyes fill with tears of anguish, Madrigal hastened to explain, "I was raised a slave, Lady. It is all the life I have ever known. It is difficult for me to overlook the difference in our stations, but I *do* love you. And I need you as well. Come, let me show you."

Madrigal took Cathelin's hands in her own and gently tugged the other woman back to the bench. This time, it was Madrigal who leaned forward and kissed Cathelin, delicately running her tongue along the other woman's lower lip,

♦ The Sunne in Gold ♦

wanting to invoke the passion she knew lay just beneath the surface of Cathelin's tenderness.

Cathelin pressed herself against Madrigal as tightly as she dared, her mind reeling; the scent of the Muslim's hair, the softness of the body that touched her own, nearly overwhelmed her. But she was careful; she controlled herself, not wanting to hurt Madrigal or the child she carried.

Madrigal's eyes were closed, but she felt her Lady's mouth open against her own, strong hands touching her back with infinite care. Madrigal explored Cathelin's mouth, tongue fluttering and sliding, her own hands pressed against her Lady's face.

Finally, when both women were out of breath, they parted, although Madrigal kept her hands on Cathelin's cheeks.

Cathelin blew out a breath and smiled radiantly. "Well, if that's how you feel when you're unquiet, sweetling, I'd better start eating liver and such, to store up 'gainst the time when your confidence grows."

Madrigal returned her Lady's smile, pleased she had been able to give her happiness again. "I am content," she answered simply, then rose with a slight grunt. "Please, Lady," she said, holding out one hand, "Come lie with me."

Cathelin leaped to her feet. "Are you sure, sweetling?" she asked nervously, "What with the babe and all. Well, I'm of a mind to rather wait until the child is born for *that*, if it's all the same to you. Not that I find you undesirable as you are," she explained hastily, "but I don't want to hurt you, or him besides."

Madrigal laughed. "I understand. Then will you sleep with me again? I miss you in the bed, Lady." When Cathelin started to demur, Madrigal replied, "You will not hurt me. Please, Lady. Will you do this thing? It will give me great comfort."

♦ Nene Adams ♦

Against that argument, Cathelin had no defense. She bent over and kissed Madrigal's swollen belly. "As you wish, sweetling. But, 'tis back to the cot I'll be going if you wish it. And don't be shy about telling me, Madri. God knows I've never borne a babe myself, but I've heard stories."

Madrigal smiled and laced her arm through Cathelin's. "Do not fear, Lady," she answered. "As I said, I am content."

Cathelin escorted her love from the room, the Irishwoman's heart felt much lighter than it had been; Madrigal feeling as if she had begun to stretch her wings, and for the first time in her remembered life, cherished the heady sensation of *true* freedom.

♦ The Sunne in Gold ♦

♦ **Nene Adams** ♦

CHAPTER NINE

hen Madrigal woke the next morning, Cathelin was gone. Quickly, the Muslim donned a dress and with considerable effort, managed to pull on a pair of soft house shoes.

Twisting up her hair and thrusting pins into the thick coil as she hurried down the hall, Madrigal met Becca, who was coming heavily up the stairs. "What is it?" Madrigal asked, spotting the worried look on the kern's face.

Becca replied, "Lady Cathelin sent me to tell you to stay within. She doesn't want you seeing this. Sorcha's about to be hung and the Lady's up on the battlements with McLeod and Drury and Father Paul."

Madrigal hesitated; on the one hand, she felt that she must obey this order, and on the other hand, she desperately wanted to be at her Lady's side during this ordeal. Madrigal thought furiously and made her decision. If she were truly free, as her Lady had said, then she should act on her heart, not on the blind obedience that had been ingrained within her.

✦ The Sunne in Gold ✦

"Please. Take me to her," the Muslim requested, biting her lip to hide the trembling.

Becca shook her head. "Nay, lass," she answered, "I'll do no such thing. I'd end up swinging right alongside Sorcha, and no mistake."

Madrigal laid her hand on the other woman's arm. "Please?" she asked. "The Lady needs me, and I wish to be with her."

Becca sighed and rolled her brown eyes. "Oh, all right," she conceded, "I'll take you up. But I'm expectin' you'll shed a few tears when Lady Cathelin tears out my guts for harpstrings, truly."

Madrigal gave the kern a reassuring smile. "I am sure she will not mind."

Becca took Madrigal by the arm and led her to a narrow, inner staircase that accessed the roof of the castle, muttering, "Aye, she says 'twill be all right, but she's never seen the Cat in a temper; Saint Brigit protect me."

By the time they had wound their way around the stone spiral staircase, Madrigal was out of breath and her back was aching. They paused at the door a moment, Becca asking anxiously, "Are you all right? Shall I fetch one of the men to carry you?"

Madrigal struggled to control her breathing and finally, the tight pain in her ribs eased. "No, I am well," she said, "Let us go on."

The day was overcast, although a few rays of sun peeked bravely through the dark, sullen clouds that littered the sky. A chill wind whipped across the battlements, snapping and fluttering the pennants that reared on poles above the towers.

Madrigal shivered a little. She should have thought to bring a shawl but had been in too much of a hurry.

Cathelin was standing with Wolf McLeod and Michael Drury. The old priest, Father Paul, was administering the Last Rites to doomed Sorcha. The chatelaine stood bravely, the rope already about her neck, blonde braids hanging on either side of her pale face. Her hands had not been bound; this had been at her own request.

Becca escorted Madrigal to Cathelin, mentally praying to Saint Brigit, the Virgin Mary and any other saint who might be listening, to spare her the Lady's wrath.

Madrigal reached out and touched Cathelin's arm; the Irishwoman jumped a little, turning her head. Her amber eyes widened in surprise when she spotted the dark haired Muslim.

"What are you doing here, sweetling?" Cathelin asked in a low tone, not wanting to interrupt the priest's droning Latin prayers. "I thought I told Becca…"

The curly-mopped kern backed away slowly, hoping to get out of her Lady's sight before she was spotted.

Madrigal caught Cathelin's attention before her Lady could spy the sheepish soldier. "I wanted to be with you," she said. "I did not want you to face this alone."

Cathelin sighed, shaking her head, then opened her cloak and drew the smaller woman against her side, covering Madrigal with the thick wool. "Madri, I would wish you not to do this. Hanging's not a pretty death. But if you insist, I'll allow it. Just please, if you feel faint, tell me."

Madrigal nodded, insinuating herself beneath Cathelin's arm, her sweet face poking out of the front of the cloak.

Cathelin's dark red hair was held back from her face by a leather band, the rest allowed to fall unhindered down her back nearly to her knees. She wore her full regalia as an Irish chieftain–a pair of silver earrings set with amber, a heavily carved torc around her neck. Around her eyes, blue woad had been dappled in a cat pattern, that to Madrigal, made her Lady seem to be a figure of legend come to life. Beneath the cloak, Cathelin wore a black tunic covered in crimson and gold knotwork, black trews and crimson boots.

♦ The Sunne in Gold ♦

Besides the torc, she also wore a crucifix on a long silver chain. A scarlet baldric stretched from shoulder to hip, bearing the phoenix insignia of her family, the black sun on its field of gold that was her personal standard, and a red cross on a white background, which signified her status as a former Crusader.

Father Paul finished, making the sign of the cross above Sorcha's forehead with an oiled thumb. The blonde chatelaine's eyes stared out over the people that had gathered in the outer courtyard, seeking one face in particular.

This crowd was a more seemly lot than they had been before; there was none of the festival air that had offended Cathelin before. Instead, the people were somber and grave, for the Lady had caused it to be known that if any of the spectators became unruly, they would be summarily ejected, if not punished themselves. The presence of her fully armed kerns around the fringes of the assembly made it clear that she was not to be denied in this command.

Sorcha's green eyes locked on a ragtag figure who stood shoulder to shoulder with a group of peasant farmers. Even from this distance, she could pick out the figure of Lord Francis and took an odd sort of comfort in knowing that her betrothed would watch her die.

The twisted hemp rope around her neck scratched and burned her delicate skin. Sorcha clenched her fists into her skirts and forced her trembling knees to be steady. She would be damned if she would show fear now.

Cathelin drew off her cloak and tucked it around Madrigal. Striding forward into the sunlight to stand in front of Sorcha, she said gravely, "'Tis not too late, kinswoman. Confess to me the name and deeds of the one you call the 'Lord' and you can be saved yet. Come, Sorchi-fach, I've no wish for you to die. Mayhap exile, but surely you've other kin who'll take you in."

Sorcha's mouth worked a moment and she spat full into Cathelin's face. "A pox on you and your mercy!" she cried. "Know that I die this day filled with nothing but hate for you and your leman. My curse on you and all you have or own. May you rot in Hell, Cathelin O'Cameron, and I pray to the Dark Ones that you'll *never* have a moment's peace or happiness 'til my Lord and my death are revenged!" Her voice rose into a high-pitched shriek that cut across the wind like a bean-sidhe's wail.

Cathelin wiped the spittle from her face with a shaking hand. Taking a deep breath, she said, "So be it," and stepped up between two of the massive stone blocks that lined the top of the roof like blunted teeth.

"Inishowen!" Cathelin shouted, and every eye in the outer courtyard turned towards the figure of their Lady. She continued in a clear voice that had been trained to carry across a battlefield, "I call ye forth to witness. Sorcha O'Reilly, chatelaine and kinswoman of the O'Camerons, has been adjudged guilty of treason. Her crimes were that she betrayed Inishowen to the usurper, Lord Francis Westfield; and further, that she attempted to murder one of our own. For that, I have ordered her life be forfeit; this day she shall hang, and may God Almighty have mercy upon her soul."

All below crossed their breasts piously as Sorcha was helped up to the Hangman's Leap–a single rectangular block of stone that jutted out from the battlements like a stunted finger. The other end of the rope had been fastened to an iron staple set directly into the stone; when she jumped, or was pushed, she would fall directly above the outer courtyard. The height was more than sufficient to guarantee an instantly broken neck.

Cathelin nodded, and pipers began to blow a plaintive melody; it was a lorica or prayer of protection, and as they played, everyone began to chant softly in time to the music.

♦ The Sunne in Gold ♦

"God with me lying down, God with me sleeping.
God with me in sunlight or in shadow.
Evil be far from me because of Brigit's cross beneath my feet,
Mary's mantle about my shoulders,
Sweet Michael's hand within my own
And his wings spread above me, a shield of light,
And in my heart the peace of the Son of Grace.
Should malice threaten me, then the White God
Stand betwixt the blackest sin and my own soul.
For a year and a day, and from this very night,
And forever, and for eternity. Amen."

There was absolute silence as the wailing of the pipes took a more martial air and a drummer began the beat. Sorcha stood still on the Leap, skirts whipped by the chill wind, and kept her own eyes on Lord Francis'.

Finally, Cathelin nodded again, the muscles in her jaw rippling beneath the skin. Wolf McLeod approached the Leap and prepared to vault up to the finger of stone, but he was stopped by Sorcha.

"Nay, whore's dog," she said to the warrior proudly, green eyes ablaze with scorn. "Ye'll not be sendin' me down. My Lord, I kept your faith. *Avenge me!*" she continued loudly enough to be heard in the courtyard, and closing her eyes, stepped off the Leap and into space.

The snapping of Sorcha's neck was shockingly audible.

Cathelin stood stock still, lips drawn into a tight line. She waited while Sorcha's body was hauled up and her kerns began to disperse the folk in the outer courtyard. One of the young priests from the abbey, Father Reuben, had come to bear witness for Abbott Benedict; he threw a length of clean white linen over Sorcha's twisted features after she was laid down on the flagstones.

♦ Nene Adams ♦

Cathelin walked over to the corpse of the one she had called her kinswoman; kneeling down, she pulled aside the cloth and softly kissed Sorcha's still brow. "God will judge thee, Sorchi-fach," she whispered, "for I cannot."

Then she stood and went back to her place on the wall. "Inishowen," she cried, "I have called ye forth to the place of execution to witness justice. Look upon this work, and remember this day. The law shall *not* be broken!"

There was a roar of approval from the folk who were being herded out of the gates, from Cathelin's kerns, and from the castle folk who had stopped their duties to watch the rare execution.

As everyone went about their duties, gossiping and chatting, Cathelin walked back to Madrigal. Her face was stony, amber eyes dulled with pain, and her breath came in harsh gasps.

Madrigal immediately hurried over and reached the Irishwoman just as she thudded to her knees, face buried in her hands, keening in a high-pitched wail of grief and unutterable loss.

Wolf McLeod, Michael Drury and the others quietly carried Sorcha's body away on a litter to prepare her for burial. Cathelin reached up blindly and buried her face in Madrigal's skirts, sobbing uncontrollably.

Madrigal put both hands on her Lady's head and spread her legs apart for balance as the Irishwoman wept.

At last, the storm of weeping eased. Cathelin raised her face; streaks of woad ran down her cheeks like jester's face paint. "Oh, Madri," she whimpered, "what have I done?"

Madrigal had closed her eyes when Sorcha had leaped; she had not watched the body being drawn up. She understood the burden her Lady was under–as the mistress of Inishowen's domain, justice and the keeping of the law were in her hands. Truthfully, Madrigal was somewhat relieved at Sorcha's death; that woman had been the cause of a great

✦ The Sunne in Gold ✦

many of her hurts, and the former slave felt she had gotten only what she deserved.

"Lady," Madrigal asked, "Did not Mistress Sorcha break your laws?"

Cathelin nodded dumbly.

"And did she not betray your father and yourself?" Madrigal continued.

Again, Cathelin could only nod in forlorn agreement.

"Then what you have done this day is justice, not revenge. Be at ease in your heart, Lady. In my country, criminals receive far worse, as you know. At least, her death was merciful as well as richly deserved."

Cathelin was shocked. "B-b-but sweetling!" she protested, "Sorcha was kin. You do not understand what you are saying."

Madrigal interrupted, her lustrous eyes full of wisdom beyond her years. "If all were permitted to receive no punishment for their crimes, then the world would burn in the fires of chaos. There must be laws; there must be punishments; there must be justice. That is all. Kin or not, if she broke your laws, and you have said that she did, then let Allah be merciful if He wishes, for you cannot. Are you not required to follow the law as well? Did you not offer her chance after chance? Surely, none could have done more."

Slowly, the throbbing ache in Cathelin's chest eased. She still grieved over having ordered Sorcha's death–never in her life would she forget that awful moment when her kinswoman stepped into God's arms–but at least, that death was justified. She had tried to be merciful, but had she allowed Sorcha's crimes to stand... *Well, that I could not do*, Cathelin thought. *I will pray for the deliverance of her soul and hope her death is not counted as sin against me when I go to my own judgment. That is all any one of us can do.*

Cathelin stood, looking ruefully at the dark blue woad stains on Madrigal's dress and her own cloak. "I've ruined your pretty dress, sweetling," she said with a sigh. "You're right. I do only what I must. Even as lord of Inishowen, my obedience of the law is no less required than that of a peasant."

Madrigal nodded. In the physician's household, she had come to know many of his patients, and some were judges in the caliph's own courts. She had heard this argument before, about the justification of dealing death to criminals; she was glad that she had remembered enough to give her Lady some freedom from guilt and pain.

Cathelin said gravely, "For what she did to you, sweetling, I could have slit her throat myself, truly. But revenge is not lawful. Justice is. The folk must have justice."

She held Madrigal's hand tightly as she walked across the lonely battlements, and the only sound they heard was the cry of a hunting hawk high above the castle and pennants snapping crisply in the smoke-scented wind.

Sorcha's body had been laid out in the small chapel attached to the castle. Despite the treason that had been the cause of her execution, Cathelin had ordered that she receive an honorable burial in the family cemetery. The chatelaine who had so zealously craved position and respect - who had so envied the honors bestowed on others – was, in death, to receive the attention and merit she did not earn in her lifetime.

Her hair and body had been washed and anointed with rose oil; a fine linen winding sheet lay neatly folded at her feet. Sorcha had been dressed in a green wool gown that matched the color of her eyes – her favorite festival dress -

✦ The Sunne in Gold ✦

and a prettily embroidered scarf wound about her throat hid the livid marks of the rope. Her face was concealed behind a veil, and a chaplet of seed pearls crowned her rich blonde braids.

A pair of expensive beeswax candles burned near the bier, and moonlight glowed through a tiny stained glass window behind the alter, bathing the dead woman in beams of sullen scarlet, blue and emerald. Father Paul, the household priest, had said Mass, praying earnestly that Sorcha's penance in Purgatory would be mercifully brief. An old man plagued by gout and rheumatism, he had long since sought the comfort of his warm bed, leaving the body alone and unattended.

The night was silent, save for skittering mice, the rustling of wind through the leaves, and a gentle pattering of rain.

When the door to the chapel was eased open and a figure slipped inside, no one raised the alarm. It was a few hours till dawn; decent folk were long abed and the sentries on the wall watched for trouble from without, not within.

Lord Francis crept quietly up to the bier, his wet cloak trailing water on the floor. His hair was a tangled mess, his hazel eyes bloodshot and swollen.

"Sorcha," he whispered hoarsely, reaching out a trembling hand to caress her hair. "My sweet lass. What have they done to you?"

He stayed motionless for nearly a half hour, staring at the corpse as if by sheer will power he could cause her to rise and live again. Finally, hands clenched into fists, he walked away and began to strike the rough stone altar again and again, smashing his knuckles with reckless abandon, panting hard between his teeth as grief and madness drove him into a frenzy.

There was barely a sound save for the harsh rasp of his breathing. At long last, exhaustion forced him to stop. He held up his hands and stared at the bloodied flesh curiously, flexing his fingers without a wince. Sunk deep within the depths of insanity, Francis felt no pain. His knuckles were scraped raw, nearly down to the bone, but he did not care.

Had he been capable of admitting the truth to himself, it was not love that drove him to self mutilation but the sheer frustration of the moment. Seducing Sorcha had been one of his more intelligent acts; using her as a direct conduit into the castle, he had been able to gain valuable information and communicate with his allies without much risk to himself. Now that she was gone, his task was made much more difficult.

He walked once more to the bier and looked down at the veil covering Sorcha's face. Whisking it away, he took in her open eyes – as green as spring, he had once told her – and her mouth, lips parted slightly as if waiting for a kiss. If it were not for her fixed stare, he could have believed her asleep.

"So beautiful," he groaned softly, suddenly full of desire. His manhood twitched and hardened as the memory of her soft, warm body – so welcoming, so tender, so ripe for passion – made him forget that he had considered her merely a tool. "You are perfect and perfectly pleasing, my lady."

Bending down, Francis pressed his mouth on Sorcha's lips, forcing his tongue inside, ignoring the stale taste of death. He whimpered when her arms did not enfold him, did not draw his head down to her breasts, did not urge him to greater heights of passion.

Nearly frantic, he pulled apart her bodice and caressed her cold breasts, sucking at her mouth like a hungry babe. He stared into her unseeing eyes, no longer indifferent but actually aching for her to return. Because he could not have her now, Francis valued Sorcha more than when she'd been alive.

✦ The Sunne in Gold ✦

A gust of foul breath from the depths of the dead woman's belly blew past his lips and he nearly retched, pushing himself away.

His erection withered at the memory of Sorcha standing so proudly on the Hangman's Leap and the brittle snap of her neck breaking when she had hurled herself into oblivion rather than betray him.

He would never forget that sound.

"It's all *her* fault!" he hissed in fury. "That murderous bitch! Slut! Whore!" He continued to rant, heaping curses on Cathelin's head in a strained whisper. He might have been insane but Francis was still not above caution. "She was mine! Mine! *Mine!*"

That he could have saved the chatelaine by surrendering himself never entered his mind. Everything was always someone else's fault – he would never cease blaming Cathelin for all his ills – and he prized his own skin too much to sacrifice his life for another's.

Running out of breath, he became quiet again and began absently pulling one of Sorcha's braids through his fingers, staining the pale tresses with blood. His unstable psyche made another shift and he beamed at the corpse, giving it his most charming smile.

"Come with me, my lady," he crooned. "Let me save you from my cousin's tender mercies. We will have our vengeance soon, you and I, my Sorcha, my love. Our friends are gathering and it will all be ours soon... soon..."

Francis tenderly gathered the dead woman into his arms and kissed her forehead. It pleased him that she stared so dutifully into his face, never blinking, as if she did not dare look away without his permission.

She was so limp, so acquiescent, so helpless that he felt his heart swell with affection.

Wrapping Sorcha's body with his own cloak to protect her from the rain, Francis left the chapel with his prize.

♦ Nene Adams ♦

"What do you mean, gone?" Cathelin frowned at Father Paul and wondered for a moment if the old man was beginning his second childhood. The chapel was empty save for the two of them; she had come running at his summons without taking time to break her fast, leaving Madrigal stuffing herself with porridge and eggs alone.

The priest scrubbed at his white whiskers. "My sorrow to trouble you with this foul business, my lady, but Mistress Sorcha's body has vanished from the chapel. There's blood on the altar as well, sweet Mary preserve us." He crossed himself and gripped the crucifix on his rosary as tightly as his swollen fingers would allow.

Cathelin was struggling with her mixed emotions at this unwelcome news. Part of her wanted to scream in frustration and tear at her hair – had the wench not caused enough trouble? – and another part wanted to howl in rage at the sheer audacity of whoever had dared to bring further disgrace to the clan. Either reaction would have shocked Father Paul to the core, so she swallowed hard and tried to compose herself.

"Was my cousin's body left alone last evening?" she asked.

"Aye, my lady." The priest looked miserable. "I'm not so young as I used to be, ye ken. I went to my wee house to lie down for a while – my bones ache somethin' fierce when the weather turns to rain – and I didn't wake up till the cock crowed this mornin'. May God forgive me for the sin of sloth," he added, shaking his grizzled head.

Cathelin stalked over to the altar and examined the bloody smears and flecks of flesh adhering to the rough stone.

♦ The Sunne in Gold ♦

"'Tis fresh enough," she muttered, running a finger across the scarlet stain. "Naught but a few hours old, or I'm no judge."

"Who would be so blasphemous as to desecrate the altar of Our Lord?" Father Paul asked, suddenly horrified as a fresh idea presented itself to him. "Who would risk their immortal soul by stealing a corpse? Could there be necromancers or witches in the village?" He crossed himself again in obvious distress. "Have there been demonic rituals in this sacred space while I slept unaware? Sweet Jesu!"

Cathelin shook her head and patted the old man's shoulder to comfort him. "I doubt it. You know as well as I that anyone dancin' widdershins or riding withy-sticks within a league of the village would set the biddy-gossips' tongues to wagging faster than a winter gale."

Father Paul considered this and looked a little relieved "Aye, my lady, I find I must agree with ye. The village is small and close; 'tis difficult to keep such dark secrets when your neighbors' eyes see all that ye do and the smallest sin finds its way into the confessional box - will ye, nil ye."

The Irishwoman went to the open door and glanced around; evening rain had turned the dirt beyond the stone lintel into a morass of mud and puddles of dirty water. A confused variety of footprints was churned into the ground – hers, the priest's, the messenger he'd sent and many others.

Cathelin cursed beneath her breath; the kerns often used a shortcut from their quarters to the dining hall, and it took them directly past the chapel. If an army twice the size of her own had done a spirited reel before the doors, it could not have made more of a mess.

She stood quietly for a moment, contemplating. As near as she knew, none of the villagers or castle folk bore such a grudge against Sorcha that they would deny her Christian burial. Not only that, but corpse thieving was a mortal sin as well as an act punishable by secular law. It took either incredible courage or extraordinary evil to risk both imprisonment on Earth and the fires of Hell afterward.

A thought struck her and Cathelin's eyes went wide.

'Twas the mystery lover who came and stole Sorcha away! It could be no other. Realizing that they had missed a prime opportunity to catch Sorcha's partner in treason made Cathelin want to give herself a sharp kick in the buttocks. No one, not even Wolf, had considered that the mysterious 'Lord' might pay a midnight visit to his dead leman.

Stupid woman! she berated herself savagely. *Had your brains not been stuffed with goosefeathers, you could have ordered a discreet watch and caught this 'Lord' of Sorcha's before he could stir up more trouble!*

The expression on her face must have been fierce, for when Father Paul tentatively touched her arm, he flinched when she turned her attention to him. "I ken that the affair's a troublesome one," he said, mistaking her distress for another cause, "but I need to know, my lady, what should I do now?"

Cathelin took a deep breath and calmed herself with an effort. "'Twas a man sunk deep in vile intentions who did this thing, Father. We know not his face or name, tho' I'd give a pretty fortune to have him in my hands this hour."

"Mayhap not this hour but another," came a new voice from outside the chapel. Wolf McLeod strode towards them through the mud and nodded politely to the priest before continuing, "I've heard o' the night's doings. May I have a moment alone with the Lady?"

Father Paul bowed his head and went away to the altar to pray. Not wasting time, the minute the priest was out of earshot, Wolf continued in a low voice, "D'ye remember how we salted the courtyard with watchers for the hangin'?"

"Aye, that I do." Cathelin raised an eyebrow. "Tell me, man, how did you hear of the theft so quickly?"

Wolf snorted in grim amusement. "The good Father's messenger is even now sittin' in state in Mistress

♦ The Sunne in Gold ♦

Shevaughn's kitchen, soakin' up ale and honeycakes, tellin' all and sundry that Sorcha's body was spirited away by the Crooked Man himself, flyin' down to Hell on brimstone fired wings."

Despite her anger, Cathelin had to grin. "I'll wager the audience is so large, they're perching on each other's heads and stacked tighter than herrings in a barrel. Well, I only hope we won't have to pry the servants out of the kitchen with steel bars and picks afore the evening meal."

Wolf's eyes twinkled. "Aye, ye've the right o' that."

"So, Master McLeod, did you come here to witness the cloven prints burned into the altar yourself or had you another cause?"

The Scottish warrior sobered. "As I was sayin' before, Lady, there were sharp eyed kerns amongst the witnesses. I've just this moment received word from 'em." He stopped and tugged his mustache, dismay mingled with triumph in his expression.

"Well, out with it, man! What's got you twisting in your breechclout like a gigged eel?"

"Ye'll not be likin' this, Lady, but ye must know what the spies uncovered. My sorry, for this is truly ill news, but I'd be a puir second if I kept it under the hedgerow 'till it rotted."

Sharply and succinctly, Wolf conveyed the information to Cathelin, sparing nothing. Although a more detailed report would come later, the initial reconnaissance revealed enough. It was ill news indeed, and the Irishwoman's face blanched in shock. Even her lips were colorless and for a moment, Wolf feared she might faint.

Slowly, color flooded back into her cheeks until they blazed. Through clenched teeth, she ground out in a cold, silky tone, "Is it confirmed, then?"

"Aye." The Scottish warrior's face might have been carved from stone. His belly muscles were clenched, as if anticipating a blow. He had rarely seen his Lady so angry. "Shall we take the whore's get now? 'Twill take but a moment to muster out a force and winkle him out o' his shell."

"So, that's the secret poor Sorcha took to the Leap. I'd feared as much, but wanted to be sure." Cathelin turned away, balling up her hands into fists. "Stupid girl. A man like that is not deservin' of such loyalty, misplaced tho' it was."

"What are your commands?" Wolf drew himself up straighter and put a hand on his sword hilt, obviously eager for the hunt. Cathelin pulled him short with a gesture.

A nasty grin spread across her face as she quoted one of her father's favorite aphorisms, "Keep your friends close and your enemies closer." Cathelin took Wolf by the arm and whispered in his ear. When she finished, the Scottish warrior beamed savagely.

"Beautiful cunnin'!" Wolf exclaimed in approval. "A huntin' party might catch a single fox, but lay a patient trap and ye'll bag the lot. Well, 'tis a mort o' work ye've laid upon my plate but I'll no complain. Leave it all to me."

"You know I trust you, man. Swear your men to silence and secrecy; there may be other traitors who would escape if they knew the sword above their necks was about to fall."

"Aye, and aye again." With a brusque nod, Wolf splashed away to obey her orders and set the plan in motion.

Cathelin's gaze followed the kilted figure until it was completely out of sight. She, too, would keep Sorcha's secret and tell no one, not even Madrigal. *Especially* not Madrigal – there was no sense upsetting the pregnant woman with such worries. She would protect her love with silence as long as necessary.

Cathelin beckoned to Father Paul and when the priest came to her side, said flatly, "Set the minds of your flock at ease and reassure them that there's no cause for alarm."

✦ The Sunne in Gold ✦

"How shall I do that, Lady?"

The Irishwoman's shoulders twitched in an almost shrug. "Tell them the truth. Sorcha's body was taken by a man – not a demon or a spirit, but a man like any other, flesh and blood, tho' black of heart. You know not why he should have done this deed, but it smacks of human evil, not witchcraft or the dark arts."

"That is so," the old man said, fingering his rosary. "I'd best summon the village hetman and call a special meetin'. 'Twould be best to act quickly and spread the truth, or within a fortnight, every herb wife will be suspected as a witch and then ignorant folk'll start pilin' up kindlin' for bonfires."

"I rely on your wisdom, Father," Cathelin murmured.

Father Paul's rheumy eyes narrowed. "And what will ye be doin' to solve this mystery?" he asked. "While the thief has no face and hides yet in the shadows, the villagers will wonder no matter what I say."

Cathelin startled the old man by giving him a beatific smile. "Why, I am going to break my fast with the woman I love," she answered lightly. "So since my stomach thinks my throat's been cut, I'll beg your leave and be on my way."

Father Paul watched her go and crossed himself slowly. He did not know what troubled him more – the theft of Sorcha's body or the mercurial change in Cathelin's attitude.

Still puzzled, the old man went back to his altar to pray for guidance, all the while wondering what dread secrets might be bubbling beneath the life current of castle Inishowen.

♦ **Nene Adams** ♦

CHAPTER TEN

It was Samhain, the Feast of All Saints, and Madrigal proudly smoothed the front of her new gown. Made of heavy wool dyed with purplish blackberry stain, the Muslim had sewn tiny bone buttons in the shape of flying birds all over the bodice, and the full skirts were decorated with braided loops of bright ribbonwork.

Cathelin walked into the chamber, carrying a mysterious sack over her shoulder. "Well, sweetling?" she asked with a grin. "Are you ready for the festival?"

The Irishwoman wore the teal blue, silver-knotworked tunic Madrigal had repaired, and a pair of light tan leather trews. Her cloak was pinned at one shoulder with a round brooch set with a cabochon beryl.

Madrigal returned her Lady's smile and settled the silver chain of her precious necklace over her head. The agate with its intaglio design of a phoenix glowed against the

♦ The Sunne in Gold ♦

purple-black of her dress. "Yes," she answered with a soft smile of her own, "I am ready."

"Hmmmm." Cathelin cocked her head to one side and studied the other woman. "Sweetling, I'm thinkin' you're a mite underdressed."

"Underdressed?" Madrigal looked down at herself in confusion. "I do not understand."

For answer, Cathelin reached into the sack and drew out a harp. Madrigal caught her breath. The lap harp was made of dark wood heavily carved with leaping dolphins set with ivory, gold spirals and polished agates. It was the most beautiful instrument Madrigal had ever seen.

"'Tis for you, Madri. I had it off a Sassenach trader a little while back. He played her for me. She's got a sweet sound, and 'tis God's truth that she'll match your voice marvelous well."

Madrigal reached out and took the harp, running a finger across the strings. The tone was high and pure, like a young boy's voice. She sat down carefully on the edge of the bed and propped the instrument against her bulging belly, head cocked to one side. Skilled fingers quickly plucked a rippling melody and she smiled. Not only did the harp have the sweetest sound she had ever heard, but it was perfectly tuned.

Madrigal rose, a beaming smile lighting up her face. "Thank you, Lady," she said, walking over to Cat to bestow a kiss on the other woman's chin. "It is a beautiful and fine gift. I will play it tonight in your honor."

Cathelin leaned down and kissed Madrigal's lips before the other woman could move away. "Will you not call me Cat, Madri? 'Tis what my friends call me, and my kin mostly; you're both and much more, besides."

Madrigal nodded shyly. "I will try, Lady Cat," she replied, compromising a bit, and was rewarded for her effort with another kiss.

♦ Nene Adams ♦

"We'd best be going, sweetling, if you're not to miss the contest. Don't forget your cloak; 'tis as cold as a witch's tit outside, even with the bonfires."

Madrigal chuckled and pulled her cloak off the hook. Cathelin fastened it around her shoulders, taking time for another kiss. .

Cathelin insisted on carrying Madrigal down the stairs, which did not embarrass the Muslim anymore. In truth, not only did she enjoy the sensation of Cathelin's strong arms bearing her lightly, but she also tired more easily these days.

There is only one small thing that makes my happiness incomplete, Madrigal thought as Cathelin put her down at the bottom of the stairs and escorted her to the outer courtyard. *And that is that my Lady still fears to touch me with passion rather than tenderness.*

Although Cathelin had begun to sleep with Madrigal again, she had attempted no further intimacy other than a few kisses. The Muslim woman was growing annoyed at this reticence. Cathelin had assured her that she found her beautiful and desirable, but... *I know she has not visited the barracks*, Madrigal thought. *Surely, her need must be strong, but her will is stronger. I must think on this and decide what to do.*

Both the inner and outer courtyards of Inishowen were filled with people. Samhain was an important festival, for it marked the beginning of winter's cycle and foretold the ending of the year. Rush torches and bonfires had been lit, and the walls of the castle were hung with colorful buntings and branches of pine and rowan.

All around there were tales and song. Inishowen's hospitality to minstrels and bards was legendary; some had come from as far away as London to participate in the contests and entertain the folk.

Cathelin led the bemused Madrigal to the inner courtyard, where a song contest was to be held. Already, the

♦ The Sunne in Gold ♦

space was filled with both contestants and interested spectators, milling about, drinking beer, ale and cider and tuning their instruments.

At the moment, the story-telling contest was winding down. An old woman with a hooked nose and tiny eyes set like raisins in the wrinkled skin of her face was concluding the ghost story, "The Adventures of Nera."

"... And so Nera, mighty hero, vanished into the sidhe, walking boldly into the mists of shadow... and was never seen or heard from again," the old woman concluded with a hair-raising cackle. There was a whoop of appreciation from the spectators and the judges smiled.

Cathelin led Madrigal to a bench that had been set up against one wall. It was crowded already, but as soon as the Lady of Inishowen was spotted, a space was hastily made to accommodate her heavily pregnant companion.

"Sweetling," Cathelin said, bending down to plant a kiss on the other woman's brow, "I'll be on the judge's dais. Don't be nervous or upset; just play and sing as if for my kerns and all will be well."

Madrigal smiled and fingered her harp as Cathelin strode away. She had been working on a very special song for her Lady. At first, she had thought to do one of the provocative songs of her homeland that had been popular in the harem, but had ultimately decided against it. Surprisingly, it had been Wolf McLeod who had recommended a particular song, and Madrigal was grateful for his help.

Her dark eyes searched the crowd for familiar faces. She spotted Becca Half-Tongue, dressed in brilliant crimson and dark blue, hanging onto the arm of a handsome minstrel; Wolf McLeod was dressed in somber black and gray, eating a roasted apple and talking to a gray-bearded old man who held a branch of wood hung with tiny bells; Shevaughn was regaling a group of children with a grisly ghost story.

♦ Nene Adams ♦

  Madrigal sat and waited her turn, listening to the other performers. Most were talented amateurs, but there were one or two whose polished performances were breath-taking. These would be the ones that Madrigal would have to outshine if she were to win.
  Finally, her turn came. Rising, she came forward and seated herself on the small bench that sat on the dais. The judges sat to one side behind their long table; all eyes turned to her as she adjusted her cloak and began to play an ancient Irish air with an oddly compelling melody.

"She is pure gold, she is a heaven round a sun," Madrigal sang,
"A wine filled cup of silver, amber and summer's light;
She pours forth honey from her mouth,
And a saint's wisdom is bound within her words.
An angel, a precious stone of charity,
Her heart burns with divine passion and right.
A sweet branch heavy with blossoms,
A glittering stream, a spear of truth, a chariot of might;
None dare pass where she has tread her foot,
Her wings spread far, feathers brushing the night.
The moon that glories holy Heaven
Is far less beautiful, for she is glitter bright.
An alter of her eyes, a shrine of her face,
A temple of her swan white neck,
She is never less than a Lady's grace.
She is white-bronze, she is gold.
She is my beloved; her virtues are untold."

  For a moment there was silence, then the crowd burst into wild shouts of approval. Most knew of Madrigal, though many had never met her. But all knew enough to recognize the Muslim's song as a tribute of love to Lady Cathelin, and although some disapproved of Madrigal's religion,

♦ The Sunne in Gold ♦

nevertheless they had to acknowledge the honor she had done their Lady and themselves.

Cathelin brushed aside a tear. Madrigal's achingly pure voice soaring in that beautiful love-lilt had touched her deeply. Glancing around, she saw from the expression on the other judges' faces that they had been just as affected.

Madrigal rose and bowed her head, then stepped lightly from the dais. She had seen the look on Cathelin's face and the tear; she smiled to herself as she went back to the bench, pleased beyond all measure that her Lady approved.

Madrigal's performance seemed to take the heart out of the other contestants. In a short time, the judges were ready to announce the winner. Sir James ap Mathonwy, a man of middle-height and dignified bearing, came forward. In his hands he held a crown made of autumn leaves bound with grasses and wound with trailing scarlet ribbons.

"As you know," Sir James said, "it is the duty of a judge to be impartial. But many of us here tonight—nay, all of us—were so moved by a particular song that we could not help but declare our favor. Need I truly tell you who has won the crown?"

The crowd roared, *"Madrigal!"* as Sir James beamed and gestured for the Muslim to take her place on the dais.

Madrigal was trembling but her face was wreathed in a glorious smile. Sir James laid the winner's crown on her head, and she turned to Cathelin, dark eyes filled with light and incandescent joy.

Cathelin was so proud of her love she thought her heart would burst. She sprang to her feet and clasped Madrigal in her arms, kissing the other woman in full view of the crowd, which snickered, sighed and clapped wildly.

Madrigal looked up into Cathelin's shining amber eyes. "Are you pleased, Lady Cat?"

♦ Nene Adams ♦

"Sweetling, I am so pleased and proud 'tis a wonder and a marvel that I can stand without falling arse-over-crown. Oh, Madri, I do love you so."

"I love you as well," Madrigal replied shyly.

Cathelin led Madrigal from the dais, unaware that amidst the throng, two pairs of eyes watched them, glittering with hate and awful purpose.

The two women wandered the festival, stopping now and then to hear a story, or speak to a visitor, or nibble a treat. Finally, however, Madrigal confessed herself exhausted.

"I am sorry, Lady Cat," she said as Cathelin carried her back into the castle, "Please, stay and enjoy the feast. I will do well enough."

"Madri, don't fash yourself. The folk will get wondrous drunk and eat themselves sick, and on the morrow, we'll be lucky to have no broken heads or hearts to tend to. I had much rather spend the time with you."

Madrigal smiled and snuggled her face into Cathelin's neck. She was tired, but not nearly as worn out as she had claimed. In fact, she had some very good ideas about the way she wanted to spend time with her Lady, and all of them involved the bed, and none of them involved sleeping.

Cathelin carried Madrigal into the master's chambers, kicking the door shut behind her with one foot. Carefully, she eased Madrigal down until the other woman was standing on her own.

Cathelin had just removed her cloak when Madrigal asked with calculated innocence, "Lady Cat? How is it that you have not been with Mistress Aoife these days?"

♦ The Sunne in Gold ♦

Cathelin nearly choked. Aoife, the rambunctious kern with whom she had shared a night of tupping in the hayloft, had indeed let it be known that she was not loathe to test her commander's stamina again. Although Cathelin had been feeling deprived of late, she had sternly curbed her libido. She did not want to hurt Madrigal by turning to another.

"Er," Cathelin replied, stalling for time, "Aoife? Who is that, Madri?"

Madrigal laughed, hanging up her own cloak. "Why, have I not heard tales in the soldier's barracks of you and Mistress Aoife and a certain hayloft?"

Cathelin flushed. She really did not want to discuss her previous sexual partners with the woman she loved. "Oh, *that* Aoife," she answered, pulling off her tunic, boots and trews in quick succession. "'Twas not a matter of any great moment, sweetling. Only for one night, and before I loved you, besides."

Madrigal stepped in front of Cathelin, her eyes slowly appraising the naked woman from heel to crown, lingering deliberately on her Lady's firm breasts and most especially, the flamboyantly red cluster of curls between her muscular thighs.

"I can understand why she would wish for your return to her loft, Lady Cat," Madrigal purred, licking her lips, "You are a very desirable woman."

Cathelin was growing increasingly warm and uncomfortable. "Um, Madri?" she asked tentatively. "Do you not want to go to bed, sweetling? You said you were tired."

Madrigal pressed herself against Cathelin, and the other woman gulped as the fabric of the Muslim's dress brushed against her legs and belly. "I do wish to go to bed, Lady Cat," Madrigal said softly, reaching up one hand and tracing Cathelin's bottom lip, "but I do *not* wish to sleep."

As Cathelin desperately tried to think of something, anything, to say–half of her wanted to ravish Madrigal then and there, the other half still feared hurting her–there came a discreet scratching at the door.

Biting back a curse, Cathelin strode to the door and flung it open to confront the disapproving frown of Abbott Benedict.

The abbot's cold gray eyes flickered as he took in Cathelin's nudity. "Lady," he said, reclining his head slightly, "There are matters I wish to discuss with you, if you are not otherwise *engaged*?" He lifted his brow at this delicately phrased inquiry, and Cathelin blushed furiously–in anger, not embarrassment.

"One moment, Father Abbott," she replied and snatched her cloak from its hook by the door. Flinging it about her shoulders, she said shortly, "What is it?"

Benedict stared down his nose at Cathelin, hands hidden in the sleeves of his voluminous robe. The ebony rosary of his office was around his neck, and a heavy gold crucifix studded with rubies, sapphires and pearls showed that material wealth was more important to him than spiritual rewards or vows of poverty. These jewels were an expression of the abbot's power, a symbol of his venial nature, and he cared not who knew it, save only that they be impressed by his status and wealth

"The matter regards Sir Alexander Wallace," he replied tranquilly.

"I see." Cathelin raised her own dark red brow and continued, "What of the pig-dog?"

"You know the Church frowns on duels, my Lady," Benedict said, a slight sneer on his lips. Behind Cathelin, he could see the figure of her Muslim whore, a hand on her mouth and eyes cast downward as if shamed and surprised. *The slave is obviously overawed by me,* the abbot thought with smug satisfaction. *Even such an unnatural woman acknowledges my authority in God.*

✦ The Sunne in Gold ✦

He drew himself up a little taller and continued proudly, "Nevertheless, I have been commissioned by Sir Alexander's surviving family to petition you for the return of..."

Cathelin interrupted flatly. "There was no duel. 'Twas an lawful execution by right of my oath as a knight, and according to the rule of our Orders. The Hospitaler's motherhouse was given due notice as well. So whatever his family's request, I say them nay."

Benedict's eyebrows shot towards his hairline and he struggled to control his dismay and surprise. "Surely you do not mean to deny his family the comfort of a Christian burial close to his ancestral home?"

Cathelin waved a dismissive hand. "The Benedictine brothers have laid the bastard's bones in consecrated soil, and I paid for the grave and a Mass, besides. I offered him the comfort of confession and shriving before my sword fell on his neck. His family inherits his horse, plate, weapons and whatever wealth he did not squander – they should be thankful that I was satisfied with his execution and haven't demanded a blood price from his entire clan for the insult he gave to one who is very dear to me. What I took from his body is unimportant, and do they wish it so much, let them come and reive it away from me if they will."

She started to shut the door, but Benedict interrupted. His face was red and his eyes dark with anger. "You would defy God, Lady? For I am one of His authorities on Earth and as such, have the divine right to order you to make restitution or imperil your immortal soul. Return what you have stolen and I will make your penance light; refuse, and I will do everything in my power as a representative of Our Holy Mother Church to see you punished."

Cathelin had been pushed too far. The good mood of the earlier evening had fled, replaced by stark fury. "You forget yourself, Father Abbott," she hissed, "and your place.

♦ Nene Adams ♦

Go back behind your walls, you gape-mouth, lolly-locked hypocrite, and wear out your knees before the altar of the God you truly worship. Or did you believe that I knew nothing of your filthy secrets?"

Benedict turned pale and reeled back a step, dignity forgotten in the sudden flash of shock and panic. "You, you, you know?"

"Of course." Cathelin tossed her head. "My walls have ears, Father," she replied with deadly sweetness, "and my village as well. I've not told the Bishop yet, but I can have a messenger on a fast horse within the hour."

"No!" Benedict said in a strangled voice. "I, I, I withdraw my petition and my order, Lady Cathelin," he continued. "Do as you will in the matter; I have already forgotten it."

"Why, 'tis thanking you I am, for all your graciousness," Cathelin said sarcastically. "Now, is this business done?" In truth, Cathelin had no idea what the abbot's 'secrets' might have been, but she knew he was the type to have many; she had used this sort of bluff before and was pleased that it had worked.

"Yes." Benedict turned to go, then stopped. "What shall I tell Wallace's family?" he asked, shoulders slumping in defeat.

"Tell them to be glad I took only his head and granted him the mercy of a quick death. Slow torture would have been too good for his sins," Cathelin answered shortly, then slammed the door shut in his face.

Benedict was shaken. *How had she known?* he thought, as he walked down the stairs. *I've been so careful. I'm certain none of the boys would have told their parents, not with the threat of hellfire and damnation hanging above their heads.*

As the abbot walked through Inishowen, surprise and fear turned into renewed hatred and a further resolve to see

♦ The Sunne in Gold ♦

that the hammer of Almighty God struck the red-haired whore with all the power at his disposal.

Madrigal stood in the middle of the room. She had overheard the conversation–there had been no choice–and now, she did not know what to say or how to act. Her Lady had slain the Inglizi ! The dark-haired woman did not know whether to laugh, cry or faint dead away in astonishment and awe.

Cathelin removed the cloak and hung it back on its hook. "Sweetling," she began, and stopped, licking her lips nervously.

Madrigal sat down in a chair next to the hearth and kept silent, her hands clasped over her swollen belly.

Cathelin scratched her head. In truth, she would rather Madrigal had not found out about Wallace's death just yet; she had been saving the tale for a special Solstice treat, and had commissioned a minstrel to write a special song to be sung in the Great Hall during the winter celebration.

"Er, Madri," Cathelin began again, seating herself in the chair opposite Madrigal. "I did not want to tell you just yet. I would have, sweetling, only, well, I wanted to surprise you."

"I am surprised," Madrigal replied, dark eyes wide. Her hands trembled slightly; she could not quite grasp that the Inglizi was truly dead, that he would trouble her no more in this life.

"Did I not swear, sweetling, that I'd make a present to you of his head? I went a-hunting Wallace and finally caught him."

♦ **Nene Adams** ♦

"And?" Madrigal asked, still reeling from this unexpected news.

" "And I executed him as an oathbreaker. 'Twas the best way, you see, for I could not involve our clan in a war with his by killing him outside the law. The whole thing was done in Dublin. Do you remember when I had to go away for a few days to settle a yeoman's dispute? Well, I lied." Cathelin looked slightly ashamed. "My sorrow for the untruth, sweetling. I did not want you to worry.".

Madrigal nodded. "I understand," she replied softly. "There is nothing to forgive, Lady. Please to on."

"There is precious little left to the tale. He was no real knight, Madri, just a callous swine with evil appetites dressed in a pretty rank. Any skill he had was long ago pawned to wine. He squirmed like an eel, trying to save his skin, but the right was mine. I took off his head with one blow and it ended there."

"He did not suffer?"

"I agree 'twas a kinder death than he deserved. I've no stomach for torture, but if you'd rather I'd taken him alive, I understand. I'd even have sharpened the knives for you, sweetling, but..." Her voice trailed off as she saw, in her mind's eye, another man's face amid sand and wind.

Madrigal felt a sudden swelling of emotion in her breast. It was not sorrow–she would never be sorry the evil Inglizi was dead–it was vindication and triumph. When she had belonged to him, there had been many times when she had fantasized about the Inglizi helpless, as she had been helpless, writhing beneath all the torments of a vengeful slave. But now she was only glad he was dead, glad her Lady had killed him, and glad many times over that her Lady Cat had not been harmed by the Inglizi's evil.

"No, Lady," Madrigal said, raising her eyes to look directly into Cathelin's own, "I did not wish to torture him." She rose and walked around the small table. Leaning down,

♦ The Sunne in Gold ♦

she put her arms around her beloved Lady's neck and kissed her cheek, murmuring, "Thank you. I cannot tell you how much."

Cathelin put a hand on Madrigal's back. "No matter, sweetling," she replied softly. "I know. I wanted to spare you. I've already told you of how I went mad after killing Irizin's master. I thought I should kill Wallace myself, cleanly, to spare you that agony."

Madrigal pressed herself as closely to Cathelin as she could, but her bulging stomach got in the way. "I love you," she said simply.

Cathelin stood up, and Madrigal's arms slid away. "As to his head... it's at the goldsmith's. I'm having his skull made into a drinking cup."

Madrigal's eyelashes fluttered. She had heard of some of the barbaric customs of her new land, but this?

Cathelin laughed at the expression on Madrigal's face. "Nay, sweetling," she said, "Not for you to drink from. 'Tis a trophy is all. There's a whole cabinet full of the things down in the Great Hall. I've never drunk from one myself, but my grandfather did. 'Tis a custom, you see, to enshrine the remains of our worst and greatest enemies, so that our children do not forget where we came from and who we are."

Madrigal nodded, although she was still slightly appalled. *Still, if it is custom*, she thought, *I will say nothing. Some of the customs of my homeland would seem equally barbaric to these Christian folk.*

Cathelin stretched, making the cloak fall to the ground and Madrigal's attention was immediately riveted to the play of muscles sliding smoothly beneath the other woman's skin. Exposure to sun and wind had given her a light tan on her arms, neck and face, but the rest of her body was as light as cream, blue veins visible on her breasts and flat stomach.

Madrigal asked softly, "Will you help me with my dress?"

"Of course." Cathelin helped pull the thick wool gown over the smaller woman's head, and carefully folded it up and placed it back in Madri's clothes chest–a tightly woven willow basket with engraved brass bosses on every corner in the shape of bulls' heads.

Turning around, the Irishwoman saw Madrigal combing out her incredibly long, blue-black hair. Her swollen breasts jiggled a little as she moved the wooden comb briskly though her hair, and the proud, high curve of her belly jutted forward like a brash new moon.

Madrigal stopped combing when she realized she had her Lady's full attention once more. Flipping back the long strands of her hair, she laid the comb aside and put her hands on her hips. "Did you not tell me once you found me beautiful?" Cathelin's mouth was dry. "Aye," she whispered hoarsely.

"And I, too, find you beautiful," Madrigal continued with a tiny smile. "Since we are two such beautiful women, should we not act upon this attraction?"

Cathelin could not say a word as Madrigal walked towards her; her love was not as inhumanly graceful as she had been, but...

Madrigal stopped, allowing her belly to press against Cathelin. "You will not hurt me. Nor the child." She picked up Cathelin's hand and placed it on the curve of her stomach. "I desire you very much, Lady Cat. I wish to show you the depth of that desire. Come," she continued, gently tugging Cathelin's other hand, drawing her towards the bed, "let us see if I can guess what pleases you the most."

With those words, Cathelin's passion erupted like an uncontrollable burst of flame. She swept Madrigal off her feet and laid her on the bed, crouching above her, legs on either side, supporting her weight on her hands. "Do you truly wish this thing?" she asked, amber eyes burning with need.

✦ The Sunne in Gold ✦

Madrigal reached up and grasped a handful of dark red hair on either side of Cathelin's face. Pulling her down for a kiss, she whispered, "Yes."

Cathelin bowed her back, fitting the curve of her body to Madrigal's, and pressed her lips against the other woman's, feeling her lover's lips open to her, so sweetly, so sweetly.

Cathelin slid her tongue into Madrigal's mouth, tasting cinnamon and cloves from the apple she had eaten earlier, moaning slightly as the other woman's tongue slipped around her own, sparring lightly, flicking and dancing.

Madrigal closed her eyes, her hands holding Cathelin's hair tightly, and they parted. Cathelin trailed soft kisses all along her cheek. Those feather-light kisses sparked prickles of fire along the Muslim's skin.

Abruptly, Cathelin swung her other leg over and settled herself beside Madrigal on the bed. She wanted to make love to Madrigal in the truest sense of the word. The fire in her blood gentled as she stared into the Muslim's dark eyes, heart swelling at the expression of trust and love she saw there.

Cathelin bent her head and kissed the soft skin of the other woman's shoulder, breathing in the scent of herbs that clung to her long black hair. Her own dark red locks slid along Madrigal's body as she shifted on the bed and put a strong arm across her love's body, supporting her weight as she leaned over to trace her tongue in delicate patterns all along Madrigal's breast.

Madrigal gasped as she felt the warm touch of her Lady's mouth, and her hands clutched Cathelin's shoulders as those tender lips descended, capturing one of her nipples and sucking gently.

The tight coiling of passion in Madrigal's lower belly vibrated more strongly and she moaned as Cathelin's lips tugged on her sensitive nipple, tongue flicking against the swollen nub.

♦ Nene Adams ♦

The Irishwoman allowed Madrigal's nipple to slide out of her mouth, and she smiled at the expression of desire on her love's face. She lowered her head again, putting more of her weight on her arm, and softly kissed her way to the other breast before giving it the same loving attention.

Madrigal's legs had unconsciously spread; she felt a trickle of hot moisture flow from her center as Cathelin released her nipple and said huskily, "Sweetling, I want to make love to you with my mouth."

Consumed by desire, Madrigal whimpered as Cathelin's kisses trailed lower down her body. The Irishwoman kept shifting on the bed, moving her head back and forth, determined to cover every inch of Madrigal's skin with warm, wet kisses.

Cathelin took her time, running her hands along the bulge of Madrigal's belly, and following those hands with her lips. She swirled her tongue around the Muslim's navel, and was rewarded with a small buck from Madrigal's hips as the other woman sought to bring Cathelin's kisses lower still, to ease the aching itch that tormented her so.

Finally, Cathelin positioned herself between Madrigal's thighs, drawing up the dark beauty's legs and resting them over her broad shoulders. Settling down with a sigh, Cathelin began licking the ebony curls that adorned Madrigal's mount in long strokes with the flat of her tongue, hands beneath her love's buttocks.

At the first touch of Cathelin's tongue, Madrigal nearly exploded with sensation. She wanted to bury her hands in Cathelin's hair, but her belly was in the way. Instead, Madrigal clutched the fur coverlet in a stranglehold. Her hips shot off the bed when Cathelin's tongue probed her more deeply.

Cathelin supported Madrigal's weight on her hands as she flicked her tongue all along the other woman's rosy folds, teasing and tasting. *Like honey*, Cathelin thought, *and rarest*

♦ The Sunne in Gold ♦

wine. She stabbed her tongue deeper, seeking and finding Madrigal's font, the vermilion gate, and eagerly thrust her tongue inside as her love cried out, thighs quivering.

Lowering her to the bed, Cathelin swept her tongue up and took Madrigal's small, sensitive bud between her lips, sucking and nibbling; Madrigal nearly screamed as the explosion of pleasure that coursed in trembling waves throughout her body became stronger, lifting her higher and higher.

Finally, the dam burst and Madrigal convulsed, a star sprinkled sky of ruby and diamonds and gold coruscating behind her tightly closed eyelids. Breath coming in shuddering gasps as she floated through a rippling sea of unbelievable pleasure, she at last fell again to the ground, toes curled, sweet sensations slowly, slowly dying.

Cathelin waited until she was sure, then gently kissed Madrigal's inner thigh. She could not see the other woman's face but imagined the expression of deep and purring satisfaction there. Cathelin carefully lifted Madrigal's legs from her shoulders and laid them back on the bed, then flowed up to rest beside her love.

Madrigal's face was covered in sweat; strands of dark hair clung to her skin. She opened her eyes and stared at Cathelin, trying to catch her breath. Her pupils were dilated so widely her eyes appeared black. "Lady," she said, wonder in her voice, "I have never…"

"What, sweetling?" Cathelin asked, lazily tracing a forefinger along Madrigal's stomach and was startled to feel the child moving against her touch, as if he, too, took joy in his mother's happiness.

"I have never felt such before. Is this magic?" Madrigal still could not believe how she had felt. *I have felt the stirrings of desire,* the Muslim thought amazed, *but I have never felt such sensations before. Truly, my Lady is a worker of miracles.*

♦ **Nene Adams** ♦

Cathelin drew her brows together in a frown. "Are you telling me you've never…"

Madrigal shook her head. "That such things existed, I had heard," she replied. "But to hear of a thing and to experience a thing, they are very different," she concluded, still marveling.

Cathelin tried to wrap her mind around this revelation. "I can't believe…" she began, then stopped. *Of course*, she thought, my poor Madri. *She was trained to please others, but never herself.* Compassion warred with pride as the Irishwoman realized that in some things, she would never be Madrigal's first lover, but in this, she was the only. "I'm truly sorry, sweetling," she said, bowing her head to kiss Madrigal's cheek, "but I take it you liked it?"

Madrigal chuckled throatily. "Oh, yes," she replied, running her hand along Cathelin's arm, "I liked it very much. Only…"

"Mmm?"

"Only, how long will it be before I can have another?" Madrigal asked plaintively, remembering her training in the harem, and how men, having reached the pinnacle, sometimes required long periods of rest before they were able to become aroused again.

Cathelin threw back her head and laughed. "Why, sweetling," she said when she was able to speak again, "you may have as many as you wish, as often as you wish. Would you like another now?"

"Oh, *yes!*" Madrigal exclaimed with the excitement of a child who has discovered a new and wonderful toy.

Cathelin chuckled deep in her throat as she captured Madrigal's lips with her own and thought, *Well-a-day. 'Tis going to be a fine, long night, indeed.*

♦ The Sunne in Gold ♦

♦ Nene Adams ♦

CHAPTER ELEVEN

The seasons turned, autumn into winter, and snow roared down from the mountains, casting a chill white blanket over the demesne of Inishowen.

It was nearing Solstice and Madrigal's belly had ballooned and dropped, so that her heavy burden hung more closely to her knees than her breasts. She was having difficulty sleeping, and only leaning her back against Cathelin's strong body in bed, and being supported by her love's strong arms, allowed her to get any sleep at all.

This morning the village midwife, Branwen mac Nessa–a tiny, bird-like woman with the smallest, narrowest hands Madrigal had ever seen–had spent a good half-candlemark with her ear pressed to the Muslim woman's belly, pale green eyes closed in concentration, fingers probing inch by cautious inch.

♦ The Sunne in Gold ♦

Finally rising, Branwen smiled at Cathelin, who had watched the entire ritual wide-eyed with excitement. "Well?" Cathelin asked eagerly.

Branwen smiled more widely, showing several missing teeth, and flipped the hem of Madrigal's dress back over her swollen belly. "Och," she replied with satisfaction, "'tis twins; both male child an' female, or I'm no judge."

Cathelin grinned. "Hear that, sweetling? Twins, by God!" She was nearly as ecstatic as a new father herself; in fact, she had come to regard the child–now know to be children–in Madrigal's womb as her own flesh and blood.

Madrigal grunted. She was tired, so tired; it seemed as if all her energy went straight to her stomach, leaving none for herself. In the last month, she had not even wanted Cathelin to perform that amazing magic on her, and she had certainly not felt like giving pleasure, either. All she wanted to do was eat and sleep, and she was grateful that her Lady Cat did not press her.

Madrigal struggled to rise from the chair and her lover hastened to help. "Madri, sweetling, are you all right?" Cathelin asked.

"Yes," Madrigal answered shortly, brushing a lock of stray hair from her brow. "I am hungry, though. Again." The Muslim woman was feeling a bit peevish this morning; she had to restrain herself from kicking the chair to relieve her irritation.

She waddled over to the bed, Cathelin clucking behind her as anxiously as a hen with one chick, and Madrigal really had to restrain the urge to kick her Lady. She did not know why she felt so ill-humored and grumpy, but she knew she would be glad when the birth was finally over.

Cathelin stifled a laugh at the petulance on Madrigal's face. At any other time, she might have tried to jolly the other woman out of her bad mood, or perhaps even given some in return, but... *Well, she's got the mulligrubs, poor mite,* she thought, *and no wonder, carrying twice the burden of another woman, and her so small to boot.*

Getting Madrigal settled, Cathelin drew Branwen out of the room. "'Tis worried I am about the birth," Cathelin said. "Madrigal is so small."

Branwen clucked. "Nay, gie it no more thought, Lady. Yon one's hips be wide enow fer th' birthin'. Now, 'tis her first, an' those be more difficult than others an' wit' twins, hmph. I'll be comin' up ta stay at th' castle after Sunday, an' Brother Ignatius will be on hand as well. So dinna fret. We'll see th' wee one through wit' th' Good Lord's help."

Cathelin nodded, slightly reassured. As Madrigal's time grew nearer, she worried more and more. She had heard of women dying in the birthing bed, each tale more gruesome than the last, and the thought of anything happening to her love was nearly more than she could bear.

Abruptly, Madrigal's voice was raised behind her. "Must I go to the kitchens myself for food?" she yelled, thoroughly out of sorts. "Will the djinn waft me down the stairs, or must I rub Aladdin's lamp first?"

Cathelin bit her lip and her shoulders shook as she laughed silently. *Oh, my sweet Madri is turning into quite the crosspatch beldam*, she thought, amused. Lifting her own voice, she shouted, "Ho, a servant for your Lady."

As a manservant pelted down the hall towards the master's chamber, Cathelin heard Madrigal grumble in Arabic, "Children of she-camels and he-goats. I starve, and they all laugh at my distress. Allah, defend Your servant from this barbarian horde."

The manservant was very surprised when the Lady laughed in his face.

♦ The Sunne in Gold ♦

Six miles from Inishowen, in a cavern cut into a cliff, a group of men had gathered.

Lord Francis had washed and cut his hair and trimmed his beard; he no longer resembled a woods-hermit. Instead, to the other men, he seemed the very image of a holy Crusader, for his hazel eyes still burned with a fanatic's light. However, it was the insanity in those same eyes that caused them to shudder and turn their faces away.

Beyond their view, in the darkest shadows of the cave, Sorcha's body lay uncovered. Cold had helped reduce the stink, but after nearly three months, the corpse was no longer in pristine condition. The flesh of her face had shrunk; the shriveled mouth made teeth more prominent; her green eyes had completely rotted away, but Francis did not notice. In his delusional mind, she had not changed a whit but was still as beautiful as when he'd stolen her out from under his hated cousin's nose. Francis liked to toy with Sorcha's long blonde braids as he sat by the fire, brooding; sometimes, he would even kiss her cold, worm riddled cheek and talk to her as if she were still alive. He had not truly loved her when she was living–he had only used her - but now that she was safely dead, his increased affection knew no bounds. To him, she had become the ultimate woman: quiet, obedient, and loyal to the end.

"Soon, my love," he crooned, casting his gaze to the corner. Abbot Benedict watched with narrowed gray eyes, but said nothing. He knew Francis was insane; he only hoped the Lord could maintain his grip on what little sanity remained to help put their plot into motion.

♦ Nene Adams ♦

Gathered in the cave were ten other men, three of them Sorcha's kinfolk from southern Ireland; they were hard-bitten sell-swords and thieves, whose stake in the venture was more than revenge. They thirsted to loot Inishowen and fill their clan's purses, and they had pledged a dozen men to the venture.

Three were lords who, for one reason or another, had cause to be disaffected by Lady Cathelin. Benedict let his eyes wander from one to another while they talked.

Sir Duncan Galbraith, Baron of Carbery; his grudge was that Cathelin's great-grandfather had, in his family's mind, cheated them of prime pastureland, and they had never forgotten, or forgiven, the insult.

Edward O'Kennedy, head of a powerful merchant clan: Cathelin, as Blacksunne, had commanded a portion of Richard's army that had included his son, killed in battle at Acre. O'Kennedy blamed her for that death.

Desmond O'Brian, Earl of Kinslainne, whose eldest son had been betrothed to Marguessan, Cathelin's younger sister; O'Brian had tried to force Sir Giles to betroth Cathelin to his son Robert after Marguessan's death, but Sir Giles had refused. When Robert pressed his suit at his father's insistence, Cathelin had challenged him to a joust that had left the boy with a permanently twisted leg from a bad fall.

Three of the other men were representatives of a certain element in the village that Abbot Benedict had been carefully cultivating. There were some who felt that Lady Cathelin was condemned to Hell for her unnatural sexual proclivities, and wanted her gone lest the same doom fall upon them by association. They were not many, and all peasants and woodsmen, but Benedict was proud of his contribution. Knowing the land as they did, these folk would be ideal for penetrating the castle's grounds and allowing an element of surprise.

✦ The Sunne in Gold ✦

The last of the seven was a Knight Templar from England, Sir John Rivenoak. He was a hired champion who had fought in many jousts, tournaments and challenges. Sir John was a pragmatic individual, who sold his sword to whosoever could afford it, and always gave satisfaction for his fees. Sir John would take care of Lady Cathelin while the rest of the men, and their personal soldiers, poured through the gates and took Inishowen.

All of the men were quietly discussing their plans when Lord Francis spoke up. "There is one more thing that must be done," he said, "before we can proceed with the attack."

Sir Duncan looked choleric. A stout man with a full beard, he suffered from gout and was in a perpetually testy mood. "What d'ye mean, sirrah?" he asked angrily. "The attack is planned for tomorrow morning. My men are shivering in the woods as we speak. Nay, we shall *not* wait upon you!"

In a move as swift as a striking snake, Francis had his belt knife pressed against Sir Duncan's throat. A thin line of blood appeared as the razor-keen edge barely parted the flesh. "You *will* wait," Francis hissed. The other men looked at each other then backed away. No one wanted to get between this madman and his prey.

Just as suddenly, Francis' knife flickered back into the sheathe on his belt. "Besides, it will not take long," he said with an ugly smile. "I just need to reclaim something that was stolen from me."

The others looked at him, and Abbot Benedict shivered, but not with fear. He shivered with glorious anticipation.

♦ Nene Adams ♦

Cathelin had gone, called to some early evening conference with Wolf McLeod and Michael Drury in the barracks. Madrigal was alone in the master's chamber when there was a discreet scratching on the door.

Calling, "Enter," Madrigal saw a red-nosed, bleary-eyed maidservant, with cornsilk yellow hair. The woman's face was scarred from the pox, and her figure stick thin. The Muslim had never seen her before, but with winter hard upon the land, some of the folk from more isolated areas had come to Inishowen for shelter.

"Yes?" Madrigal asked kindly; the maidservant looked like a timid mouse, eyes darting at shadows.

"Beggin' yer pardon, Mistress," the maid said with a clumsy curtsy, "But Master McLeod sent me ta tell yer ta come down ta outer court straight away. Been an accident."

Accident? Madrigal heaved herself off the bed, cursing slightly under her breath, and waddled across the room, grabbing her cloak. Her back had been bothering her all day, with pains that came and went with increased frequency.

"What sort of accident?" Madrigal asked sharply, fastening her thick woolen cloak with a brooch.

"Somethin' ta do wit' a horse is all I knows," the maid said, wiping her runny nose with one hand. "Ta Lady needs yer, s'all I were told."

Oh, Allah! Madrigal thought, and hurried as quickly as she could out of the chamber. Lady Cat had recently been gifted with a fiery destrier, a war-trained mount half-jokingly named Shaitan. That beast had already savaged a stableboy,

✦ The Sunne in Gold ✦

and Madrigal knew that her love was determined to train Shaitan to her hand no matter the cost.

She has probably broken her leg or her head, Madrigal considered, carefully picking her way down the stairs. Her heart almost stopped when she concluded that Lady Cat's wounding must be more acute than she had first suspected, for Master McLeod had not sent one of the kerns to help her down the stairs, according to the Lady's strict order.

Madrigal swept through the halls, not noticing the curious glances of the servants. All her thoughts were solely concentrated on Cathelin.

When she let herself out of the gate, she was surprised that the outer court seemed to be deserted. Carefully she listened–for the screaming of a horse, the shouts of men, the curses of her Lady–but heard nothing.

Madrigal's moment of confusion was short-lived. Suddenly, a sack was pulled over her face and she screamed, but the rough cloth muffled her cries. She struggled, but was picked up and slung on the back of a horse, and a man's hard body settled in the saddle behind her, arms like iron bars squeezing her rib cage until she thought she would vomit.

The horse pounded away from Inishowen, while Madrigal screamed and cried and clung to the mount's mane, until the pommel of a dagger struck her sharply behind the ear, and her head exploded with pain then blackest oblivion.

Cathelin's face was grim. "How many men does he have now, Wolf?" she asked.

♦ Nene Adams ♦

McLeod looked at his Lady, ice blue eyes bright. "Two hundred or so," he answered. "Th' bulk o' th' men trained soldiers, but a few o' our own among 'em."

Cathelin sighed and closed her eyes. It particularly hurt that some of the would-be invaders were her own people. *Still*, she thought, *if I tried to please everyone, I would please no one.* "And their plans?" she asked aloud. "Have they changed from what we learned before?"

"Our people inside were s'posed ta open the gates an' cause a distraction in th' hours o' early morn. Their warriors would slip in an' th' fightin' would begin."

Cathelin grunted. Wolf had kept her appraised of his spy operation—he had noted Sorcha's attention fixed on one particular man in the crowd the day of her hanging and instructed a pair of kerns to follow the individual. They had tracked him to the sea-overhanging cliffs that lay six miles away and discovered it was the exiled usurper, Francis Westfield.

This was the shocking news Wolf had brought to her that morning in the chapel, when she had already been staggered by the theft of Sorcha's body.

Infuriated that Francis was still plotting against her – would that whoreson's greed never be quenched? – she had forced herself to stop and assess rather than react in blind fury. Cathelin had no way of knowing whether Francis was working alone or whether he had managed to make potentially dangerous allies.

Experience in the Saracen lands had taught her that it was better to be cautious and wait for accurate intelligence than stick her head in a dark bear's den and hope for the best. Her orders to Wolf had been to keep a close and careful watch on all Francis' activities – but that doughty warrior was able by good luck to take the plan a step further.

Not only were Westfield's visitors identified, but some of their actual conversations with the erstwhile invader

✦ The Sunne in Gold ✦

were reported. A deep crack in the cliff face next to the cave provided an ideal eavesdropping point for an exceptionally skinny kern, who was wedged in this cramped spot for some fourteen hours a day, risking daily exposure and certain death should he be discovered by the plotters. Fortunately, Francis' overconfidence was infectious and neither he nor his allies ever thought to post sentries or make a simple search of the area.

Daily reports had come from the spies, and three hours ago the last had been received. Things were coming to a head; Westfield and his borrowed army, with the help of Cathelin's enemies, were to attack Inishowen a few hours after dawn.

This was the last little detail she needed. Instead of a surprise attack from an invading army, she would lead her kerns to the opposition's staging area and catch *them* by surprise, neatly turning the tables. They would be outnumbered nearly two-to-one, but Cathelin's men and women had survived Outremer–a war that had toughened them like no other. And she had an ally in particular who thirsted after the O'Kennedy's blood, so the odds were not too bad.

She pushed aside the parchment maps that littered the table and took a swallow of well-watered wine. Rising, she said, "Have my squire Thomas meet me in the armory and gather the army. Full weapons, winter cloaks and shields. Pick a few of your best horsemen and issue them mounts from the stables; they'll be breaking trail for the rest. Have you heard from the O'Fierna?"

Wolf nodded, his expression fierce. The O'Fierna clan was closely connected to the O'Camerons by blood, and Lord Bran O'Fierna had responded enthusiastically to the Lady's request for aid in her campaign when the usurper's plans were first known. Francis' ally, the O'Kennedy, had long ago made an enemy of O'Fierna over a woman and a deadly insult.

♦ Nene Adams ♦

Wolf had sent the message bird himself scarcely two hours ago, instructing the Lord in where and when the fight would take place, and the reply had been thrust into his hand right before the war council.

"Aye, Lady," he responded in his rough, deep voice. "The O'Fierna's agreed ta bring another thirty men as weel as himself; 'twill be meetin' us at Saint Wilfrid's Ford."

Cathelin nodded, and Wolf bowed and hastened away to begin the preparations. The Irishwoman turned to her chief man-at-arms, Neith Owen. "You are in charge of the castle defenses whilst I'm away," she said. "Have the archers line the walls and ready the oil pots. God willing, we will defeat this enemy, but if not, then it's up to you, Owen, and your men, to see Inishowen safe for my heirs."

Neith bowed deeply, rusty red mustache stained with purple wine. He had been called from his dinner to join this conference, and, with a sigh, he mentally consigned the remains of his meal to the cookfires. There would be no time for a leisurely feast tonight.

Michael Drury cleared his throat. "And me, Lady?" he asked nervously.

Cathelin looked at him with cold amber eyes. "My will," she said simply. "'Tis locked in my desk, and Bishop Rudolphus has a copy. In the event of my death, you're to see to its lawful execution." Seeing the confused look on Drury's face, she explained, "Madrigal's children. She and they will inherit Inishowen; I have no time for long ceremony, but you men bear witness: At this moment, as chieftain of the O'Camerons and Lady of Inishowen, I formally swear that she is kin to me and mine, and an equal of the blood."

Taking up a small paperknife, Cathelin made a careful slit in her forefinger, allowing blood to drip down on the earthen floor of the small war room attached to the barracks. "This do I vow, by earth and blood," she declared solemnly as both men watched, "That Madrigal, child of none, is here

✦ The Sunne in Gold ✦

this day of the clan O'Cameron. Saint Brigit watch over her, Mother of God keep care of her, and may the Good Lord smite without mercy if I, or my inheritors, or other kin of the name, ever dishonor her. So be it."

Drury and Owen murmured, "So be it," to complete the ceremony. True, it was far less elaborate than the usual adoption; that was more like a festival celebration. But their Lady was correct. Inishowen was on war footing, and there was precious little time to waste on ritual. Later, that blood-soaked bit of earth would be scooped up with a silver sickle and mingled with Madrigal's own blood. The result would be flung into a fire made of three sacred woods–oak, ash and rowan–and there would be a grand party to welcome Madrigal into her new clan. If there was a later.

The Master of the Hounds, David Uileand, appeared in the doorway and tugged his forelock in respect. "My lady, will ye be wantin' the gazehounds?"

Cathelin frowned at the interruption. Michael Drury said quickly, "'Twas my idea to summon the man to our council. I hope I did aright."

"No blame will fall, Master Drury. You acted for the best." Cathelin turned to Uileand and continued, "Aye, Houndmaster, all brave hearts are welcome on the field. Choose two of your best dogs – a hunting pair, perhaps – and stay out of the melee. 'Twill be enough to pick off stragglers when the fight's well up and hot."

"As ye command, Lady," Uileand replied. His face was twisted with strong emotion and unshed tears glimmered in the corners of his eyes.

"Well, man, be about your business," the Irishwoman said in dismissal, faintly irritated that he was still shuffling feet in the council room when there was work to be done. "We've scarce time for chatting when war is at the door."

"Aye, my lady," Uileand said in a choked whisper. He did not leave, however, but continued to hover nervously until the Cathelin lost her temper and snapped, "Sweet Jesu! Did a devil nail your feet to the floor? Get thee hence, Master, and to your own business at once!"

Owen rumbled through his mustache, "No shame for admitting your fears, Houndmaster." He thought Uileand, inexperienced in matters of war, was hesitating out of natural anxiety. "None shall call you coward, man, for e'en a blooded soldier suffers doubts on the eve of battle. Take courage from the clan and do what needs be done for the sake of all."

Uileand suddenly fell to his knees and drew a small knife from the sheath on his belt. Holding it so the point was pressed lightly against his heart, he cried, "Chieftan, I bring a blood grievance, and beg your ear fer th' clan's sake. An' ye fail in yer sacred duty, not a morsel of food nor a drop of water shall pass my lips 'till the burden passes from me to thee, so help me Christ, an' may all th' saints of Heaven an' th' angels their own selves bear witness to this vow."

Cathelin was visibly startled. Drury began to remonstrate, pointing out to Uileand that this was neither the time nor the place for formal petitions, but the Irishwoman shushed him with a gesture. "Go now to your tasks," she said quietly to Owen and Drury. "I will deal with this matter in private."

When they were alone, she cocked her head to one side and said in a dangerously silky voice, "So, Master Uileand. You would bring the hunger fast against me?"

The Master of the Hounds gulped but did not break his position. From time immemorial, the common folk held the tradition of publicly fasting against those whom they felt had treated them unfairly, and ancient law forbade any noble to interfere. So shaming was this custom – who would not blush when a starving man squatted on their doorstep in full view of anyone passing by – that most Irish lords would rather fight naked against a barbarian horde than have a single unarmed peasant begin a hunger fast in their name.

♦ The Sunne in Gold ♦

"Ye don't know, Lady," Uileand half sobbed, the knife trembling in his hand. "Ye dinnae ken what he's done!"

With a sigh, Cathelin sat down and beckoned for the Houndmaster to rise. "No need to stand on ceremony, David. You have my ear and my oath, as your overlord, to do all within my power to answer your grievance. Take a cup of wine and tell me what eats your guts so hardly that my army must wait upon your word."

Uileand got up and sheathed his knife. His hand shook when he poured wine into a cup, slopping it over the table, but Cathelin said nothing, just waited in silence. Finally, after taking several long gulps, he began to speak.

The Irishwoman listened, and the longer he spoke, the more her eyes glittered in suppressed rage. When he finished, she said through barely parted lips, "You did well to bring this to me. I have but one question, Master – shall it be my sword that wrecks vengeance or your own?"

Uileand wiped his face with his tunic sleeve. Now that he had unburdened himself, he was much calmer. "'Tis my blood an' my revenge, Lady, but I dared not act wit'out yer good will behind me."

"You have it." Cathelin rose and put her hand on the Houndmaster's shoulder, squeezing gently. "Do what you must. However you choose to bring death to such an unspeakable monster, I will stand firm at your back."

"Thank you, Lady." Uileand stood up straighter. "My sorrow to have troubled ye so. But he... that bastard... what he did to my..." The man broke off, overwhelmed by anger.

"Don't fash yourself, David, and don't apologize. If he escapes, then after the battle I will use every resource at my command to chase him down. Otherwise... well, as long as you don't burn the village or abbey to cinders looking for him, I'll turn a blind eye to aught else. Now," she clapped him on the arm, "you must go to your work and I to mine."

"Aye, my lady. Wit' a full heart an' a steady hand, my vow upon it. Ye'll have nae cause against me, fer I ken my duty well." Uileand strode away, a man filled with purpose instead of aimless hurt, relieved that his grievance would soon be answered - if not by his own hand, then by that of his sworn overlord.

Cathelin shook her head. "So much to answer for," she whispered. "Had I known..." But there was little use in regret or recriminations. If David Uileand did not kill his enemy, she would and with about as much compunction as squashing a roach beneath her heel.

She firmly pushed the matter aside. War was approaching and she could hear the rustling of the battle crow's wings – this took precedence over other matters at the moment. Cathelin left the room, heading towards the family chapel. She had much to do, but first, she had to confess and be shriven, and then she would say her good-byes to Madrigal.

Madrigal was terrified. She had wakened in a smoky cave, lying on the filth-encrusted stone floor; from a short distance away, she heard a voice she recognized and it sent a chill of horror down her spine.

Lord Francis was saying, "We'll march out at early dawn. By the time we arrive, the gates should be open, and we'll be able to take the outer courtyard before the alarm is raised. Sir John, do not forget. Lady Cathelin will be in her Blacksunne armor, so you should be able to spot her easily. If not, ask; the three commanders know her on sight."

✦ The Sunne in Gold ✦

Madrigal tried to curl up into a ball but was unable to. Suddenly, a sharp pain rippled through her stomach and she bit her lip to stifle a moan, both hands around the swollen mound. She knew what was happening—her children, eager to see the world, had decided it was time to begin the business of being born.

Footsteps approached and Madrigal squeezed her eyes tightly shut, pretending to be unconscious. A booted toe prodded her arm and she rolled with it, keeping her limbs limp despite her pain; then the foot drew back and kicked her viciously in the thigh. Madrigal fought to remain still but feared the next kick might be to her vulnerable belly. The pain eased as the muscles of her womb rested to prepare for another contraction.

She opened her eyes, squinting a little in the bright light of the torch Lord Francis held above his head. "So," Francis said, a slight cold smile on his face. "The bitch is awake, eh? Good. I promise you, slavey, you'll not die just yet. First, you must live to see your whoremonger mistress' head on a pike. And after..." His lips stretched into a death's-head grin. "I'll kill your brat. Would you like to hold it once before I smash its head apart on the walls?"

Madrigal shuddered. His eyes... Lord Francis had never been entirely sane, that she had known. But now... *He has been possessed by an evil djinn*, Madrigal thought with horror. *He is as mad as a foaming dog. Allah preserve me!*

She knew she would be missed eventually and prayed that her Lady would be able to track the abductors. *But if what he says is true*, she thought, *there is some kind of army outside. But my Lady Cat is the greatest warrior in the world. Surely, she will find a way. And if not, I pray to Allah and all the saints that I die before she and my children are taken to Paradise.*

Francis drew back his foot and kicked her thigh again, making her wince as the blow landed in the same bruised place as before. "What, no words of love?" he asked in mock disappointment. "Did you not miss me? I should think that warming my cousin's bed wouldn't hold a candle to the things I did to you, slavey."

Hot tears filled Madrigal's eyes, but she struggled to maintain control. She would not beg–she knew this was what he wanted–and within her heart, she held her Lady's words, repeating them over and over, "I love you" and "You are free." She would never be a slave again; Lady Cat had taught her about true freedom, and Madrigal, having at last discovered pride and love, would never be forced to that place of abject slavery again.

I must continue, she thought, as Francis stared down at her, frowning. *I must be strong. I must not give in to fear. My Lady will come for me.*

Abruptly, Francis turned away, tired of the game. A true sadist, if his prey did not respond with fear, he became bored.

Earl O'Brian cast a worried glance at Lord Francis. "D'ye think it can be done?" he quietly asked Sir John, who adjusted a shoulder vambrace on his armor and replied, "Yes. As soon as we take the castle, I'll kill him. But I'll expect half my payment in advance, my Lord of Kinslainne. And the other half when I deliver Lord Francis' head to your tent."

"Aye," O'Brian answered, handing the other man a bulging pouch. "But why wait?"

Sir John weighed the pouch thoughtfully in his palm before tucking it into a fold of his surcoat and smiling slightly. The mail coif he wore over his head framed a seamed, weathered face, criss-crossed with scars, and his light brown eyes met O'Brian's. "Because, my Lord, I *am* an honest man. I can only be bought by one master at a time."

✦ The Sunne in Gold ✦

Cathelin took the stairs two at a time, hurrying at breakneck speed. She had spent far longer in the chapel with Father Paul than she had intended, and her kerns had almost finished gathering in the forecourt. Her good-byes to Madrigal would have to be brief.

"Madri?" she said hastily as she skidded into the room. There was no reply.

Cathelin's eyes searched the chamber but there was no sign of Madrigal at all. Spinning about on a heel, she noticed the other woman's cloak was missing from the hook beside the door.

Where in God's name can she be? Cathelin thought, beginning to get irritated. *Surely she's not gone to the jakes on a night like this.* She walked to the close-stool that sat in one corner behind a screen and lifted the lid. *Nay,* she thought, *the pot's empty and the ash clean.*

Her dark red brows drew together in a frown. *If she's down in the kitchen again, I'll be skinnin' her alive*, she thought darkly. "That woman'll be the death of me yet," Cathelin muttered aloud. "Disappearing to God alone knows where, and me with my war band freezing in the forecourt." Not to mention her squire Thomas waiting in the armory to help her on with her suit of plate armor.

The sound of wild weeping drew her attention. Coming down the hall was Wolf McLeod, his face grimmer than usual, ebony brows drawn so closely together they appeared to march in an unbroken line across his forehead. In his tight grasp he pulled along a crying, stumbling maidservant, her cornsilk yellow hair straggling across her pock-marked face.

♦ **Nene Adams** ♦

"What's this?" Cathelin snapped in annoyance. "I've no time for disciplining servants!"

Wolf paused at the threshold and thrust the maidservant inside the chamber. She fell to her knees, wet face buried in both hands. "One o' the new maids, my Lady," he said. "'Twas showin' this about in th' servant's quarters." He cast a handful of silver coins down to ring and chime on the stone floor.

"I questioned her, for one so poor ta have so much is beyond an honest man's ken." He paused. This news would be no easier to deliver than it had been to hear. Taking a deep breath, Wolf continued, "Mistress Madrigal's been ta'en."

For a moment, Cathelin was certain she had gone deaf, or mad, or both. "What?" she asked in confusion. "Taken? What do you mean?"

"This one," he said, prodding the maidservant with a toe, "is handfast ta Simon Fletcher down in th' village. He's one o' them we've been keepin' a peeled eye on." Wolf waited, hoping he would not have to explain further.

Abruptly, comprehension dawned, and Cathelin closed her lips tightly against a bellow of pain and rage. *Madri!* she thought, *that bastard Francis has taken my Madri!*

She grabbed the maidservant by her shoulder, hauled her up off the floor and shook the hapless girl like a rag doll. Cathelin's lips had peeled back from her teeth in a snarl of pure animal fury and her eyes were as hot as the gates of Hell. *"Where is she?"* she shouted, oblivious to Wolf's protests. "Where is she? What have you done with my Madri?"

The maid could only stammer and wail, and finally, Cathelin threw her back down to the floor in disgust, struggling to control the instinct to draw her sword and hack the girl into a dozen or more pieces. She panted, trying to think, but her mind would only circle back to the same terrible thought–her Madri back in Francis' power. Suddenly,

✦ The Sunne in Gold ✦

she calmed. It was as if a cloak of pure ice had been drawn over her swirling, blood-maddened emotions; dimly, Cathelin was aware that she was in the grip of the most profound anger she had ever known. Not since Irizin's death had she felt this way, but instead of heat, all she felt was cold, the chill craving for revenge, and more than revenge.

"Tell me," she said through gritted teeth to Wolf McLeod.

He ran a shaking hand through his black hair. "Fletcher's wit' Francis' army. Th' maid tol' me a 'friend' gie her th' coin ta bring a false message ta Mistress Madrigal. Thirty pieces o' silver he paid the little Judas. Tell her, lass. Tell the Lady what ye've done."

The maidservant keened, "I were only tryin' ta earn enow fer th' banns; an' he were tellin' me it were a jape. S'all, Lady, I swear ta yer!"

Cathelin knelt down and forced the maid's head up. Her terrified, bleary blue eyes stared fixedly, and the maidservant quaked in terror, knowing her life hung in the balance. "Who paid you?" Cathelin asked, her tone dangerously soft, "and what did you tell her?"

The maid swiped a hand across her runny nose. "I dunno his name, Lady," she replied with a sniffle. "I only knows I were s'posed ter tell yer woman ter go down ter outer court, an' tell 'er it were somethin' about an accident wit' a horse, an' that yer needed her."

Cathelin sat back on her heels. "That's all?"

"Aye." The maidservant was so frightened that she had to clench her bowels against a burning gush; she knew full well there had been something more behind the man's excuse of a jest. No one paid good coin in a hard winter for a mere joke, but the silver had been too much to resist. She knew her life was forfeit and shivered, mouth forming a plea for mercy that she dared not voice.

Cathelin rose. Her face might have been carved from granite; her lips were pinched and white with strain. *My fault!* she screamed at herself in an agony of guilt. *I knew Francis was close and could have warned Madrigal. I thought I knew best. Jesus! What has my stupid, foolish pride done to my love? Had I told her, she might have been more cautious and this would not have happened!*

The icy control nearly slipped but she refused to indulge in an orgy of regret now. Her course of action was clear; there would be time later for self-recrimination – if later ever came.

"I'll be down within the half-hour," she told Wolf. "Have the men ready; we ride as soon as I'm armored."

"What of this one?" Wolf asked, looking pointedly at the shivering maidservant.

Cathelin was already on her way out the door. "I'll deal with her on my return," she replied over her shoulder as she walked away. "Give her to Father Paul and tell him to pray for her soul."

The maid burst into a fresh shower of tears as those ominous words struck deeply, and Wolf McLeod bestowed on her a look of angry satisfaction.

♦ The Sunne in Gold ♦

CHAPTER TWELVE

The army marched.

Through a blanket of pristine white, their breath foaming in the air, woolen cloaks held tightly against the cold, wolfskin boots crunching down the snow-clotted trail. They needed no torches; moonlight shone brightly on the scene.

Cathelin rode in front with Wolf McLeod, Becca Half-Tongue and four others, their horses' hooves breaking up huge patches of snow, and Cathelin thanked God and Saint Brigit there had been no freeze as yet. The snow was packed but not iced, and easy to break through.

Cathelin was in full Blacksunne armor and the smoke of her breath streamed from behind the grilled visor of her war helm, a frothy plume like a steel dragon from ancient myths. The mighty broadsword of the O'Camerons was on her hip, and behind her saddle hung a quiver of javelins with leaf shaped tips of razor-sharp steel.

✦ The Sunne in Gold ✦

Wolf carried aloft the O'Cameron banner, a bright crimson flag with a white and silver phoenix rising from ebony flames, while Becca proudly fingered her new badge of office–Cathelin had promoted her to the officer ranks. It would be her task to stay with the Lady during the fight and blow battle signals with the ancient ivory horn of the clan.

Cathelin had not said a word when she had arrived in the forecourt earlier, looking like the Morrighan –the Battlecrow herself –in her black enameled armor. Her new war horse, Shaitan, had bucked a little as she had swung into the saddle but her fist between his ears had put an end to his fractiousness.

As they marched, the kerns softly sang a war song, although the pipers and drummers were silent; scouts had been sent ahead to deal with any sentries the enemy may have posted, but Cathelin had promised to hang any who lost them the element of surprise. So the army marched and chanted quietly beneath their breaths:

"Fire, sun, moon or sea -
The prayer of Saint Brigit protects me!
The White Christ above me,
Host of Holies in his hand -
The Queen of Heaven's mantle
And a fiery angel's band!
My sword to the service of God!
May the blood of my lord's enemies
Be as a river beneath my feet,
And that bright red water
Be mingled with their women's tears..."

Cathelin gave a feral smile behind her war helm as the quiet verse reached her ears, and urged Shaitan with her heel to pick up his pace, while behind her, the army marched on.

♦ Nene Adams ♦

Madrigal arched her back slightly as she was squeezed in a fist of pain; she had wrapped a stick in a scrap of cloth torn from her skirts, and her teeth were tightly clenched down on it to stifle her cries.

The pains were coming more frequently now; she was bathed in sweat and beginning to believe there had never been anything in the world except this cycle of pain and purpose. *Oh, Allah!* she thought as the agony eased and she panted quietly, *protect Lady Cat and lay your merciful hand upon my unborn children!*

Campfires flickered fitfully as the men of Francis' army huddled in their cloaks, sharpening their swords or, in most cases, napping. A veteran knew to take his rest where and when he could.

Small tents had been set up in the grove; most of them were quiet and dark. Lord Francis was in the commander's tent with O'Brian, O'Kennedy and Galbraith, going over their plans for the coming morn and eating a late supper

"We must strike quickly," O'Kennedy said, tearing a roast chicken apart and licking grease from his fingers. "I'll not waste my men in a prolonged siege."

"Aye," Sir Duncan Galbraith replied, glaring sullenly at Francis. He was still smarting over the lord's attack the previous evening; that sharp knife had pricked both his throat and his touchy pride. "A surprise attack and a swift, clean kill. That's the way of it. No more of this poxy plotting and scheming, b'Christ. Real war is work for men, not an overly clever boy still tied to his mother by the birthing cord."

Rather than express fury at this insult, Francis gave the stout knight a wolfish grin. "I grant you that my mother is

♦ The Sunne in Gold ♦

a grasping whore." He picked up a cup of wine and took several swallows, runnels of liquid escaping the corners of his mouth and staining his shirt. When he finished drinking, he continued, "But at least I knew the father who begat me."

Sir Duncan bellowed in fury and shoved away from the table. "I'll not swallow such from you!" he shouted. "How dare you, sirrah! I demand satisfaction!"

O'Brian snorted. "Christ's blood! We're none of us here out of love for Lord Westfield, so put your injured pride away and concentrate on the task at hand, Duncan. There'll be time enough for duels after our work is done and the battle won."

"Aye, we'll go our merry ways once my cousin lies cold in the ground," Francis said, toying with an eating knife, "and we'll all receive our just rewards. Even you, my lord windbag. Oh, I'll not be forgetting you when the reckoning time comes."

"God curse you for an upstart puppy," Sir Duncan choked. "How dare you threaten me?"

Francis made no reply but his eyes glittered with malice.

O'Kennedy shoved a hunk of bread across the table and said, "Sit you down, my lord Galbraith, and cease this tiresome baiting. We'll not be taking the castle if we fight amongst ourselves. Common cause unites us, gentlemen. We can at least be respectful and not allow words spoken in the heat of a moment to divide us."

Sir Duncan blew out a breath and sat down hard, picking up the bread with a shaking hand. "Pax for now. But 'tis only because I hate the O'Camerons more than I hate you, Westfield. They stole my family's land and shamed us in the bargain..."

"Enough of your puling complaints, Galbraith!" O'Brian interrupted, banging his fist on the table. He alone knew of the treacherous bargain he'd made with the English mercenary Rivenoak. When the castle was taken, Westfield would cease to be a problem, and Duncan's attitude was grating on his already raw nerves. *The man's worse than a bulldog, the way he worries at a single thought as if it were a marrowbone*, O'Brian thought in disgust.

He continued hotly, "If any here have better cause to hate Cathelin O'Cameron than myself, I'll bend the knee and kiss his hairy arse. She crippled my poor son, that witch, and ruined his life."

O'Kennedy hurled the cleanly picked chicken carcass over his shoulder. "Kneel and pucker your lips, by the bleeding Christ! At least you have a son. Mine she left to die in Outremer and I suffer from the wound still!"

The quarrelling grew louder and more acrimonious until it was shattered by Francis, who threw his head back and laughed, a mocking bray with a lunatic edge that sent chills down the spine. Galbraith, O'Kennedy and O'Brian stopped bickering and eyed him with disgust.

"Do you mock us, my lord?" O'Brian asked pugnaciously. Only the knowledge that Westfield would soon be dead stayed his hand from delivering a blow that would have rattled the madman's teeth.

"Nay!" Francis exclaimed. "I just find it amusing that even when she's not here, my cousin rules us all so completely."

Sir Duncan flushed and after a long pause, said hesitantly, "Tho' it pains me to admit it, Westfield is in the right. I apologize, my lords, if my temper got the best of me. I meant nothing by it."

"Aye, there should be no fighting among brothers in war. I offer my apologies as well," O'Kennedy said.

O'Brian stared at the tent walls, gooseflesh raising on his arms as a superstitious chill raced down his spine. What if Lady Cathelin really *was* a witch? "Has she put a curse on us,

♦ The Sunne in Gold ♦

you think? She's in league with the Devil, that one, and who knows what unholy powers she may command."

"No matter," Francis said gruffly. "She'll be dead soon enough and Satan may have her as his bride with my compliments."

The other three men muttered at this statement, which bordered on blasphemy.

"I hope you've not put the ill star on our venture," O'Kennedy said. "Mayhap we should have Benedict come and bless us, to drive away the evil."

Francis opened his mouth to make a caustic reply but suddenly, the quiet night was shattered by nearly a hundred voices raised in the keening, hair-raising wail that was the Irish battlecry. Out of the dark, flaming arrows sizzled down to strike the trees and set them ablaze.

Francis scrambled out of the tent, the other three men barely a breath behind, as several trees burst into flame, becoming gigantic torches that cast a surreal light on a scene from their worst nightmares. Pipers and drummers gave the beat as a horde of screaming soldiers burst into the camp with raised swords, cloaks streaming like great wings, faces painted into devil's masks with sacred blue woad. And, to Francis' horror, they met with little resistance.

O'Brian bellowed frantic orders as the terrible figure of Blacksunne slid down from her horse, the quiver of hunting javelins empty; Cathelin had hurled them expertly as she had ridden into camp, and twelve of the enemy already lay dead. She drew her sword and whacked Shaitan on the withers, sending him flying from the fight, and settled down to begin wrecking destruction in earnest.

Galbraith, his lean face pale, hastily jammed a helmet on his head and ran, legs pumping, to rally his own men to the fight, O'Kennedy hot on his heels.

Lord Francis watched, entranced, as resistance was quickly organized and the fighting began in earnest. It was as if he dwelled apart, in a space alone, somehow above the battle, yet observing it all. His hazel eyes were wide with excitement, and he shivered as he watched a man's severed arm fly through the air to land steaming in the snow beside him. He slunk away from the scene to find a safer location to watch from; he knew his whore cousin's men would be looking for him and he had no intention of dying just yet.

Cathelin ignored the banging of swords against her armor and swept her own sword up and around, cutting a soldier in half. She was still in the grip of icy, almost detached calm. Behind the war helm, her face was rigid, lips skinned back from her teeth in a rigid snarl.

She pivoted, smashing the iron boss of her shield into another man's face and he fell, spitting teeth and blood. Cathelin stamped down hard on his exposed neck as she engaged another warrior, cracking the fallen foe's windpipe; behind her, she heard the drumming of his heels on the ground as he choked to death. *Always make sure of your enemy*, her father's voice sounded in her ears. *Never assume he's dead until you hear his death-rattle.*

She grunted, swinging her broadsword up and back until it lay in a straight line down her back. She milked the hilt as she had been taught, then belly muscles clenching with effort, swung it down in the pattern Sir Giles had called the 'apple splitter'

The soldier had been banging his sword along Cathelin's armored sides, seeking a seam he could penetrate. The blurred arc of her broadsword shot down like a bolt from Heaven, and he did not even have time to raise his shield in a futile gesture as the steel struck, and his head was cleaved literally in half, down to his breastbone.

Cathelin raised a foot and kicked the convulsing body off her blade. Her head swung around, seeking another enemy to send to Jesus' arms.

♦ The Sunne in Gold ♦

All around her, pockets of her own men and the O'Fierna's were engaged in battle. Bran O'Fierna himself was locked into a sword dance with the O'Kennedy, the two men exchanging panting insults over their shields. Cathelin spared a tiny corner of her mind to note that they were evenly matched, and sent a small prayer to Saint Brigit that O'Fierna would not be too badly injured.

Suddenly, a voice caught her ears; amidst the clash of steel, war cries and screams, it was barely audible, but to Cathelin, it had all the power of a shout from God Himself. Her eyes narrowed behind the steel grill of her visor as she searched for the source of that voice and saw Madrigal on her knees at the entrance to a cave mouth.

The ice that had held her soul in its grip fractured, then splintered apart into a thousand shards as the sight of the woman she loved hit her like a blow and her blood began to flow again. Cathelin screamed, *"Madrigal!"* and began to hack her way through the clustered knots of fighting men, determined to reach her love, until she was halted abruptly by an infuriated bellow behind her.

Turning, she beheld a giant of a man dressed in mismatched mail and leathers. He was nearly seven feet tall and bald, with a heavy blonde mustache, and his face was covered in woad tattoos. In his hands he wielded a heavy war maul, the leather covered head of the hammer dripping with blood and brain matter.

"I'll kill thee, Blacksunne!" the giant roared, swinging his maul negligently and bashing a hapless soldier to the ground. "Come an' die by Cormac's hammer!"

Cathelin settled herself behind her shield, sword at the ready, heart pounding furiously in her chest. She controlled her breathing as she had been taught, but her thoughts were not on the coming battle. They were with Madrigal, only Madri, and she was impatient to kill this Cormac and rush to her love's side.

Cormac yelled lustily and came at her, hammer swinging with deadly purpose.

Madrigal heard the ululating war cry burst from the night's silence, and then the clash of swords and ringing steel. She struggled to her knees, crawling across the cave floor to the entrance, compelled to witness what was going on. She had to know, had to find out if her Lady had come.

Her knees and the palms of her hands were bloody, rubbed raw on rough stone, by the time she gained the entrance, but she did not notice. All of her attention was fixed on the swirling, flame-lit scene before her as she searched the skirmishing warriors for the one figure she knew would be there.

Wolf McLeod thrust the crimson phoenix banner of the O'Cameron's into a mound of snow covered earth, then drew his longsword. He carried no shield, but in his left hand he wielded a hand axe with deadly efficiency, and he leaped into the fray with a blood-curdling scream.

Becca Half-Tongue danced lightly beside the black armored figure of Blacksunne, her sword flickering like a serpent's tongue and just as quickly. At Cathelin's muttered orders, she would raise the ivory horn to her lips to blow patterned notes in the code that would tell the Lady's men and allies where to gather and where to strike.

Madrigal's eyes feasted on her Lady; she was enthralled by her battle prowess. *My Lady is the greatest warrior in the world*, she thought, eyes shining with tears of love and pride.

♦ The Sunne in Gold ♦

Soon Cathelin stood alone, separated from her men and embattled, but using her sword like an extension of her arm and will, creating an ever-outward expanding circle of death and blood around her.

Madrigal watched and felt her stomach contract again. She bit her lip until the blood ran, trying not to cry out as she was gripped by pain. Curling over her bulging stomach, both hands clawed at the unforgiving stone floor, but at last, she threw back her head and howled the name of the one person she longed for, "*Cathelin!*"

Down on the battlefield, Madrigal saw through a haze of agony that her Lady Cat's head had swung around in answer, and she nearly wept when the figure in black armor began methodically chopping soldiers out of her way, heading straight towards the cave. *My Lady comes*, Madrigal thought and collapsed on her side, panting.

The terrible pain finally eased. Madrigal sat up and her dark eyes widened as she supported herself on her hands and saw something that made her heart nearly stop. *Allah*, she thought, *the size of him!* Her Lady was being challenged by a hammer-wielding giant, and Madrigal felt an icy chill of fear trickle down her spine.

"Oh, Allah!" Madrigal breathed fervently, "Let Your hand cover my Lady Cat; protect her, watch over her, let her come back to me safely."

The Muslim watched with growing apprehension as her Lady and the giant exchanged blows, the giant's hammer smashing the Lady's shield from her hands. They circled and danced, the Lady fighting like a wolf, darting in to wound and leaping out of range; the giant like a mighty bear, closing in on his prey to smash and rend.

Finally, however, the blood-covered giant roared in fury and began swinging wildly, raining blow after blow down on Cathelin, who adroitly avoided the hammer and pricked him in the thigh.

To Madrigal's horror, the giant swatted Cathelin's sword away from him with one hand, the other bringing up the war maul underhand with all his strength behind it.

The maul struck the Lady full in the chest, sending her flying backward to land with a crash on her back. As Madrigal wept and prayed, her heart in her throat, the giant closed in for the kill...

She could not breathe.

Cathelin rasped for breath but could not fill her straining lungs. The steel of her breastplate had been so severely dented that it acted like a vise, squeezing her grating ribs together. Spots danced before her eyes as she struggled to turn over. *Get up, get up,* she remembered her father saying, when as a child she had fallen exhausted to her hands and knees after practice. His commands ricocheted through Cathelin's head and her limbs automatically obeyed ingrained warrior training, lifting the broadsword in a shaking hand as she sat up with a hiss of pain and tried to gather her legs under her.

Cormac bellowed in triumph. He swung the maul up over his head, gripping the shaft tightly, muscles in his arms bulging like oak knots beneath the skin. His tiny eyes were red with fury, like a boar's; the earth seemed to shake beneath his feet as he rushed forward.

Cathelin's vision had narrowed to a small tunnel of light surrounded by darkness. The point of the broadsword wavered as she watched the seemingly tiny figure of Cormac coming towards her. With her last conscious thought, she seemed to see the smiling face of Madrigal, her love,

The Sunne in Gold

beckoning her onward, and behind her visor, Cathelin returned that smile.

Becca downed another man, twisting aside fastidiously to avoid spurting blood, and whirled around to see Cormac the Giant, hammer in hand, standing above the Lady. The kern bent, snatched her opponent's spear from his convulsing hand and cast it without pausing, praying to God and all the saints that her aim would be true. Even as the spear hummed through the air, she ran to her Lady's side, still spitting out near incoherent prayers.

Just as Cathelin lost consciousness and collapsed, Cormac stopped; the spear thrown by the desperate kern had thudded home and stood, quivering, between his shoulder blades. His eyes held a faintly puzzled expression and a flood of dark blood spilled over his lips as he choked, then fell as heavily as a mighty oak hewn by woodsmen's axes, to land with a crash on top of Cathelin, his mighty hammer driving into the earth.

Becca skidded to a stop beside her fallen commander. She snatched the ivory horn to her lips and blew a measure. Without waiting to see what effect this had on her allies, she fell to her knees and began trying to roll Cormac off the Lady, sweating and grunting with effort.

In a moment, she was joined by Wolf McLeod. As other soldiers pounded up to form a protective ring around their commander, she and Wolf managed to get Cormac off the Lady. Her squire, Thomas, wriggled his way through the massed warriors, waving a large rucksack.

♦ **Nene Adams** ♦

"Let me pass! Let me pass!" he squealed. Getting through to the inner circle, the squire hurled himself down to the ground beside Cathelin and rummaged in the sack, quickly bringing out a set of steel bars, pointed at one end and blunt at the other.

"Here," he said breathlessly, passing the tools to Becca and Wolf, "use these on the armor joints and break it apart. *Hurry!*" He drew off Cathelin's war helm gently. Becca gasped at the sight of Cathelin's pale, still face; the Lady's lips were turning blue, and the kern knew it wasn't from the cold.

The three of them worked quickly, first getting off the badly dented breastplate; Wolf whistled–the area of collapsed steel was as deep as his fist. Thomas, tongue between his teeth and a lock of reddish-blonde hair hanging in his eyes, expertly peeled the breastplate back.

All around them, the men kept back Francis' rallying soldiers, using spears and swords and shields to hurl the enemy away. But they did not break rank to pursue–they dared not. If one enemy warrior broke through, it would take only a single swordstroke to rid them of their beloved Lady, and every man and woman there was determined to sell their own lives if necessary. The O'Fierna's men began attacking the enemy soldiers, and soon, Francis' men were trapped between two walls of sharp steel.

The instant he could, Wolf laid his head on Cathelin's chest, probing her rib cage. She still wasn't breathing properly, only in shallow gasps, but there was no wheezing; it was as if her body had not yet realized it could take deeper breaths. He could not detect any sign of a collapsed lung.

Calculatingly, Wolf drew back his arm and delivered a careful blow to Cathelin's chest, making her draw a sharp, deep breath of pain as his hard fist made bruises flare in anguish. The sound of that indrawn breath was sweeter than angel's harps to him, and a rare smile lit up his face.

♦ The Sunne in Gold ♦

Cathelin's eyelashes fluttered as the pain, and the increased oxygen to her lungs, brought her up from darkness. In a moment, her amber eyes opened, and she beheld the smiling face of Wolf McLeod. "C-C-Cormac?" she rasped, a hand clutching her aching chest.

Wolf and Becca helped Cathelin sit up as Thomas worked on removing the rest of her upper armor. "Dead," Wolf said simply. Cathelin's eyes moved to the giant's corpse and she smiled faintly. "Whose spear?" she asked.

Becca flushed and could not speak, so Wolf nodded his head in her direction. "'Twas th' Half-Tongue," he replied. "Good cast, lass."

Cathelin raised a hand and touched Becca's arm. "My thanks," she said. Her disordered mind began to wake and she struggled to get up, amber eyes wide. "Madri!" she gasped.

Thomas protested, "Sit still, Lady. I've got to get the rest of this armor off you."

Cathelin ignored him. "Where's my sword, Wolf? Madri's up there." When the three paid her no heed but continued to unlace her armor, Cathelin snapped in fury, "I've no time for such! Give me my damned sword, McLeod!"

"Nay," he said, concentrating on a knot. "Just a few more moments, Lady. Ye canna confront th' enemy half-accoutered. I'm sure th' wee lass is safe."

Fuming, Cathelin allowed them to get the rest of her armor off, then stood, swaying a little as the sudden motion caused spots to dance before her vision. Beneath the armor she wore only leather trews and a padded gambeson; the cotton shirt was rust-stained, stinking of stale sweat and iron.

♦ Nene Adams ♦

Thomas pulled a mail shirt out of his sack and helped Cathelin draw it over her head, the steel rings jingling. Then he drew out a helm, the noseguard in the shape of a phoenix; the wings of the bird swept over either side of the dome.

Cathelin stamped a few times, settling the mail into place, and pulled the helm over the coils of her dark red braids. Her chest felt as if she had been stampeded over by a herd of horses, but she could breathe, and while her ribs creaked, she didn't think any had been broken. Wolf pressed the hilt of her broadsword into her hand, and Cathelin nodded her thanks.

Around them, the outer ring of kerns was holding strong. Cathelin pushed between two of them, nodding at her men's shout of "The Sunne! The Sunne!" as they beheld their Lady, and a mutual prayer of gratitude was whispered from a dozen throats, thanking God that their Lady was uninjured.

Screaming, "Attack!" Cathelin led her kerns into another charge, and the slaughter began with renewed ferocity. She swirled through the battlefield like the Cailleach, Black Annis herself, harvesting the souls of heroes; in her wake was strewn the bodies of the dead and dying.

Becca caught a riderless horse by the bridle as it pounded past and helped Thomas load the Lady's precious plate armor onto a hastily rigged litter. She boosted him up on the mare's back, saying, "Run back home, Tom-Boy, and have a pull on the wineskin for me, eh? 'Tis a fine day's work you've done."

Seeing him safely off the battlefield and on his way to Inishowen, Becca smiled grimly and wrenched the spear out of dead Cormac's back, bracing a foot on the cooling corpse. Twirling it expertly between her fingers, the scar-faced kern chanted a fierce war song as she danced back out onto the battlefield, eyes alight with unholy glee.

Sir John, the Templar Knight, commissioned to resolve both the fate of Blacksunne and then of Lord Francis,

✦ The Sunne in Gold ✦

watched the tide of battle. No coward but a cold bloodedly practical man, he could see the outcome as if it were written in the very soil and rock of the land. Quietly, without announcing his intentions, he dropped two small purses in the tents of his erstwhile allies and withdrew from the field. There wasn't enough gold in all the kingdoms of God that would make him risk his life against such certain odds. The venture was ended, and experience had made him an expert judge of when it paid to fight, and when it paid to be prudent.

He turned his horse's head in the direction of Dublin, leaving the shouts, screams and clashing of arms behind him.

Had any of the other commanders seen the Templar fleeing the scene of their destruction, they would have begged to join him.

♦ **Nene Adams** ♦

CHAPTER THIRTEEN

Abbot Benedict watched with growing dismay and alarm as the tide of battle turned against the defenders. Despite the best efforts of the Lords' combined men, they were no match for Inishowen's blood-hungry and more experienced fighters.

He picked up the skirts of his brown robe and hustled away, calculating, planning. Behind the false stone in the fireplace of his private study in the abbey, there was a sack of gold and jewels–his personal fortune, gathered over the years by skimming the offerings and taking bribes from local Lords to turn a blind eye to some of their misdoings This would enable him to buy passage to anywhere on earth and set him up for life, besides. He could live like a minor king, should he desire true secular power, but the abbot had other plans. The Church was the mightiest entity in the world; only a madman would throw away such a dream if it could be salvaged at all.

Benedict knew his heartfelt desire of becoming a Bishop, or even Archbishop, was in jeopardy, but he was determined to play this out to the end. If he could only get

✦ The Sunne in Gold ✦

away, perhaps to Rome itself and be the first to tell the story. *Well, then*, he thought, dodging a snow-laden branch, *it may yet be that I can put down the Inishowen Whore and all her ilk, and come away clean and ennobled by the Church as well.*

His steely gray eyes sparkled at the thought of Cathelin bound to a stake, being burned alive at the behest of infuriated churchmen. There were those elements in the Church, he knew, who would have no qualms about ordering such action, the political consequences be damned. Even Bishop Rudolphus could not afford a breach with Rome, nor could he ignore a direct order from the Pope.

As Benedict hurried away, his mind racing through plots and plans, he failed to notice an infuriated pair of eyes watching his exit.

David Uileand, Master of the Hounds, spotted the Abbot scurrying away from the battlefield out of the corner of his eye, and his heart swelled with renewed fury. This was the man he had sworn to kill.

As he had told Lady Cathelin earlier at the war council, his grievance against Benedict was on behalf of his ten-year-old son, Gwion. The terrified child had just that morning spoken to him of the goings-on among the choirboys at the abbey – a foul tale of rape and being forced to fulfill the Abbot's unholy lusts under threat of damnation if ever the truth was revealed.

David had been appalled. At first, he had been inclined to disbelieve the child but the story had rung all too true. Then his wife, Emer, had fearfully confessed to finding blood on the boy's sheets, and his doubts had exploded into rage. He had wanted to grab up a hunting spear and kill Benedict before he drew another breath, but the consequences of acting without his overlord's consent held him back. Not for his sake – if need be, he would have cheerfully sacrificed his own life for that of his son's – but flouting the law might have meant banishment or worse, and how would his family survive if tarred by the brush of treason?

He had not even been sure of the Lady. *God forgive me*, Uileand thought, *for believin' the high born haven't a care for aught but their own.* Lady Cathelin was wise and good; he should have remembered her compassion for all the folk equally, however logic had been buried beneath an onslaught of doubt and rage. In his mind, he had already decided that she would refuse his grievance because the Abbot was a very powerful man, and using the hunger fast against the Lady seemed the only course left open to him.

Thank the White Christ and Saint Brigit that I was wrong, and the Lady forgave me fer actin' like a puppy wit' more spleen than common sense.

Her understanding, immediate sympathy and permission to exact his own form of justice had taken him by surprise, sorely shaming him for doubting the Chieftain whose rule he had vowed to obey.

But the time for thinking was long past. Benedict was disappearing into the trees, stumbling through the snow, and the chance to avenge his poor boy's honor had come like a gift from the Almighty Himself.

"Ssssa, ssssa, me lovelies, me fierce ones," he whispered to the two enormous hounds at his side. Although scrawny and whip thin, David's musculature was sufficient to hold the dogs in check as they strained on their leather leashes.

The gazehounds were shaggy, brindle-coated monsters, bred to take down an armored foe with ease. Their

♦ The Sunne in Gold ♦

shoulders were even with David's hips; they had blocky heads with feathered, drooping ears, and their eyes glittered with feral intelligence. They bayed, paws scrabbling at the snow, fangs bared, strings of spittle hanging from black jowls.

David pointed to the figure of the Abbot; the hounds' heads swung around, their noses working to catch the scent. Unique among canines, gazehounds hunted by both sight and scent; once an enemy had been spotted, it took only a single command to set them on the hunt, and they would pursue that target relentlessly until they brought it down or were killed themselves.

"Derga, Culain," David said softly, and the hounds pricked up their ears a little at the familiar names. Their bodies quivered with eagerness as the Master of Hounds unbuckled their leashes, careful to avoid being pricked by the heavy, steel-spiked collars they wore. Both hounds were impatient to begin their lawful work.

David was sure the hounds had been fixed on the abbot; both Derga and Culain had the tail down, ferociously concentrating look he had come to know well.

He drew a breath and said, grinning fiercely, "Brave ones, *seek*!" he commanded, and both hounds shot away, bellies low to the ground as they howled after their prey.

The Houndmaster smiled to himself as he trotted after his charges. He would not miss this slaying for all the world.

Abbot Benedict's boots crunched on the snow as he turned in the direction of the abbey, following a small, frozen stream that he knew ended behind the monk's walls. He had gone far enough from the battlefield that the sounds had faded; he pushed aside an icicle-strewn branch and picked his way carefully, trying to avoid a slip. If he broke his leg now, it could cost him his life.

Suddenly, shockingly near, he heard the baying of hounds. Benedict's heart froze in his chest; surely he had to be mistaken. But the howls drew nearer and the abbot panicked, running, stumbling, catching himself against the boles of trees in his headlong flight.

He had no real warning; one moment, he heard panting and the thudding of paws along the ground; the next, he was falling forward, screaming thinly as massive jaws gripped his shoulder in a bone-crushing grip, and nearly fifteen stone of muscle and fur sent him crashing to the ground.

Derga snarled and shifted his grip, grinding the abbot's arm into a splintered, bloody mess. Benedict wailed again, his good hand clawing at the slush covered earth in an instinctive effort to get away.

Culain's head darted forward and she seized Benedict's buttocks in her slavering jaws, teeth penetrating deeply. Derga leaped off the prey and Culain picked up the squealing abbot and shook him, blood splattering the snow and spraying into her face.

Benedict's eyes were closed as excruciating pain exploded through his body. He had never felt pain like this before; even flagellating himself with a barbed whip had never caused such unbelievable agony. Both hounds seized mouthfuls of his flesh and began their work again, tearing chunks away, which steamed in the cold air as he screamed and screamed and screamed.

A shrill whistle caused Derga and his mate, Culain, to back away from the whimpering Benedict and sit down on their haunches. Both hounds' muzzles and faces were dark with blood; they panted, tongues lolling, waiting for their master.

✦ The Sunne in Gold ✦

David Uileand trotted up, a cross-barred boar spear swinging in his hand. Benedict rolled over with a massive effort, useless arm flopping to one side. The abbot whimpered when he saw the grim satisfaction on the other man's face.

David's dark green eyes shone as he surveyed the hounds' work. Derga and Culain slunk over to him; the man patted and praised the dogs before turning his hot gaze on the horribly injured Abbot.

"I'm knowin' what ye did ta me boy, ye pederast barsted," David spat viciously. "An' th' others. Ye'd best pray fer God's mercy, ye pig-dog, fer ye'll be gettin' none from me an' mine."

The abbot blubbered, tears of pain and humiliation spilling down his face. He wept and begged, but David's face was as hard as stone. He said, "I hopes ye burns in Hell, poxy whoreson. Ye'll no more make a catamite out o' any childer again." Derga and Culain whined as they waited for a further word from their master. Their black eyes were locked on the figure of the pleading abbot and they snarled, roused by the smell of blood and fear.

David smiled, a heart-stopping grin of such ferocity that the abbot's mouth clicked shut, and he began whimpering the Lord's Prayer. David pointed to the abbot and commanded, "*Rend!*"

"Nooooo!" Benedict screamed, a high, thin wail of disbelief and awful torment as Derga and Culain leaped upon him with a howl and began to tear him apart, piece by bloody piece, taking their time as they had been commanded, instead of killing their prey quickly.

David watched as his charges evoked further screams from the abbot. Eventually, there were no more and the blood-splattered scene was quiet except for the hoarse panting of the hounds, and David's jaunty whistling as he drew a broad bladed knife and set to work himself, taking a trophy from the ripped-apart corpse to show to his traumatized son –

and also prove to his Lady that the cause of justice had been served in full.

♦ The Sunne in Gold ♦

♦ Nene Adams ♦

CHAPTER FOURTEEN

Madrigal bit down on her stick again, belly heaving. She had propped herself up against the stone wall of the cave and her legs were spread wide apart as she pushed, grunting with massive, muscle-straining effort.

Finally, the pain slacked off and she relaxed with a sigh, legs spraddled on the floor. Despite the cold, her face was beaded with sweat, and her limbs trembled with exhaustion. She knew she had a while to go yet before the birth was imminent, and she wondered if she would survive.

Below her, Cathelin was frantic. It seemed that an endless parade of enemies blocked her path to her love, and although she mowed them down relentlessly, they kept popping back up, anonymous faces with all too real weapons that had to be swept out of her way.

At last, though, she disposed of a final warrior, and her eyes darted back and forth, seeking another, but there

♦ The Sunne in Gold ♦

were none. The clear call of a horn flowed over the battlefield and Cathelin looked around. Galbraith had taken his surviving men and fled back to Carbery, to lick his wounds and pray for Inishowen's downfall; the Irishwoman knew it would be a frozen morning in Hell before Sir Duncan came against her again.

The O'Kennedy was dead, his head tied to Bran O'Fierna's saddlebow, and his warriors had been slaughtered to a man. O'Brian had been captured, and even now knelt in the snow, waiting judgment and possible death at Cathelin's hands. His men had surrendered and had been let free by Wolf McLeod, to bear the news back to the O'Brian clan.

Where is Francis? Cathelin wondered, allowing her gaze to sweep back up to the cave where Madrigal waited, and she caught her breath as a wave of pure fury overcame her. Her cousin was there, his fist wound in Madrigal's hair, and he was dragging her further into the cave.

Cathelin let out a scream of pure rage and bolted towards the cave, casting off her helm and dropping the broadsword, her only thought to tear Francis apart with her own two hands.

She was not noticed by her men; they were busy giving the grace stroke to badly injured enemy warriors and organizing litters to carry Inishowen's wounded to the leeches who waited to tend to their hurts.

Madrigal yelped as Francis dragged her across the floor. Her hair felt as if it were being ripped from her skull, and she supported her belly with both hands as she was scraped across the rough floor.

♦ Nene Adams ♦

Finally, Francis flung Madrigal down in the back of the cave and drew his knife with his left hand. It was dark, but the Muslim could see ripples of light shimmering down the length of the steel. She gave a small sigh of relief when Francis used the dagger with a bit of flint to light a torch on the wall, then slid it back into the sheath.

She was lying against something brittle, with an odd, musty-sweet smell. Madrigal craned her neck to see and bit her lip hard to smother a gasp of shock.

Sorcha's body lay behind her, the woman's lips drawn back from the ivoried teeth in a hideous grin. Her eyes were hollow sockets and she was virtually unrecognizable as the vibrant chatelaine of Inishowen, except for the two long, blonde braids that had been her hallmark when living, and now served to identify the dead.

The corner of the cave was dark, but Madrigal could detect a salty flavor in the air. There was a hollow roaring, as if she held her ear to a seashell, and the Muslim squinted against the torchlight, straining to see. *Yes*, she thought, *those shadows seem less dark than the others. That must be a blind corner and an opening to the sea beyond.*

Francis was muttering, "Whore! Whore! You stole *my* land, you stole *my* Sorcha, you stole *my* army, but you'll not steal *my life!*"

He squatted down abruptly and laid a hard hand on Madrigal's belly. "I've scant time to play anymore, sweet slavey." The knife glittered in his left hand again and he grinned, the pupils of his hazel eyes expanding with excitement. "I'll have to end this more quickly than I expected. Too bad I can't stay to see the look on my bitch cousin's face when she comes to find you gutted like a pig and still squealing."

Madrigal trembled and was swept away in a ferocious burst of pain. *Not now*! was her last conscious thought before pure instinct took over and her hands squeezed the rags of

♦ The Sunne in Gold ♦

Sorcha's dress. She whimpered, helplessly tossed in a whirling storm of agony.

Francis looked down at Madrigal's grimacing face and, with a start, realized she was in labor. He grinned widely. He had never cut a pregnant woman before and wondered if her womb would still convulse with the effort of birth after he ripped her stomach open.

He licked his lips with anticipation, spinning the blade in his hand. Madrigal's eyes were closed as she pushed against the rigid muscles of her abdomen, panting heavily.

Francis lightly trailed the point of the knife along a fold of Madrigal's dress and whispered, "Sweet slavey, I'll take your heart with me when I go."

He pulled his arm back and up, his manhood growing hard in his breeches as he prepared to strike.

Cathelin skidded into the cave, nostrils flaring, breathing hard. It was empty, but a faint flickering of torchlight at the back of the cave caught her attention.

The Irishwoman walked carefully towards the light, feet making not a sound on the dirty stone floor. When she rounded the shallow corner, her amber eyes flared with renewed rage.

Madrigal lay on the floor, twisting in pain, with Francis above her, a knife poised to strike.

Cathelin's mind went up in flames.

With a roar, Cathelin tackled Francis from the side, rolling him with her momentum across the floor, fetching up with a bang against the opposite wall, her hated enemy on top. Francis was stunned until he felt Cathelin bury her teeth in the tender flesh of his throat.

Cathelin growled through the mouthful of flesh, jaws grinding, and Francis screamed, striking out with his knife. The point was deflected by Cathelin's mail shirt but the force of the blow made her release him. She sprang to her feet and waited, nursing her bruised ribs with a hand.

A trickle of Francis' blood stained the corner of her mouth and her tongue flicked out to taste it. The explosion of coppery sweetness sobered her somewhat. *All too well do I know that taste*, Cathelin thought as she controlled the urge to attack her cousin like a wild animal.

Francis got to his feet and touched the side of his neck to assess the ragged wound.

"So, my whore cousin returns," Francis said sardonically, "and such a kiss of welcome, too. Come for your little slavey, have you?" He gestured with the knife towards Madrigal. "You'll have to kill me first." His voice was hard and his hazel eyes alight with insane glee.

Cathelin suddenly smiled, amber eyes as hot as molten gold. "You'll be having your wish, cousin," she replied. "You hurt my Madri, bastard whore's get. I'll kill you with my own hands, and great will be my pleasure in the doing of it."

Francis darted forward, knife held professionally low. His right hand struck out at Cathelin's face in a feint but she deflected it easily, and the point of the knife skidded across her thigh, drawing blood.

Cathelin grunted and drove her face forward, slamming her forehead into Francis' nose. Blood spurted as he reeled backward, tripping over the sweating, panting Madrigal, and falling to sprawl on Sorcha's body. Cathelin started towards him as he scrambled backward, disappearing around the blind corner and out of sight.

✦ The Sunne in Gold ✦

Cathelin paused and squatted down beside Madrigal. "Are you well, sweetling?" she asked, keeping her eyes on the corner, lest Francis should return. She was still very angry, but her concern for Madrigal overrode other considerations. *Besides*, she thought, *he'll not escape, save he learns to fly.* She had explored these caves as a child, and knew the opening at the rear of the cave led to a sheer two-hundred foot drop, straight down to the white-foamed maw of the sea.

Her love opened her eyes; the Muslim's contraction eased, and Madrigal replied hoarsely, "Now that you are here, yes. But the children come quickly, Lady Cat. Finish it and come back to me." She bestowed a tired smile on her Lady, and mentally thanked Allah for protecting Cathelin.

Cathelin leaned down and kissed her beloved's sweaty forehead. "Rest, Madri," she said softly. "I'll be back before you even know I've gone."

The Irishwoman stood, dark red hair loosened from its braids and flowing in tangled strands across her broad shoulders. She stepped carefully over Madrigal and Sorcha and stalked around the corner, the muscles of her jaw writhing beneath the skin.

Francis was waiting, outlined in the faint ruddy light of dawn that streamed in through the small cave mouth. His shirt was stained with blood, rusty stains spotted his sandy beard, and one eye was rapidly swelling shut, but his lips were stretched in a defiant snarl.

"I'll kill you, *you bitch!*" he screamed and rushed towards Cathelin, who ignored the twinge of pain in her thigh and prepared to meet him.

The two warriors grappled, reeling across the small room. Francis drove his knife repeatedly into Cathelin's back, squalling in pain as the woman's arms tightened around his waist and she squeezed with all her strength.

♦ Nene Adams ♦

Cathelin ignored the pain of the blows against her back and heaved Francis from his feet, tightening the muscles in her arms into rigid bars as she tried to break his back with her grip alone. Her face was stony, lips pressed so tightly together they were pale and bloodless.

Francis managed to free his left arm and drove the knife towards Cathelin's face; she dropped him to dodge aside. His right hand caught the Irishwoman in a hard swipe across the throat and she gagged, staggering backward, chest heaving as she tried to draw breath through a bruised windpipe.

She felt her heels falter on the crumbling stone at the edge of the drop-off and her heart hammered in her chest. Her arms flew out to brace against the sides of the opening, strong hands gripping the rock face convulsively.

With a shrill yelp of triumph, Francis stalked towards her, and Cathelin knew she was going to die. It would take only a small thrust to break her grip and she would tumble backwards, windmilling down to the ocean and the black spines of rock below.

Goodbye, my Madri, Cathelin thought regretfully as she prepared for death. Although she still struggled to regain her balance, the stone beneath her feet crumbling and pattering away, she was also ready to take Francis with her into death. *'Tis damned I'll be if I let him live to torment my Madri again!* Cathelin thought, as time slowed down to a crawl, and Francis came at her, knife upraised, sheer hate and elation mingled together on his face.

♦ The Sunne in Gold ♦

Madrigal's pain eased and she lay her head back on the cool stone floor. She was exhausted, so tired.

The grunts of combat from beyond the corner drew her attention. *Something is wrong,* she thought, greatly worried. *Lady Cat should have returned by now.* Shakily, she crawled over Sorcha's body, wincing as the brittle bones of the corpse crunched beneath her weight, and managed to get around the corner, although her arms shook with the effort of holding herself up. Madrigal kept crawling, stubborn determination spurring her on.

As she reached the small room beyond the corner, Madrigal's dark eyes widened in shock and fear and her heart thudded into her throat; silently, she keened Cathelin's name in her mind as she took in the horrifying scene.

Lady Cat was poised on the very edge of the tiny platform that jutted out over the sea, and she held both sides of the rock face tightly. It was obvious that she was helpless, balance gone, and it was only her grip on the stones that held her there still.

Lord Francis was stalking towards her Lady; his back was to the former slave, but she could sense his gloating delight. He was going to kill her love.

Madrigal's hand desperately scrabbled on the floor, seeking something, anything she could throw to distract him—a stone, a stick. *Better I die beneath his blade than my Lady*, she thought frantically.

Her searching fingers alighted on something, and, with a sense of disbelief, she realized it was a short horse bow. She picked it up and noted with relief that it was not some old relic, but new, the bowstring taut and perfect. *It must have been left by one of Francis' men,* she thought.

Arrows lay close by and she grabbed one, cutting her thumb on the barbed head. She had never had a weapon in her hands before and the feeling frightened her to the core. Cold sweat beaded up on her forehead and ran down to sting her eyes; the taste of bile was sour in her throat.

Fumbling the arrow in her fingers in an attempt to nock it to the bow, she felt like a clumsy fool and cursed herself silently. She had seen archers drilling in the practice yard at Inishowen and it had seemed so easy! Finally, after what seemed an eternity of fruitless struggle, the arrow was placed correctly and she drew the bowstring to her ear with a massive effort that left her panting, colorful swirls of light dancing in her vision.

Madrigal shook her head, arms trembling with strain. A howling terror seized her suddenly, paralyzing her limbs and sending shards of ice racing through her blood. She could not breathe and her heart stuttered in her breast.

A vision of the future should she fail – a yawning gulf where loneliness, grief and sorrow lived in place of her beloved Cat – blinded her in a flashing instant. She stared into space, so consumed by gnawing doubt that the world fell away, leaving her trapped in the nightmare of her own mind.

Madrigal felt disconnected, bewildered and utterly alone, a tiny figure lost in stifling darkness, surrounded by devils that tore at her sanity and left her weak. She actually considered throwing the bow away and accepting the inevitable, bowing to fate and the inexorable will of Allah. She was almost limp with despair, hating herself for being weak, hating Francis for his madness, hating even Lady Cat for this impossible situation.

I cannot do this! she whimpered to herself, on the verge of agonized weeping. *It is not fair to put such a burden on me. Oh, Allah, send a warrior angel to defend my lady, for I am but a woman and have not the courage. Let me die in her place – strike me down now if it please thee – only let the task of saving her fall to someone worthy. I cannot! I cannot!*

Just when the anguish grew so keen she thought she must die, a single pinprick of golden, glowing light swam into

✦ The Sunne in Gold ✦

the blackness of her prison and a voice whispered, "I love you, sweetling, heart's delight."

As the phrase repeated and echoed, a tumbling kaleidoscope of images wheeled across the dark – Cathelin's amber eyes glimmering with desire, her face alight with wonder, mouth curved in the open and delighted smile of a child.

I love you, sweetling...
I love you, Madri...
I love you...

A sharp pang cleaved her breast and Madrigal clutched at this lifeline, realizing that she had been drowning in a sea of doubt and hesitation. The sure and certain knowledge of the ties that bound her to Cat – the profound depth of the love they shared, the bond of souls that united them utterly – dragged her out of wretched misery and fear, cast aside the nightmares and welcomed her back into the light.

Her eyesight cleared and confidence returned; after a single panic-stricken moment when she thought all had been lost, she realized that mere moments had passed while she had wrestled with her demons. Cathelin was still in mortal danger but while Francis toyed with her, there was yet time.

She picked up the bow again and drew it, this time with little difficulty. Power flowed through her veins, molten energy from the very depths of her being, and she felt alive again. The consequences of failure no longer crippled her. She would save Lady Cat if she could, die with her if she could not. *Inshallah!*

Madrigal closed an eye, sighting carefully, the feathers of the fletching tickling her cheek. Her wavering aim miraculously steadied and she drew in a deep breath. She knew she would have only one chance. The future lay in her hands – her frail, mortal and unskilled hands – but fear no longer had a claim on her. A single chance was all she had and it would have to be enough. .

Ponderously, Madrigal struggled up on one knee, knowing that if this worked, she would have to act quickly.

Francis wet his lips with his tongue and slowly drew the knife along Cathelin's cheek, a thin line of blood springing up along the path of the razored steel. Cathelin's muscles were taut as she held herself up by sheer strength of will alone.

Francis whispered in singsong fashion, "Now you're going to d-i-i-ie," and Cathelin held herself poised, preparing to whip an arm out and fasten his tunic in her grasp, pulling him over with her as she fell.

A soft sigh echoed from the cave walls as Madrigal released the arrow and got to her feet, already in motion, casting the bow aside as she hurried with all the speed she could muster. Francis felt the arrow bury itself in his back, the barbed head slamming into his kidneys, shredding flesh and organs in its passage.

He screamed and toppled forward, but Madrigal was there, moving adroitly despite her clumsy bulk, fear for her beloved Lady lending wings to her feet. She snatched him by the arm and pivoted, hurling him away from her Lady Cat with a strength magnified by love and desperation. Francis slammed into the cave wall, the force of Madrigal's arm and his own weight plunging the arrowhead deeper into his body.

As soon as she released Francis, Madrigal's hands buried themselves in Cathelin's mail shirt and the Muslim woman heaved with all her might, pulling her Lady forward and away from danger.

Cathelin gaped as she saw Madrigal moving with grace and purpose despite her immense belly; her love's sweet face was frozen in a teeth-clenching rictus of effort and her dark eyes shone with a ferocious light Cathelin had never dreamed she possessed.

♦ The Sunne in Gold ♦

'Tis as if she's been possessed by the battle madness, Cathelin thought in amazement as Madrigal sent Francis hurtling away with what seemed like effortless ease, then darted forward to seize the Irishwoman's shirt and pull, strands of black hair sticking to her wet face.

Cathelin found her balance and released her death-grip on the rocks, but then was overbalanced by Madrigal's mad tugging. She fell, taking the Muslim woman with her; Cathelin absorbed the shock on the palms of her hands, keeping her weight off Madrigal only with a gut-wrenching effort that caused beads of sweat to spring up on her brow.

Madrigal looked up at Cathelin. Now that the moment had passed and her Lady was safe, she felt another contraction coming on. "Lady," she gasped, "my children..."

Cathelin rolled away from Madrigal and sprang to her feet. She started to run towards the front of the cave, but stopped and retraced her steps. *Always make sure of a fallen enemy.*

She walked back to the small room and over to Francis, who opened his eyes at her approach. The insane light within those hazel depths had dimmed, but he smiled widely.

"God... damn... you..." he half-whispered, and a gout of dark blood bubbled from his lips. "God... damn... you...to... Hell..."

Cathelin squatted down and put her arms around Francis. Standing up with a grunt, the injured muscle in her thigh quivered as her efforts ripped the cut wider. She carried Francis to the small opening at the back of the little room, keeping her feet carefully away from the shattered edge.

His eyes widened and he whimpered fitfully, tossing his head back and forth in denial. Cathelin looked down at her cousin's face and searched her heart, but found no guilt, no mercy–just the remembrance of justice and the meaning of the law.

"You first, cousin," she said softly, then dropped him over the edge.

Francis screamed shrilly as he fell, tumbling over and over through the air, and the wet splatter of his body striking the rocks below was overwhelmed by the rushing roar of the sea.

Cathelin watched him fall and turned away. No tears burned in her eyes for this death; only grim satisfaction at a judgment given, a punishment meted, and the thought that her Madri had, at last, been fully revenged.

Madrigal cried out, and the sound of her voice jolted Cathelin from her reverie. "Sweetling!" she yelped, then absurdly blurted, "Stay there. I'll fetch help."

Madrigal grunted in acknowledgment as she pushed, her belly heaving up and down. Cathelin ran, ignoring the burning pain in her leg and the ache of bruised ribs, shouting at the top of her lungs for Wolf and Becca.

Madrigal strained, face reddening with effort, and Cathelin urged her to breathe. "Come, sweetling, 'tis not good to hold your lungs so still," the Irishwoman crooned.

Madrigal's hands were fastened onto Cathelin's, and she clutched them in a bone-grinding grip as the pain went on and on.

Cathelin looked up at the sound of horse's hooves coming towards the cave mouth. A troop of hastily assembled kerns had gotten a roaring fire going in a circle of stones, smoke wafting up through a natural chimney in the ceiling of the cave. Madrigal had been moved to the front room,

✦ The Sunne in Gold ✦

Cathelin carrying her, and now reclined in a cushioning nest of furs and donated cloaks.

Becca had been sent back to Inishowen on the fastest horse available to fetch the midwife with all speed. Cathelin knew Madrigal could not ride or be carried, even in a litter, the six miles back to her own bed, so the birthing would have to be here. Wolf McLeod had been sent to the abbey on a similar errand–the Lady wanted Brother Ignatius in attendance as well.

Madrigal relaxed as the contraction passed, gasping for breath. Her filthy dress had been cut away and she was covered by a clean fur. Cathelin had melted snow in her helm over the fire and bathed the Muslim with a soft cloth, getting off much of the dirt and grime and making Madrigal feel infinitely more comfortable.

Becca and Branwen hustled into the cave, the midwife already throwing a spotless apron over her head. The fragile-seeming woman carried a leather sack in her hand and she grinned widely.

"So, I see th' wee lass' time is come," Branwen said. She said to Becca, "Melt some snow ta boilin' then set it aside. I'm wishin' ta wash my hands o' horse sweat an' such afore I touch th' gal." She reached inside her sack, bringing out a clay jar of soft soap and a piece of folded leather.

Cathelin sighed in relief. She helped Branwen slide the softly tanned piece of bullhide beneath Madrigal and smiled down at her love. "'Twill be all right, sweetling," Cathelin said, kissing the tip of Madrigal's nose. "I love you."

Madrigal returned the smile, although her eyes were glazed with exhaustion. "I love you as well," she said softly, and Branwen chuckled.

"Glad I am ta see these bairns be born ta such a lovin' household," the midwife said with a gap-toothed smile. When Becca indicated the water was ready, Branwen soaped up her narrow hands and lean forearms, rinsing them thoroughly before flinging the slops out of the cave mouth. An idle soldier received the barrage full in his face and Branwen ignored his muffled curses with dignity.

Kneeling down between Madrigal's spread knees, the midwife said, "Now, wee one, I'll be checkin' on yer progress."

Branwen lifted up the fur to expose Madrigal's nudity, then carefully slid two fingers into her, probing delicately, head cocked to one side. "'Tis good," she said firmly. "Not much longer now. You, Lady, get behind th' little mother an' let her rest agin ye. Yer as much a part o' this birthin' as she."

Cathelin slid behind Madrigal, pulling the other woman up between her spread legs as Branwen directed. Her naked back was against the hard stone of the cave wall but she did not complain.

Madrigal rested her hands on her Lady's upraised knees, half-reclining, her head pillowed on soft breasts, feeling a vast sense of comfort at the feel of Cathelin's strong arms around her. Then another pain hit, and her hands dug into her Lady's flesh as she let out a strangled scream.

Cathelin felt her own stomach muscles clench in sympathy. She had removed her mail shirt and gambeson, as well as her tunic as the cave had grown warmer, and the sweat-soaked strands of Madrigal's hair tickled her chest. She whispered, "Softly, sweetling, heart's delight." She stroked her love's brow with one hand as the other woman strained.

Madrigal had never felt such pain in her life. As her contractions grew stronger and more frequent, she felt as if she were being torn apart. No longer fearing to raise her voice, the Muslim screamed, cried and cursed in Arabic, calling down the wrath of Allah on the one who had caused her torment, and on the breed of men in general.

Cathelin stifled a chuckle and held Madrigal as the powerful contractions racked her small body. *My Madri has quite the sharply pointed tongue*, she thought. *I pity the bard*

✦ The Sunne in Gold ✦

who tries to satirize her. The Irishwoman looked at Branwen, who was still kneeling between Madrigal's legs.

"How much longer?" Cathelin asked.

"No much a'tall," Branwen answered, passing a short bladed knife to the hovering Becca. "Pass this through th' flames 'til 'tis cherry red, then," she added, splashing liquid from a wineskin into a wooden bowl, "put it in here."

Becca sniffed at the bowl; it was pure usquebha, the potent water of life, and the scar-faced kern grimaced but obeyed her instructions, carrying the bowl back to the midwife when she was finished.

Branwen looked up, pale green eyes alight. "I'm seein' a head," she announced.

Madrigal grunted, pushing with all her might, feeling as if her pelvic bones were separating. She wept, "I cannot! I cannot!" tossing her head back and forth against the pain. It was too much, she was too tired, she felt as if she had been battling all day and wanted nothing but rest.

Cathelin put her hands over Madrigal's where they clutched her knees and said, "Take my strength, sweetling. Let our children come into this world." She pressed her lips against the top of the Muslim's head and closed her eyes, willing energy to the woman she loved and praying silently for Saint Brigit's aid.

Madrigal sucked in a shuddering lungfull of air, heaving with renewed effort. Those words–"our children"– had given her hope. She felt as if she struggled against titanic forces, but knew that as long as her Lady Cat was there, everything would be all right.

Branwen grinned widely, hands busy beneath the sheltering fur. Cathelin opened her eyes but could not see what was going on. "Well?" she croaked.

The midwife frowned in concentration. "'Tis comin'," she replied shortly.

♦ Nene Adams ♦

Madrigal screamed as the baby's head slowly emerged amidst a gout of blood and fluid. Branwen guided the infant's shoulders out with practiced skill, and soon, a squalling child was cradled in the midwife's tiny hands, the bloody cord still attached it to the mother.

"A boy!" Branwen crowed, tying off and cutting the umbilical cord with her sterilized knife. The midwife laid the squirming child down on the fur between Madrigal's breasts; her son mewled, eyes tightly closed, tiny fists waving in protest at his abrupt transference from a place of warmth and darkness into the light of the world.

Cathelin felt tears flowing down her cheeks, while Madrigal reached up a hand to steady her firstborn. Although streaked with blood, wisps of dark hair matted to his slightly misshapen skull, he was the most beautiful thing she had ever seen.

Cathelin touched the baby's cheek with her finger and said quietly, "He's lovely, our son. Must be taking after his mother." She kissed Madrigal's ear, heart swelling with love and pride.

Madrigal closed her eyes as another spasm of pain shot through her. In a few moments, Branwen said, "An' here's t'other! Come along, lassie, yer mother's waitin'."

The other baby emerged more rapidly than her brother had done, and instead of wailing, she trilled with seeming delight.

"An' here be yer daughter. A fine, healthy bairn," Branwen announced.

Soon, both babies lay wrapped in warm furs, sleeping in Madrigal's arms. Branwen had massaged the Muslim's belly to expel the afterbirth and cleaned away all traces of the birth struggle. By the time Brother Ignatius had arrived, practically carried by Wolf McLeod, it was all over.

"Well," the old monk had sighed, "at least I'll be in time fer th' christenin'."

✦ The Sunne in Gold ✦

Becca wiped tears from her cheeks as she took the astonished Wolf by the arm and led him away from the cave, Brother Ignatius and Branwen following. They left the two women alone, Becca already making plans for the birthing celebration.

Cathelin took up the baby girl's hand and marveled at how perfect and delicate it was. "Have you ever seen such tiny fingernails?" she asked Madrigal, who sighed.

"Yes," she replied softly, "I have seen newborns before." Her dark eyes gazed down at her two children, and although she was mortally weary, she had to smile.

Cathelin was still behind her, the hard-muscled body warm against Madrigal's back, and the Lady's arms were around her. Madrigal snuggled against Cathelin and closed her eyes, drifting off to sleep.

Cathelin smiled and stroked a forefinger along Madrigal's cheek. Then with a sigh of her own, she rested her chin on top of her love's head and let her eyelids close, tumbling into Morpheus' dark-feathered embrace to dream of life and love.

♦ Nene Adams ♦

CHAPTER FIFTEEN

Two weeks later, Inishowen was the scene of a huge celebration, and the castle was crammed to the rafters with members of the clan, visitors and guests. The festival had a tri-fold cause—to celebrate the Winter Solstice, to welcome Madrigal and her new children to the O'Cameron clan, and to rejoice in the news that Lady Cathelin and Madrigal would be handfasted next Beltain in a ceremony that, while it lacked the blessings of the Church, would nevertheless be considered valid by the laws of ancient Ireland.

Cathelin sat at the high table beneath the gold embroidered Canopy of State and watched the revelers with a smile. There had been a feast—Shevaughn and her crew had worked nothing short of a miracle to get all in readiness—and her people were dancing, singing, and making merry with high-spirited abandon.

Madrigal sat at her right, blushing with shy pride each time one of the folk came up to wish her happiness, a Merry

♦ The Sunne in Gold ♦

Solstice, and to praise her babies. She wore a dark crimson gown with contrasting black queen's sleeves that fell into a point at the wrist that swung nearly to the floor. The neckline was trimmed with black ribbon knotwork, and around her neck she proudly wore both her Lady's welcoming gift of the silver phoenix necklace, as well as a new gift: a heavy silver collar of intertwined swans set with amethysts, dark garnets and exotic black pearls. Matching earrings swung nearly to her shoulders. Every inch the gracious hostess, she thanked the excited clansmen and women for their kindness; her dignity and quiet pride were visible to all.

Cathelin hitched at the hem of her own new tunic and sighed. The tunic was black with crimson trim, and Madrigal had studded the front and sleeves with white bone beads and embroidered silver moons. The Irishwoman's dark red hair swung in its customary twin braids as she turned her head and contemplated the children that had made such a difference in her life.

Currently, the babies were in the lap of the new nursemaid; a plump, cheerful, heavily freckled young woman named Crimthan Oengus, whose fiery orange hair exploded in a profusion of corkscrew curls over her shoulders and proved her mother had been right in naming her "Fox."

The boy had been christened Padraigh Giles O'Cameron. Madrigal had been very pleased when her Lady had expressed great pleasure over their son being named after her father. Though only two weeks old, the child had already earned the nickname of 'Wee Dragon', being quite fierce in his temperament and not at all shy about expressing himself.

The little girl, on the other hand, was sweetness itself. The naming of this baby had nearly caused the couple's first fight. Madrigal had insisted on naming the baby after Cathelin, who had categorically refused to countenance it.

Cathelin sighed again when she remembered the argument. "But sweetling," she had said, trying to be reasonable, "'twould be too confusing, having two of me about the place."

Madrigal had been stubborn and equally implacable. Finally, however, they agreed on a compromise; their daughter now bore the name of Brigit Cathbadh O'Cameron, but the folk called her "Honey-Cat." She was a loving baby, and her dark eyes were constantly filled with wonderment and delight at all the marvels in the world.

Privately, Cathelin was relieved that neither of the children had Francis' coloring, or, in fact, anything of him in their looks she could detect. While it would not have made her love them any less, still, the reminder of their father would have been a hurtful one. "Crimthan, lass, let me have my sweetness," she said aloud.

With a broad smile, the nursemaid passed Honey to the Lady. She, and many others of the clan, found it a source of private amusement that their fierce warrior Lady should have taken so to the little girl, while shy Madrigal, who insisted she loved both children equally, clearly had a slight preference for the boy. Crimthan chuckled, plump freckled shoulders shaking. *The Good Lord worked in mysterious ways.*

Cathelin cradled Honey in her arms, making nonsense baby talk and tickling the baby's snub nose with the end of a dark red braid. Madrigal smiled indulgently; she, too, found Cathelin's delight over the girl baby amusing. Crimthan raised an eyebrow at Madrigal in inquiry but the Muslim shook her head. Her breasts ached slightly, being full of milk, but the children were not yet hungry.

While her Lady cooed and kissed the baby in her arms, Madrigal's deep purple eyes swept over the gathering.

Wolf McLeod, resplendent in tartan kilt, sporran, blue tunic and his black hair in a braid, was engaged in a vigorous sword dance with heavy claymores against a visiting member of the O'Fierna clan–a well-muscled warrior with a pale

✦ The Sunne in Gold ✦

blonde thatch of curls and charming dimples in both cheeks named Lugh. The two men yelled lustily as their swords flashed and clanged.

Shevaughn was dancing a wild reel, the skirts of her brilliant scarlet gown held high as her feet kicked and skittered, the hearth chief twirling with unbelievable grace, face wreathed in a broad smile. Her partner, a much smaller woman with a fox-like face and wavy blonde hair named Ceridwyn, panted to keep up. Bets had already been taken among the kitchen staff as to who was seducing whom, and speculation ran rife as to whether or not Shevaughn and Ceridwyn would end up in the storeroom, the hayloft or perhaps even the wine cellar.

Becca Half-Tongue sang along with a group of her fellow kerns to an old drinking song played with enthusiasm by a minstrel. She leaned her head on the shoulder of a one-eyed veteran, and ran her hand down his lean muscled chest, keeping time with her mazer of wine with the other hand. He leaned his head down and kissed her, and Becca wondered if the war room in the barracks was occupied.

Even the hapless maid was there, drinking small beer and chattering with a group of servers, her bleary blue eyes alight with happiness. Cathelin had spoken to the pox-scarred maid for a long, long time, and having determined that the girl's crime was greed and inability to avoid temptation rather than true treason, had forgiven the girl in a burst of parental joy.

But Father Paul had not been so lenient; the old priest had laid a penance on the maidservant–to clean his small house, and bring his firewood, and cook his meals–and generally kept her about the chapel, where he could keep a fierce eye on her doings. Her betrothed had been killed in what was now known as the Battle of the Trees, and while she had wept for his death, the maid had been forgiven by the Lady, and the payment for her crimes was a light one.

♦ Nene Adams ♦

Cathelin handed the now sleeping Honey back to Crimthan, leaned over, and kissed Madrigal's lips. "Sweetling," she murmured, "What about your song?"

Madrigal nodded. Her hair had been pinned into a coronet around her head, and a crown of gold ribbon-wrapped mistletoe was pinned on top. She pulled her harp into her lap and softly strummed the strings, the dark wood with its carved dolphins glistening in the torchlight.

Cathelin stood and raised her voice in a bellow, "Silence. Silence," she shouted until the merrymaking ceased and all eyes turned towards the Lady.

Cathelin smiled. "Madri has promised to sing us a special song tonight." She paused for the wild whistling and clapping to die down, then continued, "Now, let all be silent and respectful whilst she plays. Or else," she added fiercely, amber gold eyes raking across the throng. She sat back down, certain that even the hardened drunkards would pay attention.

Cathelin nodded to Madrigal, who drew a lovely, slightly martial melody from her harp and began the Lay of Long Life:

"Seven daughters of the sea I invoke,
The salt-rich weavers of the threads of eternity!
From my beloved, may three deaths be taken!
May she be dealt seven waves of fortune fine
And spirits of evil be defied, denied in durance vile!
O, perish not her fame, nor pierce her corselet,
For she is an indestructible stronghold
And the fires in the tower of her soul shall burn fore'er!
Through seven turnings of the Wheel,
I invoke fairy wives to ring a binding seven times!
I summon to her these boons–
May she live a hundred hundred years
And may Saint Brigit's grace be upon her
From beginning to ending to beginning again,

✦ The Sunne in Gold ✦

So mote it be!"

As soon as the last strains of the harp died away, the assembled folk roared their approval, led by the new Abbot, Father Dominicus, who had lived in Inishowen as a boy before taking holy vows. He clapped enthusiastically, and even went so far as to place his fingers in the corners of his mouth and blow a shrill whistle of appreciation.

Madrigal smiled at the new abbot; Father Dominicus was much more concerned with the welfare of his flock then Benedict had been, and furthermore, had very strong ideas of his own which contradicted Church policy.

As he had explained to the Muslim upon their first meeting, "I care not whether God's children love themselves, nor yet one another, save only that there is love somewhere." His merry blue eyes had twinkled. "An' if you've ever a mind to convert, lass, then I'm your man. So," he had added with mock casualness, "when will you two ladies be publishing the banns, eh?"

Madrigal had laughed, completely at ease with the middle-aged priest. They had already had a few long discussions over the chess table, and Dominicus' attitude towards her relationship with her Lady, not to mention the fact that the priest had a very sharp mind, and a great deal of good-natured curiosity, had made the Muslim consider him a friend.

Madrigal grabbed Cathelin's hand and gave it a squeeze. "Tell me, Lady," she asked mischievously, "are you full of magic tonight?"

Cathelin grinned slyly and cocked an eyebrow. "Aye," she answered, "and near full to bursting with it, too."

"We will have to do something about that, then," Madrigal said, rising and tugging Cathelin to her feet. "I do not wish you to burst just yet, but perhaps later..." She ran her tongue along her lips and continued, "Come, Lady Cat.

♦ Nene Adams ♦

Come walk with me, come lie with me, come and share my bed."

"Sweetling," Cathelin replied, amber eyes beginning to shine with warm desire, "You've no need to be asking me twice."

The two women snuck away from the celebration arm in arm, while Crimthan rocked the babies on her lap and laughed softly.

And all the people of Inishowen sent up a prayer that night, wishing their Ladies happiness, joy, and boundless love for ever, and ever, and aye.

The End

Coming soon from Shady Ladies Press, Inc!!!

Victim of a terrible accident, famed composer and pianist Graham Yardley loses her sight, her heart and her soul. Wealth and fame mean nothing after the devastating loss of her beloved music; her life is reduced to silence, darkness and bitter regret. In a bleak mansion atop windswept cliffs, the blind woman withdraws from the world, her once consuming passions now a source of anguish and fear. Then Anna, a lost woman seeking a place in the world, comes into her life and awakens feelings she thought were dead forever. A fragile melody of love is played between these damaged souls, a song made sweeter and stronger by the day... but will their blossoming romance be destroyed by an outsider's greed or will it succumb to the discord of Graham's tormented heart? Can she find happiness with Anna, caught up in the fiery overtures and darkly gothic strains of...

Love's Melody Lost

by Radclyffe

Available March 2001

For more information, see our website at:
www.shadyladiespress.com

An excerpt from Love's Melody Lost

"Graham asked that you join her in the music room when you're free," Helen called to her as she passed through the kitchen.

"Yes, thanks," Anna replied absently, still disquieted by the scene she had just witnessed, unable to say exactly why. She showered quickly and was soon knocking on the closed doors of Graham's study.

"We need to deal with some of the personal correspondence," Graham said perfunctorily when Anna joined her. "We have been getting too many calls lately."

"Certainly," Anna answered, instantly aware by Graham's tone that she was disturbed about something. She wished she could ask her what troubled her, but Graham's unapproachable demeanor prevented even that simple inquiry. Ignoring her disquiet, she crossed to her usual seat at the desk and began to peruse the letters Graham had obviously ignored for months. Anna was amazed at the scope of the solicitations. She began to read aloud at random, for all the letters were similar in theme.

"These two conservatories have written several times in the last two years requesting that you teach a master's class," Anna informed Graham, who had begun pacing soon after Anna began reading messages to her. Anna had never seen her so agitated before.

"Tell them 'no'," Graham replied curtly, her face grim.

"There are a number of inquiries regarding your concert availability," Anna said quietly, subdued by the well-known companies seeking to engage Graham as a guest performer.

"Throw them away," Graham said flatly. She stood with her back to Anna in the open terrace doorway, and the hand she rested against the frame was clenched.

"There's a graduate student at Juilliard – she's written and called several times. She says she's writing her doctoral thesis on your early works-" Anna faltered as Graham caught her breath sharply. "She would like to arrange a meeting with you, and perhaps discuss your current-" Anna was stunned to silence as Graham whirled toward her, her face furious.

"I don't perform, I don't compose and I don't give goddamned interviews. Go through whatever's there and deal with it! I don't want to hear anything more about it!"

Anna stared as Graham searched for her walking stick with a trembling hand. She had never seen Graham misplace anything in her surroundings before. It was heart-wrenching to see her falter uncertainly as she tried to orient herself.

"It's against your chair," Anna said quietly. She looked away, giving Graham time to compose herself. She knew Graham could not see her, but it seemed wrong somehow to watch her private struggles.

"Graham-" she ventured tentatively, not wanting to add to Graham's obvious distress. "These things look important- I can't just throw them away. I don't think I can answer them without your help."

Graham paused at the door, her back to Anna, rigid with her struggle for control. "I've given you my answer to all of them - 'no'. Word it any way you want, but handle them yourself in the future. That's what I'm paying you for. Don't bring them up to me again."

Anna risked Graham's ire with one last attempt. "If you could just give me some idea-"

"Enough Anna," Graham said wearily as she pushed open the heavy door to the hall. "It's done."

Also slated for publication in 2001:

These Dreams
By Verda Foster

Cobb Island
By Blayne Cooper

The Sunne in Scarlet
By Nene Adams

See us on the web at
www.shadyladiespress.com

Cool Stuff!

Shady Ladies Press Merchandise!!!

T-shirts
Mouse Pads
Coffee Mugs

(More artwork by Corrie Kuipers can be seen at www.corrieweb.com. Check it out!)

www.cafepress.com/shadylady